# A Horse of
# Her Own

# A Horse of Her Own

Annie Wedekind

New York

**SQUARE FISH**

An Imprint of Macmillan

ISBN 978-0-312-58146-6
LCCN 2007032769

Originally published in the United States by Feiwel and Friends
First Square Fish Edition: September 2009
Square Fish logo designed by Filomena Tuosto
Book design by Amanda Dewey
mackids.com

7  9  10  8

LEXILE: 1040L

*For Mum and Dad*
*...and for Araby (my Lily)*

# Contents

Chapter 1

# The Beginning of Summer

There was no doubt that Alyssa Taylor was an excellent rider. Slim and poised, with a straight, relaxed back and lower legs like iron, she had a casual way of sitting on a horse like it belonged to her, as if she were favoring it with her seat and hands. This easy dominance was of a piece with the rest of her life—her tanned good looks and mature figure, her super-low-cut jeans with perfectly frayed cuffs, her expensive school, and her natural popularity.

As she watched Alyssa canter her dainty Arab mare, Ariel, over a combination jump, Jane Ryan admitted to herself that, as she'd been for so many years, she was still jealous. It was impossible not to be, she thought, unless you were already in Alyssa's inner circle of friends who rode at Sunny Acres farm. Jane had ridden here since she was eight, but the following six years of summer camp and Saturday lessons had not brought her any closer to the chosen group. She had always been steady Jane, willing to stay late to walk the horses and muck out the stalls, just for the chance to spend more time at the stable, and, of course, to ride the school horses since she didn't board or lease a horse of her own.

Luckily, one of these school horses was Beau (pronounced "boo"), and Jane thought he was the best horse in the world. She often allowed herself to pretend that he really *was* her own—a fantasy all too easily burst when Beau was given over to another girl to ride. But now, as she watched Alyssa and Ariel sail over the last jump, Jane patted Beau's strong brown neck and whispered to him, "As long as we're together, I'm happy as a clam, I promise." Beau flickered his ears, listening, and stamped his hoof, as if he agreed with her.

It had been a fine lesson. Jane had worried that Beau would tire early in the humid late-May heat, but he was in a particularly good mood this morning, lengthening his fluid strides as she asked him to stretch out his trot, and arching his neck rather grandly as he went on the bit without a fuss. Some days he simply pretended not to understand what she meant when she gathered the reins and gently urged him to lower his head. Though his nature was gentle, his spirit was independent, and he was certainly no "push button," as the horses who would do anything their riders asked were called. Jane liked the challenge and liked that Beau kept her on her toes. Still, she'd ridden him for so many years that she knew his repertoire of moods and could respond accordingly.

Today, their trainer, Susan McCormick, had noticed this. "Jane," she'd called out from the center of the ring, "we're going to have to find you a new horse to ride—you and Beau are starting to look like a centaur. You know each other so well, it's hard to tell you apart." It was a typical Susan compliment—accurate, nice to hear, but with a warning attached to it. Her trainer had no qualms about separating a rider from her favorite horse if she felt they were no longer learning from each other.

Susan was one of the best hunter-jumper trainers in Kentucky, and Jane felt very lucky to work with her. She reminded herself of this as she watched Alyssa finish the course flawlessly and knew she had a tough act to follow. Ariel, a glossy light chestnut with a beautiful dished face and a high-sailing, cream-colored tail, had a delicacy and quick action that looked glorious in the ring, and Alyssa pushed her hard, willing her through a perfect course.

"Jane, take Beau next, please," Susan said, and her face was stern as it always was when she watched her riders. Jane brought Beau to a canter and looked toward the first jump, a simple cross-rail. She counted strides under her breath, and Beau took the jump neatly. "Good release!" Susan shouted. "Now look ahead to the next one." Jane guided Beau around the turn, deepening her seat as he had to shorten his stride, and he glided over the high oxer with no difficulty. Beau was interested now, and he swished his tail and pricked his ears in anticipation of the combination. "Slow him down a little, keep him steady," Susan called, and Jane tightened her reins and talked soft nonsense to her horse. He flickered his ears back to her and settled into his stride, cruising over the two jumps with the cocky ease that Jane loved in him.

As soon as he landed, Jane looked over her left shoulder to the last jump, which, at a little more than three feet, was also the highest—the coop. It was only her second time jumping it, and its triangular bulk, wide at the base, narrow at the top, loomed ominously at the end of the ring. She eased her reins and let Beau gather speed, trying not to convey any hesitation through her seat and hands. Beau swayed a little out of his line as he neared the jump, and Susan shouted something that Jane couldn't hear. Her heart raced and her breath came quickly as they took the last three strides. She felt Beau gathering himself underneath her, and she rose in her stirrups, staring straight between his ears, looking anywhere but at the weather-beaten green hulk that they were now sailing over. Beau landed, snorted, shook his head, and Jane laughed with relief, patting his neck and praising him as he spun out his canter and returned to a trot. "Good boy!" she said. "What a good boy!"

"Nicely done," was all Susan said when she and Beau rejoined the other riders in the center of the ring. It was all that Jane needed to hear.

There were seven other girls in the Advanced group

with whom Jane had ridden for years—they'd all been promoted from Intermediate the previous summer. But last Saturday, she'd overheard Susan say that the group had gotten too large. For camp, which started in two weeks, she'd divide them into Advanced I and Advanced II. The stronger riders would be in Advanced I, and Jane looked at the girls around her, wondering who would make the cut. Alyssa, certainly. Then there was Jennifer, a petite brunette who was Alyssa's best friend. Her parents had bought her big gray gelding, Thunder, last summer, and he'd already placed well in several autumn shows.

Jane wasn't as worried about Liz and Shannon—she'd been surprised when Liz had been promoted to Advanced in the first place, and suspected that it had more to do with her horse than with her riding skill. Lady Blue was a perfect example of a push button—her training masked Liz's laziness; she could go on autopilot with little input from her rider. She had a sweet temperament as well, and Jane worried that eventually she would coarsen under the indifferent hands of her owner, especially since Liz had missed several weeks of lessons over the winter and early spring, forgoing the chilly farm for a series of unspecified "school projects." Shannon, on the other hand, had been a strong rider until the past March, when she'd had a nasty fall off her skittish bay, Bebop. He'd shied before a jump, and Shannon was thrown into the rails, spraining her wrist. It wasn't a serious injury, but Shannon seemed to lose her nerve. She refused to get back on Bebop, and when she finally did, three weeks later, she was tentative and easily

5

spooked by his slightest hesitation. It did not bode well for her chances of getting into Advanced I.

There were two girls who Jane wished she would be able to ride with this summer—Robin and Jessica. Robin was her best friend, a quiet girl with large hazel eyes and long, light brown hair who didn't seem to realize how pretty she was. Because she was lovely, and her family was wealthy, Robin was automatically invited to all of the popular girls' activities, from after-lesson swimming parties at Jennifer's house to movies, shopping expeditions, and Friday night private-school mixers that Jane heard about on Saturdays. But Robin rarely went—her parents were strict but, more than that, she seemed to prefer the company of horses and books, just like Jane. So "the clique," as Jane and Robin called them, had pretty much decided she was hopeless, and Robin didn't care one bit. Jane never told her that she couldn't understand why Robin wouldn't want to be a part of this bright, shining group with their late parties and their wild older brothers who took them out in the new cars they got for their sixteenth birthdays. Some of them even had boyfriends, though they were all only thirteen or fourteen. Jane was embarrassed to tell Robin how much she wanted to be a part of what Robin could be, if only she chose.

Jessica was another story. She was a funny, frank girl who went to the same school as Alyssa, Jennifer, and Robin and happily accepted her natural place with the clique. But although the other girls treated Jane with indifference or condescension, Jessica was, remarkably, often nice to her. She seemed to like Jane, and she was brave enough to show it when the mood struck her. They were not close, but Jane could count on Jessica to be friendly and even to sometimes include her in the gossip sessions after the lessons. She wasn't particularly loyal, but she didn't pretend that Jane didn't exist, or comment on the fact that Jane went to a backwater all-girls Catholic school, or that her family lived in a ramshackle house in the middle of downtown Louisville, far from the plush suburban villages nearly all the others called home.

"Time to go in," Susan said, and the riders turned their horses toward the barns. Jane stroked Beau's mane and dropped her feet from her stirrups, letting him walk with a long, relaxed rein back to the stables.

"Nice course," said a voice on her left. "For a school horse."

Jane looked up to meet the eyes of the girl she feared would be her biggest competition for a slot in Advanced I—Emily Longstreet. A stocky, athletic girl with an oddly ill-matched, narrow face, she was an aggressive rider and vocal about her own abilities. This would be her second summer at the farm—her family had moved to Kentucky from Atlanta—and she was a dogged fourth wheel to Alyssa, Jennifer, and Jessica. Jane hadn't liked her since camp last year. Besides her frequent complaints about how much cooler and more interesting Atlanta was (which, Jane noticed, Alyssa and company tired of as well) and her short temper toward both her horse, Georgia Belle, and her friends, if she felt left out or slighted, Emily also seemed to believe that being nasty to Jane was part and parcel of keeping her place in the clique.

"Hey, that rhymes, Emily," Jane said shakily. "I didn't know you were a poet."

Jessica, pulling her horse, Quixotic, next to theirs, laughed. "I can think of a better subject for you, Em: 'Oh, Matt, my heart goes splat. When I think of you, I turn to goo.'"

Jane flushed, smiling as Emily scowled, though she had no idea who they were talking about. But Emily was noticeably boy-crazy.

"That's completely retarded," she said coldly.

Jessica threw Emily a look of innocent surprise. "*Hmmm*. I don't think poets say *retarded*. You might need to work on the vocab." She turned Quixotic back toward Alyssa and Jennifer, and the triumvirate started talking about their plans for that evening, leaving Jane and Emily in an uncomfortable silence. Jane broke it by nudging Beau into a trot, pulling away from Georgia Belle.

She stopped him in the shade of the barn and dismounted, pretending to be absorbed in pulling up the stirrups, undoing his girth, and taking off the saddle and pad—she didn't want the others thinking that she cared about their plans or about what Emily had said. But she did care, almost desperately, she thought now, both about having a horse of her own and being a part of a group. "I'm so *tired* of being different," she whispered to Beau as she pulled off his bridle and he began rubbing his head vigorously on her arm. She turned, offering him her back, and he almost knocked her over with the force of his happy nuzzles. The other girls rarely let their horses do this—"Ugh," Liz would shout at Lady Blue, "you're making me filthy!"—but Jane loved Beau and would do anything for him, including getting a shirt full of horsehair and sweat and slobber. Riding, she often thought, was not for those afraid of a little dirt.

After walking Beau until he was cool, Jane turned him out in the big pasture behind the barn and watched as he trotted toward a group of horses swishing flies under a copse of trees by the pond. The hazy, rich green of the grass and the heavy branches of the oaks curving down over the gently sloping pasture were Jane's ideal of beauty. She'd found a painting by Thomas Hart Benton in one of her mother's art books and thought that he must have been painting Kentucky. When she'd told her art teacher how much she liked his work, the teacher laughed, calling her "old-fashioned."

*Maybe that's what's the matter with me,* she thought, folding her arms over the white fence rail. *Maybe I was meant to be living in the turn of the century or during the Depression or World War II. When horses were a part of everyday life, either riding them or watching their races. Man O'War, War Admiral . . . they were heroes, and they had Kentucky blood running through their veins.* She shivered happily, picturing herself as a groom, or even a jockey, in what seemed like such an uncomplicated time. *And if I'd been a boy, I wouldn't have to worry about being popular.*

*And I could wear one of those gray felt hats.* Jane tried to picture Alyssa or Emily feeling this way and laughed out loud—at herself, at how crazy they'd think she was if she ever actually said these things.

"Did Beau just tell you a good joke?" Robin had walked up and joined her at the fence.

"No," Jane said, "I was trying to picture Emily in a fedora and trench coat, like in *Casablanca*."

"Okay, I'm not even going to ask." Robin chuckled. "I don't think I want to know the train of thought that got you there."

"So only one more Saturday lesson before camp...." Jane said, knowing Robin would understand her meaning.

"And only one more chance to be judged for which group we'll be put in," Robin finished. They'd discussed this endlessly on the phone all week, creating different scenarios and unlikely lucky breaks. If Emily fell ... if Jennifer suddenly lost all interest in horses ...

"I know who it's going to be," Robin said firmly. "Alyssa, Jennifer, Jessica, and you. You're the best riders, and that's all there is to it."

"But what about Emily? And you? You're a great rider." Jane looked at her friend with concern. All of their previous conversations had ended by deciding that, somehow, both she and Robin would be in the top group.

"You know I get scared on the big jumps, and Advanced I is going to be really tough. I think I'd rather be in Advanced II." Robin spoke with such certainty that Jane couldn't believe her ears.

"But don't you *want* to be chosen for Advanced I anymore?" she asked.

"Not if it means not having a good time. I've been thinking about it a lot this week, and all I really want this summer is to hang out with you, and to ride Bess and hopefully keep getting better with her. And I don't think I will if I'm always worried about what Susan's going to make us do next."

"Wow" was all Jane could think of to say. She couldn't imagine not wanting to be promoted to the top group, no matter how scary or tough the lessons were going to become. Despite her solitariness and her reluctant awareness that she wasn't quite like the other girls, a desire to win was hardwired into her. She didn't talk about her ambition except jokingly, with Robin, or sometimes with her sister, Lily, but it burned in her like a deep, sure flame. She wanted to be the best.

"Well," she finally said, "then we'll both have to be happy in Advanced II, because Emily is going to make it, not me. I'm the only one who doesn't have my own horse, and it wouldn't be fair for Susan to always let me ride Beau. They're going to need him for other lessons. You heard Susan today—she practically said that she didn't think I should ride him all the time. She's probably preparing me for this summer, when I'll have to ride whoever's free. And I can't exactly picture Brownie or Fleur making it over triple combinations and water obstacles."

Robin couldn't help laughing at the picture of two of the oldest, most sedate school horses trying to keep up with the likes of Ariel and Thunder. "Well, at least we'd get to ride together, but I'm still betting that Susan puts you in the top group," she said loyally.

"Nope," Jane said, affecting a breezy tone, "it's me and Brownie and you and Bess in the minor leagues. Beau's not my horse, and I have to stop pretending that he is."

She smiled bravely at her friend, but she hated saying the awful truth out loud.

*Chapter 2*

# Worry

Robin hadn't really answered her question about Emily, and Jane knew she had reason to worry about her chances at beating her for a spot in Advanced I.

The next Friday night, she sat at the kitchen table, sketching a picture of Beau standing under the oak trees, trying to capture the half-wise, half-comical glint in his eyes. Her mother peered over her shoulder.

"Is that our hero Beau?" she asked, leaning her chin on her daughter's shoulder.

"Mm-hmm," Jane replied. "He's so handsome, though, I can't do him justice." *Handsome* wasn't really the right word for Beau, she knew. His slightly Roman nose, over-size ears, and shortish neck prevented him from being a traditionally beautiful horse, but to Jane his personality and ability, and their longtime comradeship, more than made up for what others might consider his plainness.

"When I was your age, the only boys I thought were handsome were of the human variety," Grace Ryan said, then smiled at the skeptical look on Jane's face.

"Mum, please, I don't want to know." Jane redoubled her efforts, shading in Beau's mane and forelock.

Mrs. Ryan sighed and went back to drying the dishes. She understood her daughter's love of drawing better than her love of horses. She was a painter herself and taught at the local university, where Jane's father taught history.

Trying for a combination of dignity and mischief, Jane realized that her drawing made Beau look half-asleep, so she got up to help her mother, wondering for the thousandth time why her family was the only one she knew that didn't have a dishwasher. Even their toaster and coffeepot were older than Jane, but at least the Ryans had those. Still, as she stacked the blue-and-white plates in the cupboard, she also knew how much she loved their old house, with its wide pine floorboards, high ceilings, and enormous windows with their wavy, imperfect glass. It was a big house in a run-down neighborhood in downtown Louisville, where many students and professors lived. Mr. Ryan claimed that he bought it for the willow tree in the front yard, and Mrs. Ryan said it was for the wavy glass.

Everything about 648 Chestnut Street felt like home, from the overburdened bookcases to the small screened porch in back, where they ate during the summer. The house was so drafty and difficult to heat that in the winter they had their meals on a low table in front of the fireplace in the living room, sitting on cushions on the floor. When Jane had dinner with Robin's family for the first time and they'd gathered around the dining room table, she'd blurted out, "Why are we eating on chairs—it's not Thanksgiving!" and Robin, who'd been over to the Ryan house many times, had nearly collapsed laughing, while her parents looked on in confusion.

No, Jane was glad she didn't live in the Winding Falls subdivision with Robin's grand, chilly family in their perfectly appointed, almost-new brick mansion. She was glad she had the sort of parents she did—funny, impractical, absentminded people who talked to her and her sister about ideas and books and art, as if they were grown-ups, too. She wouldn't trade any of it, not really, not even if it somehow guaranteed her admittance to the clique. Of course, it was much easier to remember that here, in the snug yellow kitchen with her mother, than it was at Sunny Acres. Yes, she'd keep the lack of a dishwasher, the pipes freezing in the winter and making hills in the kitchen floor, even being downtown, and thus an hour away from the farm—if only they could figure out a way to afford for her to have a horse of her own. For her to have Beau.

And soon this house that she loved was going to change irrevocably, and Jane couldn't bear to think about it. Lily would be going away to college in the fall. Everything was going to be different. No longer would she hear Lily singing in the bathroom every morning, her voice carried through the vent to Jane's attic bedroom, waking her up. No longer would Lily fling herself dramatically on Jane's bed, recounting tales of disastrous dates and nerve-shattering auditions, beastly high-school teachers, and her dreams of becoming a famous actress. No longer would Jane be able to knock on Lily's door late at night, slipping into her sister's messy, clothes-strewn room, and tell Lily all of her fears about not being popular, not being pretty enough, not fitting in. Part of Lily's magic was that she always seemed to know what to say and could always make Jane laugh.

Tonight, Jane couldn't think about it. Tonight, all she could think about was the next day's lesson.

Tonight, all she wanted was to be named one of the best riders at Sunny Acres.

But could she do it without a horse of her own?

*Jane tore up* the drawing of sleepy Beau, walked down the narrow hall that connected the kitchen to her father's study, and pushed open the screen door leading to the porch. She could smell her father's pipe and saw his profile emerge from the large wicker armchair, where he sat and listened to the crickets and birds on summer evenings. Looking out over the leafy, still backyard in the dusk, you could forget you were downtown.

"Ready for a game of slipper in the fan?" he asked,

and their small speckled mutt, Hopper, pricked his ears. It was his favorite sport: Mr. Ryan would turn on the porch's ceiling fan, throw one of his ancient leather slippers up to its blades, and Hopper would madly scramble to catch the flying slipper wherever it was tossed. On the small porch, it couldn't go far, and Mrs. Ryan had learned long ago not to keep any breakables or delicate plants in the vicinity.

"Sure," Jane said, and reached up to pull the fan's cord. But something in her voice made her father pause, slipper in hand, and turn to her.

"Maybe not just now," he said to Hopper, and lay an apologetic hand on the dog's head. Hopper put his chin back on his paws and seemed content to resume dozing. Jane slumped into a chair next to her father and stared out into the firefly-speckled square of dark beyond the screens.

"Are you glad school's almost over?" Geoffrey Ryan asked.

"I guess," Jane said. She was, in fact, looking forward to the last day of school and, more important, the last day of eighth grade. Next year she would enter high school, and she still hadn't decided where she was going to go. For weeks, her parents had been reminding her that she had to make a decision. She could stay at St. Anne's, where she'd been since fifth grade. Although the Ryans weren't Catholic (in fact, they never went to church at all), they'd enrolled Jane because of the school's academics, and because it was the only private school they could afford, convinced Jane wasn't "challenged" enough at the public elementary school she'd started in. Jane was bored of St. Anne's, though she liked the nuns and her classes for the most part, and liked teasing her parents about saying Masses for their souls. But she hadn't grown very close to the girls there—who had known one another since kindergarten, and who sometimes admired her drawing in Art but otherwise left her alone—and the school was a long bus ride away. Plus she'd worried to Lily that if she never spent time with boys—after all, Sunny Acres was almost all girls as well—she'd soon be even more of a social disaster than she already was.

Then there were the two other schools where she had a place—one was Collegiate, the prestigious high school Robin, and Alyssa and her friends, would be attending next year, and where she'd been offered a partial scholarship through the Ryans' affiliation with the university. The other she had discussed with her parents only in passing: Martin Luther King Jr. High, called simply "MLK" by the bands of students that Jane often saw rambling down Chestnut Street in the afternoon, was her local public school (at only five blocks from her house, very local). Camouflaged by the dull blue-and-green plaid of her own school uniform, Jane thought these clutches of teenagers looked like shaggy, rather exotic birds: students of all races in all possible manners of styles and clothes.

"I want to go someplace new," she said, thinking aloud. She could always do this with her father.

"Well, I can understand that," Mr. Ryan said. "But don't you think being in high school will be new enough without changing schools?"

This was logical, but still Jane wanted to shout, *No! I*

*want to go somewhere that I can be a new person! Where I can start over and walk down halls where I'm not the Jane who never quite fits anywhere.* She'd fantasized about Collegiate, the rolling, manicured green lawns of the campus, the mellow brick buildings trimmed with white, and the funny school traditions and catchphrases Alyssa and Jennifer always referenced. About actually having Robin with her every day . . . and that suddenly (somehow, miraculously) she would be accepted into the clique. The dances. The swimming parties. Knowing, for once, what everyone was talking about . . .

But what if it didn't work? What if she remained the misfit, just like she was at Sunny Acres? And what if Robin tired of Jane and decided to accept Alyssa's invitations, leaving her out? Why *would* she want to stay friends with the Gayle M. Rapley Children of Faculty Fellow who had to study all the time to keep up her grades? Not to mention that even with the scholarship, Collegiate would still be more expensive than St. Anne's, the possibility of a horse of her own even more remote. . . . Jane got tired just thinking about it—it was all too complicated, too impossible to sort out.

"Dad, I don't want to talk about it right now, okay?"

"Okay," Mr. Ryan replied softly, and Jane silently thanked him for saying nothing else. She knew her father was beginning to worry about her school choice, and she felt a warm surge toward him for understanding that she needed time to decide—and that she wasn't going to decide tonight. She had something else to ask him, however hopeless it might be.

Jane took a deep breath. "There's something else I wanted to talk about."

"I had a feeling." Jane could hear the smile in his voice.

"It's just that camp is coming up soon. And it's going to be different this year—it's going to be much more competitive, and Susan's dividing my group into two. And Dad, I've got to be in the top group, I just *have* to, and I don't think I will be, and"—Jane felt unwanted tears welling into her eyes—"and I just wish that I could have my own horse, more than anything. I don't care *what* school I go to next year, really, I just want to be able to ride my own horse this summer, more than anything I've ever wanted in my whole *life,* Dad!" She stopped, unable to continue.

Mr. Ryan sighed. "Honey, you know we've talked about this before—" he began.

"I know! And you always say the same thing!" Jane tried to keep her voice calm, like his, but all of her emotions came rushing up, and she felt powerless to stop the tears that began coursing down her cheeks.

"It's because that thing is true—we simply can't afford it," Mr. Ryan said with finality. "I wish we could, but we can't. It's hard enough paying for school, and for your lessons and camp. And now with Lily going to college, even with her theater scholarship, it's going to be even tougher. I know how much you want a horse, but—"

"You don't know!" Jane cried. "Nobody understands at all!" Jane ran from the porch, knowing she was being unfair, but filled with such a painful ache and frustration that she had to be alone. They couldn't understand that riding was to her what acting was to Lily—the thing that made Jane herself and no one else. The thing that was hers.

She shut herself in her room and pretended to be asleep when her mother, then Lily, came to say good night. Finally, her father opened her door, and she peeked out from her covers. His worried face framed in the doorway, he whispered, "Good night, Jane. I love you." He turned off the hall light, and Jane surrendered to tears of remorse and longing.

## Chapter 3

# The Nutty Knight

J anoo, time to wake up!" Jane opened her eyes and
found Lily sitting on the edge of her bed, softly shaking
her.

"Hi," she murmured. "What are you doing up so
early?" Lily was a notoriously late sleeper on the weekends,
declaring Saturday mornings "sacred." Now she looked
half-asleep still, her wavy dark brown hair sticking up at
alarming angles, her eyes drowsy. Jane—and too many
boys for their father's peace of mind—thought Lily looked
like a movie star: petite and curvy (unlike Jane, who was
tall and stick-straight), with enormous deep blue eyes and
a wide, full smile.

"I thought I'd make you breakfast. Today's a pretty big day, isn't it?" Lily said.

Jane grinned at her. Of course Lily hadn't forgotten. Even with graduation in just a few days, she'd remembered that Jane had told her that today she'd be judged for which group she'd ride in at camp. Jane sat up and hugged her sister. "You're my hero," she said.

"This is indeed one of my nobler sacrifices. You'd better get ready. I'm making French toast and Oeufs à la Lily." These were Jane's favorite—eggs fried over so hard that their father always complained that they were like eating leather.

The phone rang as Jane was swirling her eggs in syrup, causing more groans of protest from Mr. Ryan. "Have you heard?" Robin asked breathlessly.

"What? No—heard what?" Jane felt a sudden burst of hope. Maybe Emily had decided to go to the beach this summer! Maybe Alyssa had come down with the flu! Robin's next words brought her back to earth.

"Emily got a new horse. They brought him to Sunny Acres two days ago. I heard he's this huge chestnut warmblood, and he's, like, almost seventeen hands. . . . Jane, are you there?"

Jane's mind *had* actually wandered. "But what about Georgia Belle?" She was picturing Emily's other horse, a lithe black Thoroughbred with a big white blaze running down her face.

"Her parents sold Belle to one of their friends. They

have a daughter who wants to start riding, I guess. But Jane, this horse is practically a champion. He's won big competitions already."

"But how can she just sell Georgia Belle like that?" Jane asked incredulously. "Like she's just a . . . a . . . *chair* or something?"

"I know," Robin said. "But I don't think Emily felt about her the way you feel about Beau or I feel about Bess. She was just a horse."

*Just* a horse?

And then it hit her. "Rob, if Emily's . . . if the new horse . . ."

Her voice trailed off. But she was sure Robin could guess what she was thinking. With a new horse, a champion, Emily might be impossible to beat for a place in Advanced I.

*Unfortunately,* Jane had a long car ride to think about it. Sunny Acres was in the true farmland of Kentucky, on the road to Lexington and an hour from downtown. It was half that distance for Robin and the other girls, who lived in communities like Winding Falls, which had such similar names (Willow Creek, Oak Bluffs) that Jane always got them confused. Because of the distance, and the Ryans' budget, during the school year Jane only rode on Saturdays, but the girls who boarded their horses at the farm went several times a week. Luckily for her parents' patience, and their aging car, Robin's family drove Jane back to their house after lessons, and she got a ride the rest of the way with the Zimmermans' silent, somewhat forbidding housekeeper, Mrs. Lakovic, who lived a few blocks over from Jane.

When Jane's mother dropped her off, the sky was gray and low over the farm, threatening rain, and the warm early-summer air smelled of electricity. It made her heart race, the brewing feeling of the day, the way the green of the fields and trees stood out against the dark and light clouds scudding across the sky. An intermittent breeze tossed up sawdust around the entrance to the first barn. Jane felt as unsettled as the weather.

Jane squared her shoulders and tried to put the thought of Emily's horse from her mind, but it stayed with her, knotting her stomach. What was going to happen today? Had she just lost what slim chance she had?

Emily was at the center of a group of riders standing around the door of the second stall, talking loudly. "Isn't he awesome?" she exclaimed.

"Absolutely," Alyssa said brightly and hugged her friend. "I'm so glad you finally have a horse that's as good as Ariel."

Jane saw Emily's face twist with annoyance.

Jane stood at the edge of the group, her presence unacknowledged, and peered into the stall. She caught a glimpse of strong, tall, brilliantly chestnut hindquarters, saw a flash of white-stockinged legs restlessly pacing. Then the horse swung around suddenly, almost charging the door—

Enormous liquid eyes, flaring pink nostrils, a neck

arched like a bow. A short red mane that bristled from the muscular curve of his neck like brushfire. Ears pricked forward, then pinning back as the magnificent horse lunged, snorting furiously at the girls hovering outside, his hooves banging against the door.

"What a sweetheart," Jessica muttered.

"Oh, he's just stirred up," Emily said nonchalantly. "It's being in a new place. He should settle down soon. You know, he's pure Hanoverian, and they're, like, the best ever."

"I heard your first ride wasn't that smooth," Jessica said. Her voice was casual, but the sharp look she gave Emily made the chestnut horse's new owner flush.

"He'll be fine today."

"Mm. Well, we should get tacked up. You behave yourself, big boy." Jessica reached in to stroke the white swirl of hair, like an elongated question mark, on the giant horse's forehead, then quickly drew her hand back at his bared teeth. "Good lord!" She laughed, unperturbed.

Jane caught up with her at the tack room.

"So what happened when she rode him?"

"We-ell," Jessica drawled, "he was a nightmare. Keep this to yourself"—Jane was sure she was the last person to hear the story, but she appreciated Jessica's mercurial camaraderie—"but Liz came out to ride with her yesterday, and she said he was crazy. Tried to kick Lady Blue, totally spazzed out in the ring, almost threw Emily. Finally Susan had to get on him to settle him down." Jessica rolled her eyes.

"But I thought he had won shows already," Jane said.

"That's the thing—he has. A bunch. His owner only sold him because she's going to college in California. Or so she said. She hadn't shown him since last fall, though, and the rumor is that she was having problems with him, too."

"Then why did Emily's parents buy him?" Jane wondered.

"Because their darling daughter wanted him. She only saw him for a second, over at Long Run, and fell for the flashy look and the blue ribbons hanging from his stall. She's been whining at her parents nonstop, but her dad kept saying they couldn't afford it. She must've worn him down. Lord knows what's going to happen. He could be the best horse here—or he could break her neck."

"I guess we'll find out," Jane said, gathering one of the beat-up saddles that belonged to the barn and taking Beau's bridle down from its peg. A saddle of her own would be nice, she thought, as she always did, like the gleaming, padded leather Jessica held over one arm. Each week she used one of the pancake-flat, hard saddles that she shared with the beginners. Still, she was used to it. It was odd hearing of Emily being denied, at least for more than a second, something she had her heart set on. But she'd gotten the horse in the end, whatever the price.

"Exactly," Jessica said, with a small, mischievous smile. "In fact, this could be your chance, right?" Jane blushed. Jessica never missed a thing. But even if Emily's new horse acted up, she doubted that Susan would drop her to

27

Advanced II. The horse was supposed to have enormous potential, and Emily was a good rider.

She decided not to take the bait. "So what's his name, anyway?" she asked.

"Lancelot," Jessica replied. "The noble knight. Scratch that—the *nutty* knight."


*Beau nickered as* Jane entered his stall. "It's just like any other day," she told him, and herself. She stood for a moment with her cheek against his neck, feeling his warmth and taking deep breaths of his dusty summer smell. He turned his head and nibbled ruminatively on the end of her T-shirt. She stroked his muzzle. He had a large, plain face—an honest face, Jane thought, and a very intelligent one. "Time to get beautiful," and as Beau sighed, she laughed. "I swear you speak English, boy."

She started with the currycomb, moving in broad circles over his back and hindquarters, avoiding the sensitive skin on his legs. Then she ran the hard brush in vigorous strokes over his coat and finally used the soft brush over his head and legs. She combed out his mane and did the best she could with his tangled tail. Beau leaned heavily on her as she raised his right foreleg to pick his hoof, and she reminded him that she was not a crutch. He relaxed further, and Jane resigned herself to propping up his weight with her shoulder as she tugged at the clumps of grass and mud.

Yes, taking care of a horse was a lot of work, she

thought, but it was work Jane loved. She remembered the very first time she came to Sunny Acres, and how Jose, the barn manager, had taken her hand and led her into Brownie's stall. "If you want to ride horses, you must first learn to care for them," he'd said, his kind face smiling but serious. "Remember that anything really worthwhile takes a lot of work, a lot of love. And being around horses is just about the most worthwhile thing there is." Jane remembered how enormous Brownie had looked—Jane's head barely reached his chest. Jose had placed a soft brush in her hands and showed her how to brush as much of Brownie's coat as she could reach, then helped her up on an overturned bucket so she could clean his back and mane. "Talk to him," he'd instructed. "Get him used to your voice and hands. Let him know you're going to be friends." And Jane had been talking to—and caring for—horses at Sunny Acres ever since.

"How's Beau today?" Jane let the horse's leg down and looked up to see Jose outside the stall, pitchfork in hand. He and his family were from Mexico, and he often told Jane stories about the Tijuana track, where Seabiscuit raced, and the great Mexican horses and jockeys. His grandsons Ricky and Gabriel worked at Sunny Acres, too.

"He's fine. His tail's a mess, though," Jane replied.

"You take real good care of that horse," Jose said.

"Well, you taught me."

"I taught just about every girl who rides here, and not all of them learned the lessons. They just want to ride—let someone else do the work."

That was true, Jane knew. Not everyone liked Sunny Acres' policy that riders must care for the school horses they rode as if they were their own, from grooming to mucking out their stalls to cleaning their tack. She often saw the other girls, especially the ones who boarded their horses, giving their mounts to Jose or Ricky or Gabriel to groom and to cool out after riding. "Well, what are they paid for?" Alyssa had said once. But Jane thought that the Reyes family had plenty to do anyway; after all, they did the real, everyday work with the school horses and the barns, in addition to the maintenance of the fields and riding arenas, and a myriad of other chores.

"It's not really work for me," Jane said gamely, then laughed as Jose raised his eyebrows, looking pointedly at Jane's dirty fingernails, the dust and slobber on her T-shirt, and the sweat that beaded up on her forehead.

"Sure," he said, and winked at her.

*Jane's muscles were burning*, and sweat poured down her face. They'd been doing a posting trot without stirrups for ages now, it seemed, but still no word from Susan to walk. Beau had a big, jogging stride, and Jane concentrated on rising and falling evenly, not being bounced around by his natural springiness of step. She checked the position of her lower leg, tight and behind the girth, heels down as if they were pressing into stirrups. She tried to keep her upper body steady, her hands in position.

The other girls looked tired, too—Jane saw Liz and Shannon sneaking a few moments of sitting when Susan's back was turned—but Emily looked positively frazzled. Lancelot was trotting fast and choppy, his head high, fighting Emily's tight grip on the reins. He kept trying to break into a canter, and Jane could hear Emily calling to him to slow down. He fought her, desperate to run, his vibrant chestnut coat growing dark with sweat, his mouth starting to foam at the corners where the bit dug in. "I'm getting this crazy horse a curb bit tomorrow," Emily said to Alyssa through clenched teeth as she passed her. Alyssa smiled serenely back, posting easily on Ariel's liquid stride. Emily glared at her, then yanked on the reins, hard, and shouted, "Whoa!"

"I don't think shouting is going to work, Emily," Susan said with a warning note in her voice. "Okay, everybody walk. Emily, let's think about what you're doing. You need to calm your horse down, take it slow and steady. No yelling and no punishment. He's in a new place with strange horses—have some patience with him."

Emily took a deep breath and nodded, but Lancelot continued to tug at the reins, shying and skittering into a fast jog, his whole body like a coiled spring about to be set loose. He champed on the bit, tossed his head, looked at the other horses in wild-eyed challenge. He was paying no attention to his rider, who grew more and more tense and stiff in the saddle.

"Pick your stirrups up and knot your reins, everybody," Susan said, and seeing the look of disbelief on

Emily's face, she added, "You, too, Emily. Just give it a try. If you can't control him, you can take them right back."

Jane tied her reins just above Beau's withers and let her arms relax at her sides. She loved this exercise—riding without reins, guiding Beau with only her legs, seat, and voice. It made her feel tall and free, and when Beau responded well, it was like they actually were, as Susan had said last week, a centaur. The pressure from the bit relaxed, Beau stretched his neck down and snorted.

"Posting trot," Susan said, and the riders urged their horses forward again. The group was a bit chaotic at first; Bess took a corner sharply, and Bebop decided to wander to the center of the ring and stop under the shade of the trees. Beau was going well, though he, too, would not go deep into the corners until Jane applied a strong inside leg. Susan noticed. "Very nice, Jane! See how he responded when you corrected him? Next time use that leg before you reach the turn and see if you can keep him to the rail all the way." Jane focused, sweat stinging the corners of her eyes, entirely absorbed in Beau and his position along the rail. She no longer had any sense of the other riders, except when she approached their horses and either guided Beau around them—a tricky business with no reins—or slowed him down with her voice to stay behind them. She felt so good, she stretched her arms up above her head, then windmilled them from side to side, eyes straight ahead, keeping her balance well. "Very nice indeed," Susan said approvingly as Beau jogged by her.

Suddenly Jane heard the pounding of hooves behind

her, a thunderous tattoo, and Beau pinned his ears back and jerked his head up sharply. In a flash of red, Lancelot was beside them, bounding in a great leap around Beau and shooting past them down the long stretch of the arena. Emily was thrown up onto his neck, clutching at the reins, trying to stop him. Beau had startled, and Jane grabbed the reins and brought him to a standstill, watching the blur of flame in the trees at the far end of the ring.

"Everybody halt!" Susan yelled. The magnificent horse was now galloping back toward them, his head high, his eyes showing their whites, the face of his rider pale and tense above his blazing mane. She leaned back, sawing at the reins, and he stopped abruptly and reared. Emily screamed, and the other horses stirred uneasily; even Ariel pranced under Alyssa's firm hand. It was all over in seconds—Lancelot's forelegs sawed the air, then he plunged back to earth, took a mighty but awkward leap sideways and forward, and Emily, precariously balanced on the very back of the saddle, lost her stirrups and fell to the earth as Lancelot sprang forward, racing his shadow around the ring.

Susan ran to the fallen rider, but Emily was already up, dusting off the seat of her britches and looking at the enormous chestnut horse with an unattractive mixture of disgust and apprehension.

"Holy-moly," Robin said to Jane, pulling Bess up beside her.

"That's the first time I've seen Emily look scared," Jane replied.

"I would be, too," Robin answered truthfully. "That horse is acting like he's totally untrained. But at least she's not hurt." Indeed, Susan was checking Emily over, and Emily was shaking her head and gesticulating with her arms, obviously indicating that she was fine—but furious. Susan left her and flagged down the galloping horse, walking calmly toward him with her left arm out to the side, as if blocking him from afar, and her right hand stretched out, palm cupped, like she had something in it for him. Lancelot stopped and, surprisingly, allowed himself to be caught with a minimum of fuss.

"You're smart, but you're acting dumb," Jane heard Susan say to the horse, surveying him with her keen, observant eyes. She checked his girth, the fit of his bridle, and ran her hands down his legs, searching for any discomfort or injury that might be causing the horse's behavior. Apparently, she found nothing, and she led him back to his rider, who was staring at him with a very grim expression on her face.

"Can you get back on?" Susan asked. Emily nodded, and Susan gave her a leg up, then led Lancelot to the center of the ring, where he stood, trembling, sweat darkening his brilliant flanks.

"She's got serious guts," Shannon said, but Jessica shook her head.

"No, she wants to get even," she said. "If I were that horse, I'd look out."

Susan set up two simple cross-rails on opposite sides of the ring. "Okay, everybody, take the first one at a trot and the second jump at a controlled canter. Emily, you stay here, and if you feel like you want to try it, go ahead and bring Lancelot out after Lady Blue. Robin, take Bess first, please."

The riders filed out behind Bess, picking up a trot and all going easily over the low jump. Liz kept Lady Blue well behind the others and looked nervously over her shoulder at Emily as she finally asked her horse to trot. For a moment, Emily hesitated, and Jane felt sure she was going to stay where she was, but then she brought Lancelot behind Lady Blue, and he picked up a fast, nervous jog. They approached the jump and Lancelot suddenly burst into a canter, exploding from Emily's hands like a cannon, and he bounded toward the jump in three huge strides, sailing over it with several feet to spare.

"Well, now we know he can jump!" Susan shouted, but Emily didn't reply. Her lips were set in a grim line as she tugged at the reins, trying to slow Lancelot down. He stopped abruptly, and now she had to switch tactics and urge him forward. He went into a fairly controlled canter, but as he neared the second jump he shied abruptly, almost unseating her. Jane had just cleared the first jump for the second time, and she saw Emily pull up next to Lady Blue and ask Liz something. Liz handed Emily her crop, and Emily gave Lancelot a heel in his ribs.

He started forward immediately, heading again for the second cross-rail. Jane, her stomach knotting, brought Beau away from the rail and stopped him in the shade, hoping that Susan wouldn't notice her with all the dust and commotion of the other riders trotting and cantering around the arena. Lancelot eyed the jump warily, his ears pointed forward, his head tossing. "You just went over one exactly like it, you big silly," Jane whispered to herself. "Why make such a production now?" Emily had a death grip on her reins, but she was simultaneously digging her heels into Lancelot's sides, and the big chestnut was in a frenzy of confusion, springing forward, then coming to a sudden halt five strides before the jump. He froze, stock-still, and Jane found that she was holding her breath. "Turn him around," she whispered. "Let him get into a nice easy trot, let him look at it again from farther away." But Emily seemed determined to take the jump from a near-standing position. She kicked Lancelot again, he took three jolting strides, then ducked away to the right, hitting Emily's leg against the rail.

What happened next seemed to take place in slow motion, the seconds stretched out unendurably. Jane later realized that she'd shouted, "Wait—" even before Emily's arm raised high above her head as she grabbed her reins in her left hand and slashed at her horse with the crop, bringing it down again and again on his hindquarters. Lancelot wheeled and plunged and gave a shrieking neigh of pain and perplexity. Before he could bolt, Emily swung off his back, flinging the reins over his head, and bringing the crop down again with all her strength. Lancelot reared, and Emily fell backward in the dust, letting go of the reins and rolling over to avoid the hooves that came plunging earthward once more. She was back on her feet in a flash, and before Lancelot had time to escape, she grabbed the reins and brought the crop down on his neck.

Then Susan, running all out, reached her and grabbed her wrist, shouting, "That's enough!"

All of the other horses had stopped, their riders frozen in their saddles. Everyone stared at the frenzied chestnut, trying desperately to get away from the girl who stood before him, crop clenched in her right hand, staring at him in crimson-faced fury.

"Emily, walk away. Now!" Jane had never seen Susan so angry. But neither had she seen any rider at the farm treat her horse like this.

Emily threw Lancelot's reins to Susan, turned on her heel, and stalked toward the gate. Suddenly she turned. "It's your fault," Emily said in a low voice.

"What did you say to me?" Susan demanded.

"I said it's your fault. I never should have ridden that horse without reins. I'm going to tell my father you put me in danger. It's *your fault.*" She turned and stomped out of the ring, and Susan opened her mouth to yell after her, then took a deep breath and turned back to the sweat-drenched horse, standing with his head held high, his great chest heaving.

"This lesson is over," she said quietly, and placed her hand on Lancelot's neck. He started back, as if she were going to hit him, and she shushed him softly, then led him away. As they passed Beau, Jane looked at Lancelot's chiseled head, still held high, and saw to her amazement that water was pouring from his eyes.

## Chapter 4

# The First Long Night of Six (Long?) Weeks

J ane found the note tucked inside her sleeping bag as she unrolled it over the mattress on the top bunk of her bed in the cabin she'd call home during the next six weeks of camp.

*Dear Jane, Please don't go to camp. Love, Lily.*

Jane smiled and squeezed the piece of paper tightly in her palm before putting it inside one of the leaves of her sketchbook. The note was part of a long-standing tradition between Jane and her sister—one that Jane had started when she was six years old. Lily, then ten, was going to camp for the first time, a dramatic arts program that was only a week long, but it was the first time she'd been away from home alone. Jane remembered the cold pit in her stomach as she'd watched their mother pack Lily's things the night before she left. So Jane had written a note in a childish scrawl and hid it in one of Lily's tennis shoes, packed in the bottom of her duffel bag. *Dear Lily, Please don't go to camp. Love, Jane.* Lily found the note her first night at camp, burst into tears, and called her parents, begging them to come and pick her up immediately. Mr. and Mrs. Ryan dissuaded her, scolded Jane, and then let Jane and Lily talk on the phone for an hour, until Jane fell asleep, the phone curled under her arm like a teddy bear.

Jane and Lily had been writing these notes to each other ever since. Now they were funny, especially ones that said things like: *Dear Lily, Please don't go to the school lock-in. Love, Jane* and *Dear Jane, Please don't spend the night with Robin. Love, Lily.* But although the notes had become a joke, and the sisters prided themselves on the ones tucked into each other's backpacks on the shortest of overnight visits, Jane also knew that part of them would always miss each other when they were separated—no matter for how short a time. And this was certainly the longest time Jane had ever been away from home. This six-week session was something of an experiment. Since starting the camp nine years before, the owners, Mr. and Mrs. Jeffrys, now had a group of skilled riders on their hands and had decided that a longer course of instruction for the older girls, in addition to the one- and two-week sessions for the newer riders, might be popular. It was: Everyone from Jane's group had immediately signed on. But six weeks was nothing compared with Lily's upcoming separation from her family—gone until Thanksgiving, and then only home for four days!

They had never gotten into each other's hair the way so many other siblings did—their interests were so different, *they* were so different, that they were actually interested in what the other was doing and were genuinely admiring of each other's talents. Lily hung Jane's pictures in her room, and Jane never missed a single one of Lily's plays. Jane thought it was amazing how her sister could *become* another person so fully, inhabiting a character like growing a new skin. She sometimes shivered as she watched Lily transform into Helen Keller, or Alice in Wonderland, or Juliet. And Lily thought Jane was astoundingly brave just for getting on a horse. Of course, Jane knew there was no bravery in it—but she still appreciated Lily's wide eyes and open mouth as she described difficult jumps and near escapes from branches and fence rails. To Jane, these things were easy compared with the thought of being on a stage, hundreds of eyes on you, expected to perform. Now *that*, Jane thought, was true bravery.

The cabin door banged open, and Jane heard footsteps coming down the hall. Alyssa sauntered in, carrying a package wrapped in noisily crinkling plastic, which she put at the foot of the bunk opposite Jane's, then collapsed gracefully on the bed. "Bring the bags in here, Mom," she called out, yawning. A very thin, tan woman with wrists wreathed in gold bracelets and a slim gold watch entered, holding a navy blue duffel bag with the initials AFT monogrammed on the side. "Where are the speakers for my iPod?" Alyssa demanded, rolling over on her side.

"Your father has them, if he hasn't lost them," Mrs. Taylor said.

Mother and daughter exchanged knowing looks. "Well, if he has lost them, he'll just have to buy me new ones and mail them here," Alyssa said flatly, and her mother nodded, a short, emphatic gesture that set the crown of her immaculate hairdo quivering.

"Sweetie? Sweetie, where are you?" a voice sounded in the hall.

"We're in *here,* Robert, *honestly.*"

Alyssa laughed, then yawned again as a tall, stooped man appeared in the doorway.

"Hello there," he said, blinking around the room, then settling his eyes on Jane. "And which one of Alyssa's friends are you?" he asked, smiling.

Alyssa snorted. "That's just Jane."

Jane blushed fiercely and made to get up and leave the room, but to her increased embarrassment, Mr. Taylor held out his hand and she had to shake it. "Well, I'm sure you'll be one of her friends soon enough. Your first year here? Everyone's a friend of Alyssa's. She'll show you around."

At this, Mrs. Taylor laughed as well. "Robert, Jane's been coming here for *ages.* You know—her parents are teachers. Don't you live . . . where is it, dear?"

"Chestnut Street," Jane managed, feeling Alyssa's bored eyes drilling into her.

"Ah," said Mr. Taylor. "A wonderful historic part of town. You have to be either in the city or else out at a place like this farm to get any real old houses with some soul in them. Though some of that history might not be all that pleasant. For instance, there's another plantation down the road from here—"

"Daddy, *please*," Alyssa moaned in protest. "Where are the new speakers for my music, did you remember them?"

Mr. Taylor started, blinking more rapidly. "Oh, yes, here they are, sorry, sweetie. . . ."

Jane finally made it out of the room, escaping the drone of complaint that continued behind her. Her face was still burning; Mr. Taylor had always seemed nicer than his daughter, or his wife, but every time she saw him, he introduced himself to her again, as if she had never made the slightest impression. Jane hated that she blushed so easily—sometimes she wasn't even feeling that shy or that awkward and she blushed anyway. Then, of course, someone would tease her about it, and the blush would just get worse. Jane sighed with exasperation at herself as she walked to the pasture.

Twilight hung softly over Sunny Acres, turning the grass emerald and making the outlines of the bright white fences circling the fields glow faintly in the evening colors of lilac, gold, and dark, dark green. As she walked toward the big pasture where most of the horses were turned out at night, she could see the main house, really a mansion, where Mr. and Mrs. Jeffrys lived. It was an imposing three-story antebellum manor with graceful white columns and large bay windows that overlooked the sweeping drive, lined with dogwoods, that curved up from the main gates, past the pond and the dressage ring. Behind the house were the two barns, white with dark green and red trim, and one with a covered passage that led to the indoor riding arena. To the right of the last barn was the older girls' small single-story cabin, with its irregular pine floorboards and ceilings braced by rough wood beams.

Robin, whose little brother had some epic, all-day soccer tournament in Cincinnati, wouldn't arrive until much later, so this evening Jane was alone with the other girls or, more likely, with her thoughts. Walking along the curve of the gravel path toward the main pasture, she could hear behind her the slam of car doors and shrieks of reunion as girls who had just seen each other a few days before threw themselves into each other's arms, squealing, *Omigod!* And *I can't wait to tell you—!* She turned to look at the cabin, the warm glow of its windows illuminating the old bowed oak before it, and the white headlights of cars catching the barns. She could make out the voices of Shannon, Jennifer, and then Jessica's husky laugh. She kept walking.

"Beau," she called out softly, lest the girls overhear her. "Beau, are you out there?" She could see dark shapes moving under the trees. She clucked more loudly, then called out again, "Beau?" One of the shadows detached it-self from the dark mass, and she heard the pressing of hooves against grass, a deep, quiet swish in the still twi-light. "Beau?" she called again, but then she recognized his long, loping stride, and a rush of gratitude filled her chest. Here was someone who was glad to see her.

He approached the fence, his ears perked, looking quizzically and somewhat sleepily toward her. "Hi, boy," Jane whispered, and she climbed up onto the fence. Beau stopped before her and blew into her outstretched hands. Jane reached into her pocket and found a carrot, warm and battered, but still edible. She felt his whiskery muzzle on her hands as he daintily took the snack, then she buried her hands in his mane, her throat suddenly scratchy and her eyes hot. *If only it could just be this way,* she thought. Just her and Beau, and nobody else to worry about, and no problems with money or placement in Advanced I. She wished that she could take Beau tonight, just saddle him up and start riding across LaGrange County. Was it still possible to just ride a horse across America? "We could do it," she told him. "I bet we could."

But there was the tug of recognition, she knew. The need to have their accomplishments acknowledged. She felt guilty about wanting this—wanting to be noticed by the other girls and wanting to be noticed as a rider. She did not know how to strike a balance between her soli-tude and her loneliness—her need to be with Beau alone and her wish to belong.

"Well, I'm not going to figure it out tonight," she said.

It was becoming a familiar phrase. Beau nuzzled her hands in the hope of another carrot, and Jane hopped off the fence to put her arms around his neck. When she released him, he shook his head and cantered back to the other horses.

## Chapter 5

### Divided Up

A pale ribbon of orange shone through the single window of the room as Jane opened her eyes. It was just dawn, and for a moment she didn't remember where she was. The low-ceilinged, snug cabin was similar to her room at home, and Jane rolled over, thinking sleepily, *I don't have to get up yet.* Then the bunk bed's mattress gave a loud squawk, and she sat upright with a start, looking around at the sleeping forms of her cabinmates, their strewn clothes and towels and toiletries. The first day of camp!

In the golden morning light, the night before seemed a loud, discordant blur. Girls talked excitedly about rock bands she'd never heard of, fought for a place in line for the shower, showed off tan lines and new boots. There'd been hardly any talk of horses; mostly, Alyssa and Jennifer held court on their bunk, with Jessica a lounging third, throwing in sarcastic remarks to gales of rollicking laughter. They talked about kids at their school—boys, mainly— whom Jane didn't know, but also about shopping expeditions to the upscale Plaza Court and all the new clothes they wished their parents would have let them bring to camp. At one point, Jennifer asked Jane, "Don't you wish you could bring all your cool clothes? Doesn't it *kill* you to have to wear these rags for six weeks?" Jane, however, had gotten a little wiser over the course of many summers with this crowd and knew when she was being mocked. She didn't care about clothes, and she figured that must be fairly obvious to everyone else by now. "It's devastating," she replied, poker-faced, and was rewarded by a hoot of laughter from Jessica. On that note, she'd curled up on her bunk bed and opened her book.

Since last summer, Mrs. Jeffrys no longer sent anyone over to wake the girls up—they had no counselors, per se. They were expected to rise at seven and to bring the horses in from the fields, a chore usually grumbled over, but which Jane secretly relished. Now, as she pulled on her worn jods, an equally ratty T-shirt, and her boots, she was already looking forward to the walk through the wet grass, watching the world wake up as she did. She tiptoed through the cabin to the bathroom, washed her face and brushed her teeth, and fixed her dishwater-colored hair in a ponytail. Her nose was already starting to freckle, and her large gray eyes, just like Lily's but the color of clouds instead of blue sky, looked back at her in the mirror. On top of everything else, it would also be nice to be prettier. Jane sometimes felt that all she did was long for things that weren't so. It was tiring to live in imagined yet unimaginable futures.

There was still a hint of cool in the air as she swung off the porch and headed for the stable to collect a halter and lead shank, but the low, blurry orange sun on the horizon promised a "scorcher," as her mother would say. She looked to the windows of the big house and could see Maria, Jose's wife, in the kitchen starting breakfast. She was a small woman with lean, strong arms and surprisingly big hands, and she prepared all three meals for the campers. Besides Jane's group of eight, there would be two more classes of riders—beginning and intermediate—usually about ten other younger girls, who stayed in the larger cabin nearer to the house. They had two live-in counselors, a rotating series of college students who took them through the other activities Sunny Acres offered: canoeing and swimming lessons in the pond, archery, and campfires at night. They were obviously halfhearted stabs at being a "real" camp—everyone came to ride.

The advanced students wouldn't follow their schedule. Instead, they'd ride in the mornings, break for lunch and free time probably spent swimming in the glassy-green pond, then ride again in the afternoon. Susan had told them she'd mix up the lessons: Sometimes they'd jump in the mornings, then do dressage later; sometimes they'd ride mini cross-country courses or practice obstacles. The goal was to prepare them for three-day eventing: the apex of English riding. Jane was especially looking forward to learning more about dressage, an advanced form of equitation that was hard to get the hang of riding only once a week.

As Jane approached the barn, her stomach lurched as she realized that Susan might already be writing their names on the green chalkboard that hung on the door to the tack room, where she divided students into classes and assigned horses. But the barn was empty except for the large tabby, Zelda, sleeping on a hay bale, and the German shepherd, Rocky, who seemed to feel that it was his personal responsibility to protect the girls and the horses in equal measure. He was a solemn, impressive dog, but very friendly, and he wagged his tail happily as Jane scratched his ears. "Hey, guy," Jane said as his tail thumped across her legs. "What do you think my chances are today? Will you keep your paws crossed for me?" Rocky blinked up at her reassuringly.

"Maybe he'll knock on wood, too," said a voice from the stall opposite the tack room. Jane jumped, and Rocky stood at sudden attention, his ears pricked. "Jose?" she said, then she saw that it wasn't Jose at all, but a boy about her age, leaning on a pitchfork and dusting off the front of his jeans with one hand. He was tall and skinny with longish black hair pushed back behind his ears, and something in his brown eyes did indeed remind Jane of Jose. She blushed, as usual.

"Nope. Ben," he said. "Jose's my granddad."

Jane ducked her head, concentrating on petting Rocky. "I didn't know there was anyone in here," she said.

"Obviously," the boy, Ben, said, smiling. "Otherwise you wouldn't be talking to the dog, right?"

"Well, maybe not out loud," Jane said, then blushed again as Ben laughed.

"So you're a hypocrite," he said in a friendly tone.

"No . . . I just . . . ." Jane began.

"You just don't want strangers overhearing your conversations. I know. I hate it when people listen to what Zelda and I talk about." His voice was teasing, but not mean. Jane ventured another look up at him, her growing-out bangs falling into her eyes.

"Right," she said with more confidence than she felt. "After all, Rocky might be about to confess to eating a rabbit or some other crime."

"No, he's a good boy," Ben said, and he suddenly swung forward, placing the pitchfork against the wall and leaning to pat the dog on the head in one easy motion. Jane stepped backward and banged her elbow against the tack room door.

"Um, so, Ricky and Gabriel are your brothers?" she said, trying to cover up her gracelessness.

"Cousins. Their mom was my aunt Teresa, but they were raised by our grandparents. I guess you know that, though."

"No," Jane said, feeling a little ashamed. "Are their parents . . ."

"Yeah, they died in Mexico City, in a car crash. So my granddad and grandma brought them out here when they were teenagers. My family came, too. I was eight. But this is the first year my wise elders have decided I'm old enough to have a summer job."

Jane didn't know what to say. She wanted to say, "That's great," but she couldn't, considering Ben had just told her that Ricky and Gabriel had been orphaned, which she felt she should have known. They had worked with their grandfather at the farm for as long as Jane could remember, but she'd always been shy around them. They were young men, thus naturally intimidating, and somewhat aloof, especially Ricky, mostly speaking in Spanish with Jose and Maria, and not interacting very much with the riders. Jane realized that they might feel like strangers here, too.

"Well, I better start getting the horses in," she said abruptly, and turned away to hide her deepening flush.

"See you," said the boy, and Jane heard him return to mucking out the stall as she grabbed a halter and lead and hurried from the barn.

*Jane decided* not to bring Beau in first; somehow, she thought it might jinx them. Instead, she easily caught gentle Fleur, treating her to a carrot and telling her that she was sure all of the beginning riders would be very nice to her. They were usually a mixed lot, the midgets, as Susan affectionately called them. Some arrived at camp starry-eyed at the prospect of riding a *real* horse, only to be terrified by the enormous, dirty, hoofed creatures that confronted them, so different from their toys with purple manes and silvery eyelashes. Others expected horses to behave like cars, obedient to their every demand, and grew frustrated and bossy when the animals acted like living creatures and not like machines. Then there were the awestruck girls, who might be nervous, might even be scared, but to whom fear was nothing compared with the bliss of being astride a horse. They were the ones who would work for their pleasure, and who would treat their horses kindly. Jane tried to encourage the horse-worshiping midgets whenever she had the chance.

"'Morning," Robin called out as Jane and Fleur approached the barn. She looked impeccable, as always, her hair combed into a sleek braid, her polo shirt tucked neatly into her jods.

"Time to bring in the beasts," Jane replied in the very bad fake British accent she and Robin often joked in when they were alone.

"Aye, 'tis time," Robin said. "I think everybody's in the barn," she added, lapsing back into American.

Jane's pulse leaped. "Is Susan there?" she asked.

"No, I haven't seen her." Robin squeezed her arm. "*Don't worry*," she whispered.

Jane wished she had an iota of Robin's optimism as she led Fleur into her stall and turned her loose. Instead, her hands started sweating as she walked toward the tack room. *This is idiotic,* she told herself. *It's not like it's the Olympics or something. It's just one class versus another. Maybe Robin and I will both be in Advanced II, and we'll be away from Alyssa and Emily.* This thought actually did give her a measure of comfort, and she took a deep breath as if literally trying to force down the other voice inside her head that told her that she wouldn't become a great rider unless she was in the hardest class.

Sure enough, there was a group of girls gathered around the green board in the tack room as Jane walked up. She moved forward slowly, registering the look of disgust on Emily's face, Jessica's sly smile, and Alyssa's odd smirk.

Shannon, flushed and obviously embarrassed, moved out of the way to let Jane see the board.

| Advanced I | Advanced II |
|---|---|
| Alyssa—Ariel | Liz—Lady Blue |
| Jessica—Quixotic | Shannon—Bebop |
| Jennifer—Thunder | Robin—Bess |
| Jane—Beau | Emily—Lancelot |

Jane couldn't help it—she felt an enormous smile stretch across her entire face. She blushed and turned to find Robin, relieved that her friend was smiling, too.

"See, I told you," Robin said. "And before you start plotting Susan's death, I *am* glad to be in the other class."

"You're positive?" Jane asked, giving her friend a searching look.

"One hundred and twelve percent," Robin answered, then drew Jane away from the other girls to give her a quick, surreptitious hug.

As Jane glanced at her best friend's open, good-humored face, she suddenly thought how *she* would feel if the tables were turned. *Would I be as nice as Robin if she'd made it in the class and I hadn't?* She wondered, in the midst of her happiness, exactly what sort of a friend she really, deep down, was. But then another wash of bliss came over her: Wasn't this also a sign that Susan would be letting Jane ride Beau all summer and not making her share him with the other classes? She could pretend, for six whole weeks, that he was her very own. . . .

"Listen up, everybody!" Susan, standing outside the tack room, a clipboard in one hand and the enormous thermos of coffee that was her perpetual companion in the other, interrupted Jane's reverie. She looked like everyday Susan—at least the everyday Susan that Jane knew, in loose-fitting dark blue jods, one of the do-gooder T-shirts of which she seemed to have an endless supply (this one said FRIENDS DON'T LET FRIENDS EAT FARMED FISH!), and her salt-and-pepper hair in a long braid down her back—but she was smiling somewhat mischievously. Jane suddenly wondered what in the world she'd look like in a ball gown. She put the disconcerting image (taffeta, farmer's tan) from her mind as she and Robin joined the rest of the group standing around their trainer.

"So I've been planning something a little different for this year's camp," Susan began, then paused as the inevitable whispers and questions broke out among the girls. "Since I've got you guys for six whole weeks, I thought we could put some of your training to the test. Hopefully what I've come up with will also be a help to those of you who plan on showing this fall, and who might be interested in trying for the Junior Hunter-Jumper Competition in the spring." She caught Alyssa's eye, and Alyssa gave a small, tight smile.

"At the end of camp, we're going to have two competitions: a hack and jumping show for the Advanced II riders, and a dressage, jumping, and cross-country event for the Advanced I riders. I'm going to be training each group to get ready for this, and I'm bringing in two other trainers to help me judge." Susan smiled broadly, obviously taken with her own idea. "I'll even go get some ribbons. This way those of you who haven't been showing can get a feel for what it's like, and those of you who are ready to get serious about eventing can get some more practice in. Sound good?"

A resounding "Yes!" echoed down the barn's corridor. Jane's heart was pounding and she squeezed Robin's hand. She and Beau would have a chance to compete—really compete, in an event—at last!

*The next week* of camp was the happiest, the busiest, and the most exhausting week Jane had ever spent at Sunny Acres. When the next Friday came, Jane was shocked to realize that she'd entirely forgotten to write to her parents, and she sat down under the old oak tree in front of the cabin after lunch and broke open the packet of stationery and addressed, stamped envelopes that her mother had tucked into her duffel bag. The addresses always had some silly twist to them, like using *Monsieur et Madame Ryan* for her parents' names, or including ridiculously lengthened locations, reminding the postman that the Ryans lived in the United States, North American Continent, the Earth, near the Milky Way. Jane chose one that spelled out *The Revered and Honored Parents of Jane Ryan,* leaned back against the tree, and thought about what she could tell of her week.

> *Dear Mum and Dad,*
>
> *I'm sorry I haven't written yet. I've been so busy because…I got into Advanced I!* (Here Jane drew a sketch of herself dancing a jig on the margin of the paper.) *It's me, Alyssa (you remember her—the snobby girl with the really great horse), Jennifer (Alyssa's best friend), and Jessica (the only popular girl who's nice to me) (sometimes). Robin is in the other class, which is terrible for me, but she says she's glad to be in the easier class. (???) And our class is hard. Yesterday, we practiced water obstacles—*

Jane smiled, thinking about yesterday's morning lesson. Susan, with Jose's help, had built two jumps on the bank of a wide, placid creek that wound through the farm's main pasture. Jane had to admit that they looked very intimidating when she and the other girls got to the site. The first obstacle, set on the gentler incline, was a massive heap of logs that looked like some sort of beaver dam, and the second was basically a deconstructed picnic table. Susan, borrowing Ariel, had showed them the course. She swung in a wide, cantering loop around a copse of trees, then pointed Ariel toward the creek, shortening her strides as they approached the slope leading down to the logs. Ariel floated unconcernedly over the bristling pile, snorted with insult at the spray of water that was flung up in her face as she landed neatly in the creek, then bounded like a jackrabbit up to the second jump, cleared it, and lunged relatively gracefully up the other, much steeper side. Susan had an almost preternatural stillness in the saddle, and the intensity of her focus seemed to inspire whatever mount she was on—whether a recalcitrant school horse who was giving one of the midgets trouble or a show horse like Ariel—to reach for its personal best. Of course, she had made these jumps look like a piece of cake.

They weren't, as the riders soon discovered. Jane had always known that Beau didn't like being ridden in water. She'd often taken him down to the pond and tried to get him to swim, and he'd always refused. Still, he wasn't as bad as Quixotic, who shied three times before the first jump, nearly unseating Jessica, until she finally got him into the creek. Then he careered off to the side of the second jump, actually running down the creek before he abruptly stopped, sighed heavily, and bent his head down to drink. Jane cracked up, and as Jessica walked her sheepish horse back to the group, she was laughing, too. "What do I have to do, carry him? Drain the stupid creek? Build a bridge?"

Susan smiled and arched an eyebrow. "No," she said, "just do it again."

"Or learn to ride your horse," Alyssa half-whispered to Jennifer, who coughed dramatically.

Jessica swung on them. "Do you even know what a sense of humor *is*," she asked conversationally, "or are you too perfect to need one?" She nudged Quixotic with her heels, brought him to a canter around the grove, and this time (Jane silently cheering her on), she started singing the national anthem while firmly guiding Quixotic over the first jump: *"And the rockets' red glare! The bombs bursting in air!"* Quixotic appeared so distracted by his rider's apparent loss of sanity that he forgot to refuse the second jump. He cleared it, slowly and shakily, and Susan whooped with delight. Alyssa and Jennifer stared at Jessica as she rejoined them, clearly basking in Susan's praise and Jane's laughter.

"Sometimes," she told her two best friends, "I think Jane's the only person here who gets me."

Jane smiled, but she knew better than to take Jessica's words at face value. Sure enough, she'd ignored Jane for the rest of the day.

*"Beau refused once, but then we did okay. I've been able to ride him all week, except once, when they needed him for the intermediate class."* Jane's heart had plummeted when Susan told her that she'd be riding Brownie—*Brownie!*—for their dressage lesson Wednesday afternoon. It was a joke. Brownie had

never learned to go on the bit, and at age twenty, he wasn't about to start. Jane basically trotted him around the ring, following the complicated series of turns, circles, and diagonals that Susan had plotted out, but with none of the movement that was supposed to happen in real dressage: the smooth communication and oneness of horse and rider. Jane was frustrated, but she tried to hide it. "And here," she shouted to Susan as she urged Brownie into an unwilling canter, "is where a lead change would happen, if it wouldn't break Brownie's legs."

"Don't try it," Susan sighed. "It probably would."

"You know, this is really a waste of all of our time, Susan," Alyssa complained, and Jane blushed, silently cursing Brownie as he collapsed ungracefully into a jolting trot.

"Not for me," Susan retorted. "I like watching Jane trying not to actually hate a horse."

Jane smiled gratefully, and painfully, through her clenched teeth. "I can't—hate—come on, *canter*, Brownie!—a horse that—thinks—he's a cow. . . ."

*"Emily Longstreet got a new horse, Lancelot, who was supposed to be really great, but he acted up so much that Susan put them in Advanced II."* Except now, Jane thought, a warm thrumming quickening her pulse, she didn't know that that was altogether true. She'd overheard something very odd in the barn that morning, and she still wasn't sure what to make of it. Jane had just put Beau in his stall and was about to fetch his saddle and bridle when she heard Emily's voice, loud with injury, coming from the tack room.

"There's no *point* in me riding in the other class,"

Emily whined. "I mean, in Atlanta I was the best rider in my barn, and it's completely *unfair* to hold me back—"

"I'm not holding you back," came Susan's voice in response. "I'm giving you and Lancelot the chance to get to know each other and to take things a little more slowly. I don't want you—or your horse—to get hurt, Emily."

"But it's not my fault he's so crazy."

"Well, what do you propose?" Susan asked reasonably. "I can't give you another horse—they're all being used for the beginner and intermediate lessons."

"But it's no problem that *Jane* uses one of the barn's horses. I mean, it's so unfair that she's taking the best horse away from all the other kids who should be riding him. And the only reason she's in Advanced I in the first place is because you won't let me be because of my stupid horse."

Jane clenched her fists. Part of her *did* feel guilty that Susan was letting her ride Beau so much, but she hated Emily saying it aloud. And, worse, a cold little voice inside her *did* wonder if the only reason she was in Advanced I was because Lancelot had turned out to be such a handful.

"That's actually not the only reason, Emily," Susan said quietly, and Jane froze, straining to hear. But Emily obviously *didn't* want to hear what Susan was about to say.

With a loud sigh and a syrupy, ominous lilt to her voice, she said, "Well, I promised my dad I'd call him today, so . . ." The tack room door swung open and Jane jumped back into the stall, grabbed a hoof pick from the grooming tray, hauled Beau's leg up, and busied herself with freeing a piece of gravel from his shoe. As Beau settled into his customary heavy lean, Jane's mind was racing: *What was Susan's other reason?*

"*Emily's really mad, especially since the big shows are coming up in the fall. I wonder if she'll be able to ride in them.*" Jane knew her own chances of competing were slim. She'd gotten to show Beau twice last year, but the entry and trailer fees made it expensive, and her parents didn't see the point. Jane had to admit, she didn't really, either. She could hardly hope to win the Junior Hunter-Jumper championship with a borrowed horse that she could only take out when he wasn't needed by the barn.

"*Otherwise, camp's pretty much the same—working in the barn, swimming, teaching the midgets, sketching, Maria's cooking.*" Jane stopped, thinking. There *was* something else new this year. But she wasn't sure she could find the right words for the tall boy who leaned on the pitchfork and made fun of her, and whom she'd exchanged a few more "Hi"s with.

Jane hastily finished the letter and sealed it.

## Chapter 6

# Triumphant Poop

Hot and bedraggled after class on Saturday, two weeks into camp, Jane walked wearily to the kitchen of the main house to get a glass of lemonade from Maria. Like her, Beau had been especially sweaty and tuckered out after their jumping class, and Jane had spent an hour sponging him off and walking him until she was sure he was cool and dry.

Jose had kept her company as he demonstrated to the midgets how to properly sponge and scrape off their mounts and to walk them dry. "No, no," he'd call out, "do not wipe them like your nose, *press* down and squeeze the sponge out. Tha-a-at's better." He was a gentle and patient teacher, as Jane had every reason to know. One of the young girls was obviously nervous about getting too near her horse's hindquarters—she gave tentative swipes to the back legs, then jumped back.

"Jose, do you remember how scared I used to be of picking Brownie's back hooves?" Jane called over, and Jose winked at her. "Ohh, sure, Jane, and I told you what I always say: A horse doesn't kick as long as it knows where you are and what you're doing. Just keep talking to him, and keep your hands on him, and everything is fine."

The little girl looked over at Jane with big eyes, then whispered up to her horse, "Okay, I'm going to go to your back legs now to make you nice and cool." She paused, looking up doubtfully to Jose, who nodded his encouragement. "Yes and now I'm going by your tail but I'm right here and you can still hear me, and now I'm . . ." She kept up a running commentary throughout the entire sponge bath, misremembering most of the parts of the horse and calling Rick Rack's knees his elbows and his hock his ankle, and Jose and Jane laughed silently to each other as the tired horse flicked his ears back and forth, listening to the happy prattle of the tiny girl buzzing around him.

Jane took her lemonade to the ring and leaned on the fence to watch the Advanced II class in full swing. She saw Robin and Bess go through a series of trotting poles nicely, and she waved to her. She admired her friend's quiet seat and motions, her gentle way with Bess, and told herself to remember how good Robin was at coaxing, never forcing, her mount. "There are lessons everywhere," Lily often said, throwing her arms out dramatically to encompass the world, her eyes large and wet with meaning. "Everywhere you look, you can learn something!" Jane suddenly missed her sister and wished she could talk to her. *If I miss her after two weeks, what will it be like when she leaves for college?* The thought made her throat sore, and that, too, reminded her of Lily. Her sister always said, if she didn't like something, "Oh, it gives me a sore throat." Bad movies, bad dates, they all, according to Lily, gave her the symptoms of strep. Jane caught Robin's eye and waved again.

"What's up?" Jane turned to see that Jessica had joined her at the fence, chewing gum and critically examining her dirty nails. "Watching the losers?"

"Jessica!" Jane exclaimed, shocked.

"Oh, whatever, I'm only kidding. But it's nice to be number one, right?"

"You say the *worst* things ever," Jane replied, but she felt a half-smile tugging at the corners of her mouth.

"No," Jessica said, "I say *true* things—you just don't like to hear them. Hypocrite."

That was the second time Jane had been called that— once, teasingly, by Ben, and now, not so teasingly, by Jessica. "So how am I a hypocrite?" she finally asked.

"Oh, you're supercompetitive but try to be all nice to people you beat out. You think all sorts of nasty things about our crowd but you don't say them—"

"Hey, that's not hypocrisy, it's common sense," Jane interrupted, and Jessica burst out laughing.

"That's why I like you, Jane." She chuckled. "You know they're all intimidated by you, right?"

Jane stared at her as if Jessica's head had just caught on fire. "*What?* You've got to be kidding me. They've frozen me out since we were practically toddlers."

"I'll explain it sometime," Jessica said, yawning, "but right now I've got to take a shower and lose about ten pounds of dirt." She ambled away, leaving Jane to gape after her. Somehow, she knew Jessica never would explain what she meant.

*There wasn't much* time to ponder Jessica's mysterious comment that afternoon, however. Yesterday evening, Susan had spent an hour walking the slopes and knolls of Sunny Acres' pastures, plotting out the first cross-country course the Advanced I riders would tackle. She'd told them to eat a snack and take it easy, as they wouldn't tack up until six o'clock, giving the horses enough time to rest after the morning's lesson and avoiding the sweltering heat of the afternoon. Susan passed out copies of her hand-drawn course, and Jane and Robin claimed their favorite shady oak to lounge under and discuss the map.

"This doesn't look too bad," Jane said, frowning as she studied Susan's carefully drawn tracks and arrows. Jane was, of course, intimately familiar with the land depicted, having either ridden or walked practically all of it over the years.

"Do you go right or left first?" Robin tilted her head to get a better look.

"Umm—right. The first jump's that log that we've done a million times, but then it looks like we go all the way around those trees at the lower end, and it says 'double rail,' so she must've set up something new there ...." Jane traced her finger along the dotted tracks. "Then the easy part of the creek"—a narrow and shallow bend of the farm's waterway that Jane knew Beau hopped over without a qualm—"then through the gate of the far paddock." This was a grass paddock with a small three-sided shelter and hayrack. Because it was some distance from the barns, it wasn't in regular use, but sometimes Susan broke young horses there, or stabled a rambunctious stallion that the Jeffrys would bring in to breed with one of their mares. "I guess I better hope there's no lovesick stallion in there, right?"

"My dear," said Robin, going British, "simply remind the poor suitor that Beau is a gelding, and that he won't get very far with his advances."

After their giggles subsided, Jane pointed with a groan to the next obstacle on the map. "Do we have to jump those *bushes*? Beau's not going to be happy about that at all."

"*Shrubbery*, old chap, *not* bushes, *shrubbery!*"

Jane's lemonade nearly went up her nose. "Well then, after we surmount the *shrubbery*, we'll canter calmly over the noxious and hideous creek obstacles, where Beau will *not* refuse or otherwise behave in a manner unbefitting to a fine gelding. ..."

"Then you will bravely traverse another old moldy log." Robin pointed to the map. "Gallop posthaste through the pond, leap with a mighty bound over yonder coop"—Susan must have moved it to the field for the course, Jane realized, unless there could be another, even bigger coop awaiting her?—"and fly with triumphant poop back to your noble comrades!"

"With triumphant *poop*?" Jane howled, doubling over.

"What—wait, what's that wo-ord, from the gra-aduation song?" Robin managed to gasp out, wiping her eyes.

"Pomp!" Jane shouted, and they both fell over again.

Jane's stomach was aching when Robin finally had to depart for the cabin, and she clambered to her feet and staggered to the barn to tack up. As she clutched the stitch in her side, she realized that Robin's banter had made it physically impossible for her to feel nervous, and she silently thanked her friend as she waved to her, fist in the air, shouting, "With triumphant poop!" across the driveway, into the summer dusk.

*Jane and Beau* were the last to join the group of riders gathered at the gate to the main pasture. Beau had given her trouble saddling up; he kept holding his breath, extending his stomach so that when Jane forced the last buckle of the girth through its hole, he relaxed his sides, and the girth bagged loosely again. She'd finally given him an annoyed poke and, looking at her reproachfully, he sighed, allowing her a few seconds to tighten the girth.

"C'mon, you," she said as she swung into the saddle and urged him into a trot. "The creek, the coop, jumping shrubbery—what's not to like?"

The fierce heat of the day had subsided, leaving a mellow amber glow over the farm. As Jane looked over the soft green slopes and ambling creek that framed Sunny Acres, she remembered her wish to ride Beau across the country, or at least across Kentucky, over miles and miles of the deep green that was both mysterious and comforting, an ocean of summer color, with that precarious happiness of summer—beauty that is so full, but contains its own ending, like a song.

"Jane, are you listening?" Susan's voice broke into her daydream. Jane nodded, blushing. "I was just saying that you're up first."

"Okay, right, I wasn't listening," Jane said sheepishly, and Jessica laughed.

"Let's focus. I'm going to be timing you, but just as an exercise. Don't race over this—take your time and ride a nice relaxed course, okay?"

"Got it," Jane said, and turned Beau to the gate. They walked past Thunder and Jennifer, who was involved in a whispered discussion with Alyssa that Jane caught snatches of as she looked out over the slopes of what would be her course: "I was like—" "Seriously, what did he—" Jessica was a little ways off, looking down the line of the fence, apparently lost in her own, and Jane was sure inscrutable, thoughts. No one seemed to care much that she was the first in what would be for all of them their first full cross-country course, and Jane was relieved. Normally she hated her invisibility, her irrelevance, but right now she didn't want to feel their eyes on her, judging and appraising. She lined Beau up at the gate and glanced over at Susan, who was studying her watch. "Ready," she called, "and go!"

Jane squeezed Beau's sides and he picked up a trot, then, with a sassy swish of his tail, a canter. Their route led them slightly downhill, and Jane scanned the field toward the copse of trees beyond the decrepit log that was their first jump. Beau took it casually, and Jane guided him to the right of the thicket of slender young birches, looking for the double rail. It came up suddenly around the bend, giving Jane little time to square her horse, but it was also low, and Beau managed it well. Jane decided to pick up the pace as they approached the shallow crossing of the creek, and Beau lashed his tail again as they cleared the water in a bound. This, Jane thought, was not bad at all.

As they neared the far paddock, Beau pricked his ears and slowed his gait, obviously wondering why they were careening toward the gate of a small enclosure where there might be another horse. Jane muttered a low prayer that there wouldn't be, and sure enough, the paddock appeared empty, the gate propped open, and the late-evening light pouring through the small, neatly kept shed. They trotted through, then Jane looked to the "shrubbery" that she was supposed to cross. It was enormous.

"Whoa!" she yelped and, though it wasn't what she'd meant, Beau halted. Could Susan really mean for them to jump this thing? The bushes, thickly gnarled and impenetrable, formed the western wall of the paddock. Jane had never sized them up for jumping—it had never occurred to her—and they looked at least four feet high, if not more, with thin shoots of new growth sticking up. Jane was sure it would be—if she made it—the highest jump she'd ever done.

Jane looked over her shoulder toward the main gate, but the trees by the creek blocked her view of the other riders and the reassuring form of Susan. She'd never done anything like this without Susan's watchful presence and encouragement. Then her heart gave an unpleasantly loud knock as she realized that she was letting the seconds tick by while she walked Beau in circles of indecision. Susan might have said that the timing was just an "exercise" but Jane still didn't want to be the slowest rider of the course. Swallowing hard and tightening her reins, she turned Beau toward the menacing briars. "Okay, buddy," she whispered, "let's do this."

She swung Beau around the shed, picking up a trot, then a canter. As they rounded the corner, she straightened him with her seat and hands and applied a strong leg; then, two beats before the bushes, having taken a good look at what Jane was asking him to do, Beau threw his head up and swerved sharply to the left, toward the open gate. Jane felt her right boot slip from its stirrup, and she grabbed hard onto Beau's mane. Luckily, he stopped when he reached the gate, and Jane stayed on. Now, on top of her jackrabbit heart, her hands were shaking, and she felt a little sick. How was she going to convince Beau to go over this, when such an obvious exit was just to the left? She briefly considered closing the gate, but then she'd have to open it again, eating up more time. She didn't stop long to think; her every impulse was toward getting in motion, getting this over with, and not allowing Beau, or herself, any time to really think about what was increasingly seeming like a bad idea.

And then suddenly an odd memory, one that almost made her laugh in spite of her predicament, floated across her mind's eye. Jane wondered. . . . Well, it was worth a shot, she decided quickly, before she could feel more foolish than she already did. She cleared her throat.

"O SAY does that star-spangled ba-anner yet wa-ave...." With an earful of off-key patriotism for encouragement, Beau cantered around the shed again. This time, as Jane felt him already starting to look and to shift to the left, she applied an even stronger left leg and a firm right rein and continued to sing, which seemed to give her courage. "O'er the la-a-and of the freeeee and the ho-ome..." She felt him swerve, veer back into line, slow slightly, then suddenly, and with a great bound that almost caught her unawares, he was off, launched up, and over, and Jane was thrown up on his neck, missing both stirrups, and gasping, "Triumphant poop, darn it, triumphant poop!" as she slowed him down, hugging and patting his neck, and fumbled for her stirrups. Her heart, still pounding, swelled within her, filling with emotion for this brave, so brave horse beneath her.

"I love you, boy," she told him. "I love you so much."

Then Jane heard a sound behind her—what was it? Clapping? In a blaze of confusion, she looked over her shoulder to catch a glimpse of a tall, slim figure in jeans and cowboy boots, his dark hair falling over his grinning face, emerging from the shadowed corner of the shed, clapping and giving a low whistle.

"*And the home of the bra-a-ave!*" Ben's husky tenor floated down the field, completing the song, as she galloped toward the trees. Where in the world had he come from, Jane wondered, and what was he doing there in the first place? She felt a quick burst of pleasure from his applause, then urged Beau forward once again.

*The rest* of the course went in a flash. Beau, apparently swollen with pride over his heroic effort, tossed off the water jumps, the second log, and even the splash through the pond with aplomb. Jane's heart was soaring as they rounded the last corner of the field and headed toward the coop. She could hardly restrain herself from whooping, or singing again, as they tore up the grass and charged toward the last jump. She could see the group now, and Beau picked up even more speed as they headed toward the other horses. Funnily enough, the coop didn't look nearly as intimidating as it once did, and with some self-consciousness, Jane assumed a serious riderly attitude, determined to make the jump that Susan could see come off well. It did, and then they were back at the gate and done.

"Eight minutes and forty-three seconds," Susan called out. *Eight minutes?* Jane stared at her trainer in disbelief. It felt as if she'd been gone at least an hour.

"Everything looked fine from here, Jane. How'd Beau do?"

"He was great. But that paddock jump—" Jane stopped in confusion. Susan was frowning and gave her head a quick shake. Jane looked at her, then at the other girls, who were looking at her, not at Susan. "It was fine," she finished lamely.

"Good girl. Take Beau back to the barn and get him cooled down. And put your face under the hose—you're bright red." The curse of her complexion—Jane resembled a tomato after any strenuous ride in the heat. As she turned a jaunty and self-satisfied Beau toward home, Susan winked at her. She obviously didn't want the other girls to hear about the shrubbery, and this gave Jane a measure of satisfaction. Unless they remembered the exact dimensions of the green giant, they were all in for the same surprise that she'd had.

*After sponging* and scraping and walking Beau, Jane had just turned him out into the pasture when Alyssa, who'd ridden last, and Susan approached the barn. "Great," Jane heard Alyssa mutter to Jennifer as she slid off Ariel, "so glad I get to be the last one out of the barn tonight." It was true that all the other girls were done or nearly done caring for their horses. Alyssa so rarely was last in anything that Jane allowed herself a brief moment of gloating that she might actually get to be one of the first in line for the showers tonight.

"You could always pull an Emily and just throw Ariel in her stall still hot," Jennifer said with a small laugh.

Jane glanced back from the field, where Beau sauntered off toward the salt lick. She had an idea what Jennifer meant—Jane, too, had noticed that Emily didn't seem to take much interest in the care of her new horse. She looked worriedly to Ariel, tied to a hitching post at the barn door and obviously tired and flecked with sweat, but Alyssa, after searching fruitlessly for Gabriel or Ricky, finally fetched a full bucket of water and began sponging down the lovely Arab mare.

Jane was thinking of finding Robin and getting something to eat when she heard Susan calling them to the front of the barn. When the worn-out group assembled, their trainer looked them over, smiling, but, Jane thought, with a hint of steel in her expression. There was a long pause while Susan seemed to be lost in thought, and Alyssa nudged Jennifer and rolled her eyes.

"So," Susan finally said, "what did you think of your first cross-country course?" A smattering of "Fine"s and "Okay"s came in response.

"That's interesting," Susan said, the smile wiped from her face. "Because for two of you, it was more than fine, and for the other two, it was much less." Jane looked at Susan in bewilderment, then saw to her great surprise that Jennifer had turned dark crimson—surely the first time Jane had ever seen her blush. She glanced at Alyssa, who looked haughty and bored, which was normal.

"Here are your times," Susan continued. "Alyssa was

first, coming in at six minutes and five seconds. Jennifer was second, with six minutes twenty seconds. Jessica took seven minutes and thirteen seconds, and Jane finished at eight minutes forty-three seconds."

Jane stared at her boots, her mind echoing her trainer's words: *And for the other two, it was much less.* How could she have felt so good about the course? How could she have been so happy after her ride, when she was *last*? She dared not look at the other girls and stood hot and miserable, her fists balled against her sides. She heard Jennifer, sounding back to her usual self, whisper to Alyssa, "Not a surprise." Susan heard it as well.

"It was a surprise to me, Jennifer," she suddenly barked, "because you and Alyssa did not complete the course. Had this been a real event, you would have been disqualified. I am disappointed, to say the least, in both of you." Jane's head snapped up. "Neither of you," the trainer continued, "jumped the hedge. You both circled the shed and left through the gate. Jane's horse refused the first time but she made it the second time, and Jessica cleared it on her first attempt. You two should feel very good about the courses you rode. I'm proud of you." And without another word, Susan turned on her heel and stalked away, striking her long crop against her boot with a loud crack.

*So* this *was* why getting first in line for the showers was so fought over, Jane thought as she let the scalding-hot water pour over her sore shoulders and back. Usually by the time she said good-bye to Beau and reluctantly left the barn, the cabin's water tanks, exhausted, only gave about five minutes of lukewarm water. She stood for a while more in a happy, exhausted daze, lazily watching the steam swirl off her freckled arms.

Afterward, she joined Robin on the front porch, where her friend was leaning comfortably against a porch beam and reading *Watership Down* by the soft light filtering from the cabin window. Jane smiled—she had read it for class the previous fall, and, a voracious rereader and unrepentant book thief, she'd been swiping it from Robin's bunk bed. This was probably the first time Robin had had the book to herself in days. But now she put it down quickly and looked up at Jane, her face bursting with questions.

"Alyssa and Jennifer have been holed up in the room for an hour, not letting anyone in," she said. "And Jessica, of course, isn't saying anything at all. Liz and Shannon have been trying to get in to talk to them, but they won't open up."

Jane wondered how they would handle being, for once, in the wrong. It was an interesting question, and after she explained to Robin what happened during that evening's lesson, they discussed at length what, if anything, Alyssa and Jennifer would say about it. "Probably nothing," Jane finally decided. "Somehow I get the feeling that they really don't care."

"I'm sure they care," Robin said quietly. "But I'm not sure if I can really blame them for what they did."

"*What?*" Jane exclaimed, and Robin put out a placating hand.

"All I meant is that I can understand why they'd be scared to jump that thing. I don't think I'd want to try it."

"But Robin, when have you ever known either of them to be *scared?*" Jane asked skeptically. "Remember the coop? And the race we had last summer? And that hayride when Gabriel told us those horrible stories about the house down the road that's supposed to be haunted?"

"You're right," Robin sighed. "I guess that was my last attempt not to think the worst of them." They laughed softly. After several years of trying, and failing, to ingratiate herself with the clique, Jane was more apt than good-natured Robin to view them with a jaundiced (*and jealous,* a small interior voice whispered) eye. Lily had once told her that you often end up disliking people with whom you've acted your worst, and Jane sometimes thought back to her earlier years of trying obsequiously to fit in, to flatter, to make herself popular, though they were dismally unsuccessful efforts, as the times she acted her absolute worst. *If you can't join 'em, beat 'em,* she thought now, but didn't say it aloud to Robin, as she had a feeling that that wasn't quite a noble sentiment, either.

"I wonder if they planned it," Robin said thoughtfully. "I mean, they both circled the shed, right?" Jane nodded.

"Yep, they planned it," came a voice from the doorway, and Jane and Robin turned to see Jessica's lean silhouette framed against the light in the hall, toweling her hair. "God, Jane, the water's *cold* when you shower last. Do you like that or something? I still feel dirty." She swung open the door and sank down on the steps next to them, rubbing the ends of her long blond hair. There was another creak of the door.

"Jessica, what are you doing out here?" came Alyssa's voice. "C'mon, we want to talk to you." This silhouette had a hand on a cocked hip and was waving the fingers of the other impatiently.

"Why didn't you jump the shrubbery?" The sentence hung in the air, blurted out and unretractable, along with the stupid British word, and Jane couldn't even remember forming the thought to say it. Nevertheless, heart thumping, she waited for the answer. Robin coughed.

"Because it was completely irresponsible for Susan to include the *shrubbery* in the course," Alyssa answered disdainfully. "Especially when she wouldn't be there to watch us or to help us if we had trouble."

"But Ben was there. . . ." Jane found herself arguing.

"And that's another thing, actually," Alyssa said. "It was totally wrong for her to have him spying on us. He sure wasn't there to help—what's some Mexican kid who probably doesn't even know how to ride going to do? But I suppose he's useful to her as a snitch."

Jane was stunned into silence. Jessica growled, "Oh, *please*, Alyssa."

But Alyssa ignored her and swung back on Jane. "Listen, Miss Goody-Goody, maybe you've forgotten that some of us have valuable horses that we don't want to risk on a meaningless course during *camp*. Some of us have much bigger competitions to think about. I'm sure this meant a lot to *you*, but it didn't mean anything to anybody else. Okay? Come *on*, Jessica!" But Jessica didn't move, and Alyssa turned away in disgust, slamming the door behind her.

She left a long, pregnant silence in her wake. "Well," Jessica finally sighed, "I guess they've got their story straight. Susan was irresponsible, Ariel and Thunder are too good to waste on camp, and Ben's a spy. It's perfect."

Jane and Robin nodded slowly: It actually was. The situation could be twisted so that Alyssa and Jennifer's actions seemed mature and rational, and Jane and Jessica were the foolish ones for taking the course seriously. She couldn't stand it.

"Do you think they're *right*?" she asked Jessica.

"Of course not," Jessica retorted. "They got caught and now they're lying. Don't tell me you fell for it, Jane?" Jane didn't say anything.

"I don't know what to think," Robin said. "But she shouldn't have said those awful things about Jose's grandson. I haven't talked to him, but he seems nice."

"No, she shouldn't have," Jessica said shortly, and rose from the steps. "And if you want to know what I think, here it is. Jane rode great today and Alyssa and Jennifer cheated. Period."

"What about you?" Jane asked.

Jessica smiled wryly. "Well, I did okay." She waved casually at them from over her shoulder and went inside.

Jane heard footsteps crunching up the gravel path that led to the cabin and looked up with surprise to find Susan approaching. She half-hoped that she had thought of some more things to say to Alyssa and Jennifer. But Susan stopped before the porch. "Hi," she said simply, and Jane and Robin said, "Hi, Susan," together. Their trainer looked at them uncertainly, then sat on the steps in the place Jessica had just vacated. She was still carrying her crop and drummed it lightly against her boot as she stared out into the firefly-sparked darkness before them. Robin looked at Jane questioningly, and Jane shrugged.

"Jane," Susan said softly, "I've got some bad news."

Jane's heart gave a sickening knock. "What—is someone, is Lily—" she started, but Susan cut her off.

"No, no, not about your family. It's about Beau." There was an awful silence.

Susan cleared her throat. "Jane, I'm sorry, but he's been sold." She slapped the crop against her boot again, and another silence fell. Jane's mind went curiously blank and there was a slight ringing in her ears, as if she were deep underwater, everything muffled and moving very slowly. She found she couldn't speak; even if she'd wanted to desperately, she was quite sure that she couldn't make a sound come from her tight, dry throat.

"Megan rode him in the Beginner class all spring, and she'd been doing really well on him. I moved her up to Intermediate for camp. Apparently she was disappointed that she hasn't been able to ride him, except that one day, when I put you on Brownie. . . ." Susan's voice was flat, and she wasn't looking at Jane. "Her parents called a few days ago and told Mrs. Jeffrys that they wanted to buy Beau to surprise Megan for her birthday tomorrow. Since they're going to keep boarding Beau here, it means that the Jeffrys get both his purchase price and the cost of up-keep, and they agreed. They . . ." Here Susan faltered. "Of course they know you, Jane, but I don't think they under-stood about you and Beau."

Suddenly Jane couldn't be on the porch anymore. She stood abruptly, catching a glimpse of Robin's horrified face, and like a sleepwalker she moved to the cabin door.

"Jane?" Susan called, and her normally gruff voice was gentle, which somehow made it worse.

"He . . . was never my horse," Jane began, and then her voice, and her heart, broke.

Chapter 7

Nighttime
at the Barn

The pale green glow of Jessica's travel clock showed one o'clock and Jane thought confusedly of fireflies, of how their light looked like this clock's light, and how their hum, when captured, was like the noise in her ears. She rolled over again, trying to find a place on the pillow that wasn't damp from her tears. She tried to shut her thoughts off, staring at the blank wall before her, then went back to the clock and its silent stare. Her mind moved like a broken thing, giddily fast with images of stealing Beau, setting off across the dark, still fields of the farm to ride across the country as she'd dreamed, then slowing down to a crawl as she imagined watching Beau with another rider, with an *owner*, cantering the same fields on which they had just done so well. Then her thoughts halted at the image of a phone, and her finger dialing her own number as she called her parents and asked them to come and take her home.

It was all over, she thought. She could never come back to Sunny Acres again.

As the tears, the seemingly unending tears that hurt her throat and her eyes so terribly, swelled again to a crescendo somewhere in her chest, threatening a new outbreak, Jane sat up, struggled out of her sleeping bag, pulled on her jeans and her sneakers, grabbed her sweatshirt, and fled the cabin.

The night air brought some relief to her hot face and swollen eyes, and she walked quickly down the gravel path toward the fields. She had to see her horse one more time before he was, in the morning, not her horse. It was a nightmare, though she hadn't slept: the porch, Alyssa's cold, biting words, Susan's sad face, then the loud nightly confusion of the campers and their music and shrill conversations and laughter, Robin's arms around her shoulders, Jennifer saying, *What's wrong with Miss Goody?*, apparently having cottoned on to Jane's awful new nickname. And Jane, huddled in her bunk with her face to the wall, ignoring her best friend and her enemies alike. She felt like an alien, like an outcast. *They are my enemies,* she thought savagely. *They'll laugh when they find out, but I won't care, I'll be gone. Maybe I'll move with Lily, find a high school in New York.* Her mind whirled and whirled. Then her feet stopped.

There was a light on in the main barn, and Jane saw

a shadow move across the doorway. She wondered dully what was happening. Maybe a burglar, or horse thieves (were there any horse thieves anymore? Her aching brain conjured ruffians in black frock coats and stovepipe hats, vengeful Comanches, and filthy-whiskered outlaws spitting chew). *Perhaps I'll join them,* she thought, and changed her course wearily to the lighted barn, not out of any real curiosity, but to get a handful of sweet feed for Beau. What she saw when she reached the door shook her abruptly awake.

The corridor of the barn was flooded with light. A high-pitched whinny came from the far end. Jose, his hat cocked back on the crown of his head, kept a firm grasp on the lead rope of a horse who looked in considerable distress: sweat streaked over distended sides, hooves pawing, eyes rolling white as the chestnut tossed his head, struggling to break away from the steady hand guiding him.

"*Shhhh, shhhhh,* my friend, my darling, my dear, *shhhh…*" came Jose's caressing voice as he turned Lancelot. He caught sight of Jane, standing uncertainly in the doorway, and shook his head at her.

"What's the matter with him?" Jane asked.

"It's a bad night for Lancelot—and for you, I think, little Jane." He paused the mighty horse before her, petting his strong, slender neck with even, soothing strokes. Lancelot, betraying his usual ferocious dignity, twisted his upper lip and gave what looked like an enormous yawn. "They do that, with colic," Jose told her.

"He's got colic?" Jane whispered. "How?" Colic had many causes, though the most common was overeating.

"Yes, my grandson guessed, and I think he's probably right." Jose glanced behind him, and Jane saw Ben standing in the frame of Lancelot's stall door, looking much as he did when Jane first met him, holding a pitchfork. "You got all that hay up?" Jose called, and Ben nodded.

"It's clean," he said.

Lancelot suddenly jerked his head, trying to nip at his flank, and Jose started him toward the stall. "We'll let him have a roll. Watch that he doesn't start thrashing his legs around." Jane walked with them, distracted by a fellow creature in more pain than she. Then she saw Beau's stall. It was festooned with red and gold streamers, and a banner hung above the door, proclaiming HAPPY BIRTHDAY, MEGAN! Although she felt weak and stupid with tears already spent, they came again, hot and unwanted, coursing down her face. She turned abruptly away, then felt an arm circle her shoulders, pulling her around, and she flung herself against Jose's broad chest, sobbing as he held her.

"Is Big Red okay?" Jose said over her head to Ben. Jane moved to let him go, but he held her close. "Ben will look after him right now." Jane wondered miserably what Ben would think of her, crying like a baby to his grandfather, her face a swollen wreck. She let Jose guide her to a stool by the tack room and sit her down. He brought her a cup of water from the pump, and a clean saddlecloth, dampened, to wipe her face and blow her nose. She struggled to catch her breath, and slowly, with a few relapses, stopped crying.

"*Abuelito,*" Ben called, "I think we should get him up again." Jose patted her knee and walked quickly to Lancelot's stall.

"That rolling won't hurt him, as long as he doesn't bang into the walls. We don't want to tire him out walking." He rejoined Jane and sat next to her again, taking her hand and searching her eyes for a long moment. "*Bonita,* I need you to help me," he said, and paused. "I need you to help *us.*" Jane, not knowing what else to do, nodded. "I called Doc Hallman, but he's with another horse. His assistant is calling around to other vets for us, but it's a busy time, lots of mares foaling. I hope with Big Red it's not too serious, but right now we don't know. I'm going to make up a warm mash for him with a little aspirin in it to help his bellyache. Will you keep an eye on him with Ben and help him get Red up if he starts banging around?"

"Of course, sure." Jane nodded again and blew her nose. Jose winked at her and patted her knee. He gave her a hand up and walked swiftly to the feed room.

Jane hung back from Lancelot's stall. Ben was leaning with his arms over the door, apparently concentrating on Lancelot. She didn't know what to say, and her embarrassment mounted with each passing minute of silence, broken by the restless thrashings of the sick horse.

Finally Ben glanced over at her, and she realized he looked as embarrassed as she felt. "I'm, um, sorry about

Beau," he said, his voice cracking a bit. He cleared his throat and frowned.

"It's okay," Jane said, and he nodded and turned back to Lancelot. The lie, and his acceptance of it, helped somehow. At least, it closed the subject for the evening, and Jane was so exhausted by her own thoughts and feelings that she actually felt some relief. She joined Ben at the stall door.

Lancelot was on his side, his crimson flanks dark with sweat. His large, pink-tinged nostrils were extended and his breath was ragged. He moved his legs in place, as if he were trying to outrun his pain. "How did he get like this?" Jane whispered. Ben glanced quickly at her. "You know Emily left, right?" he asked.

Jane shook her head in confusion. "What? Why?" And then she suddenly remembered something from earlier that afternoon, a lifetime ago: *You could always just pull an Emily and throw Ariel in her stall....*

"I don't know. Her parents came and picked her up this afternoon. She left class early. I was setting up jumps in the ring, and Red got out of hand when they were cantering, and she got mad at him again. Susan told her to call it quits for the day. Red looked really worked up and he'd kinda been freaking out all morning. Then—" Ben paused. Lancelot was getting heavily to his feet. They waited while he clambered up and watched him uneasily. He stood, head low, breathing loudly. But he seemed calm. Ben resumed his story.

"I had to go help my granddad unload all the feed because, you know, my cousins are gone picking up a new school horse for the Jeffrys." Jane registered with a painful twinge why the Jeffrys needed a new school horse. "So I didn't see exactly what happened. But my guess is that she just put Red in his stall and left, and he had a full bucket of oats in there waiting for his dinner later on and a pile of hay and water. He must've drunk the whole bucket of water, and he ate almost an entire bucket of oats *and* half of his alfalfa. Granddad and I were busy all day and Red is usually in his stall anyway because he's not so good yet in the field with all the other horses around. Granddad didn't see he was sick until about midnight when he came back to the barn because he left his glasses in the tack room." In spite of herself, Jane smiled. Jose was notorious for losing his glasses—usually when they were on top of his head, perched in his thick gray hair. Ben chuckled.

"I know, right? Total Granddad. But I'm glad he lost them tonight."

"Me, too," Jane said. A silence fell between them.

All of a sudden, Lancelot pitched forward onto his knees, rolled over, and started pawing at the sawdust. But he'd landed too close to the wall, and with a loud cracking sound one of his hooves struck it, leaving a crescent-shaped chip behind. Without thinking, Jane sprang forward and threw back the stall door. Lancelot was lying with his head facing her; his long legs, so delicate compared with the rest of his massive form, struck out and met the wall. Jane ran to his head and tugged at his halter. Lancelot groaned and tried to roll toward her. He wasn't getting up.

*Bang!* went a knee against the wall as he lost the mo-

mentum of his roll. Jane tugged and tugged, pleading with
him to rise, cradling his neck with her left arm as she pulled
at his halter with her right. Then, "*Hyah!*" came Ben's voice,
and Jane, startled, looked up to find him at the other end
of the stall. "Watch out!" he yelled, and brought his hand
down, hard, on Lancelot's rump. Jane just had time to leap
out of the way as the great chestnut surged to his feet. She
made a grab for his head, lost her balance, and stumbled
forward, throwing her arms around Lancelot's neck to
catch herself.

"I think," she panted, "it's time to walk him again."
And then, before she knew it, her face was buried in the
rough red mane and she was laughing helplessly, and Ben,
holding on to the bars of the hayrack, was looking at her
like she'd lost her senses.

Oddly enough, Lancelot seemed not to mind her near
hysteria, born of relief and built-up strain. He let Jane lean
into him, and for her part she'd forgotten, momentarily at
least, that she was using the wildest horse in the barn as a
combination of Kleenex and pillow.

"Okay," Jane choked out as she led Lancelot from the
stall, "this really actually isn't funny at all . . . I'm just so
glad he's up . . . and your *cowboy* call—*Hyah!*" She doubled
over again.

"That wasn't a cowboy call—they're the ones that
hanged all my ancestors for stealing back our own horses,
remember?" Ben replied, with affected offense. "That was
the cry of the great Mexican . . . the great Mexican . . .
um . . ."

"Weirdo!" Jane gasped, and this time they both cracked up.

"Indeed. The great Mexican weirdo! I get it from my granddad."

"What do you get from me?" Jose wanted to know, looking at them with bemusement as he reentered the barn, carrying the bucket with mash.

"Um, nothing," Ben said hastily, and explained what had happened in the stall. Jose ran his hands over Lancelot's legs, paying particular attention to the knee that Jane told him had collided with the wall. "No damage done," Jose pronounced. "You two did good to get him up."

"It was Jane," Ben said. "She went right in as soon as she saw he was in trouble."

"But I wouldn't have been able to get him up without your help," she protested. They looked at each other and smiled, and Jane blushed and turned back to Lancelot.

"Well, you seem to get along pretty good," Jose said.

Jane didn't know where to look. How could Jose be so *obvious*? What was the matter with adults, even really wonderful ones like Ben's grandfather, that they would say and do these incredibly embarrassing things without batting an eye? She would never forget the time that her mother, on being introduced to a certain important boy who was costarring with Lily in a play, actually said, with, it seemed to the sisters, an almost gleeful emphasis, "Oh, Lily's told me *so much* about you!" The boy had given her a look like, *Why?* and Lily hadn't spoken to her mother for two days.

Now Jane decided to pretend she hadn't heard and concentrated on walking the horse. "He doesn't seem too skittish around you," Jose called after her. "He's not such an easy one, but maybe you two will be friends." Jane contemplated leading Lancelot straight out of the barn and away from Jose's evident and totally insane determination to interfere and matchmake. What had come over him? She paused by the door.

"Yeah," she heard Ben say to his grandfather, "Lancelot seems cool around Jane." *Oh god,* she thought, *that's who he was talking about!* Shaky with relief, and on the verge of another fit of giggles, she turned the horse around.

What with the excitement of getting Lancelot up, Jane hadn't really paid that much attention to his behavior now that he was safely out of his stall and moving around. But it was true, she realized, that she felt comfortable around the big horse, and he seemed to be calming down. *It's probably because he's feeling better, or worse, and I've been too busy to be scared by him,* she thought. The middle idea—that he might be feeling worse—made her hasten back to Jose and the mash with aspirin.

And so began the long night at the barn. Jane and Ben took turns walking Lancelot and allowing him mouthfuls of the warm bran and swallows of tepid water. They watched over him in the stall, but there were no further alarms. They talked in spurts, about horses, and Mexico, where Ben's great-uncles and aunts still lived and where he visited every year, and Jane told him a little about her parents and about Lily going to college in the fall. As the hours passed, Lancelot seemed to grow more and more easy, and Jose fell soundly asleep, leaning against a hay bale, a slightly solemn expression on his kind, weathered face. Every once in a while he'd snore and Jane and Ben would put their hands over their mouths to keep from laughing and waking him up.

Finally Lancelot showed no interest in either the mash or the water, but plainly wanted to go back to his stall, where he lay down heavily, stretched out his long neck, and went to sleep. The sweat had dried on his coat, leaving salty streaks like the tracks of waves on a beach. Jane watched his quiet breathing for a few moments, then stretched her own aching arms and back and walked to the barn door. Someone flipped off the light switch and the barn receded into still darkness behind her, while before her the deep blue light of morning embraced the farm in a quiet but electric glow. It was as if a painter with a phosphorescent brush had visited Sunny Acres, brightening and highlighting the forms of bushes, fence posts, and trees.

She yawned, her whole body shuddering with sleepiness. She felt a kind of numbed quietude, physical exhaustion displacing all of the previous night's tumult. A hand squeezed her shoulder.

"*Bonita*, Big Red is asleep, and it's time for you to go to bed as well."

Jane turned to Jose. "You think he's going to be all right?" she asked.

"He's fine now. Just tired out. Doc Hallman's going to stop by soon—he got that foal delivered."

"That's go-o-od." Jane yawned again. "So he'll check him out and make sure he's completely okay?"

Jose nodded. "I won't forget your help tonight, Jane."

She blushed.

Ben joined them, standing a little apart, chewing on a piece of hay and studying the awakening landscape before them. The sun was now cresting the horizon, and Jane saw Maria hail them with a big wave as she mounted the steps to the kitchen to start preparing breakfast. They all waved back, and Jane felt a rush of gratitude toward Jose and Ben, and Maria, too, for this sense of camaraderie, of belonging, which stole up on her like the morning light.

"Well . . ." she said, glancing shyly in Ben's direction. He stepped forward, reaching out his hand, which she took. They shook, hard.

"Thanks for helping out," he said. "It was, um . . ." He stopped.

"We couldn't have done it without you," Jose finished.

Jane's and Ben's hands dropped.

"Good night," Jane said. "No, wait a sec, I mean—good morning!"

"Good morning!" Jose and his grandson replied, and, with a last look back at the barn . . . and at the pale gold rays of light just now reaching the stall festooned with streamers and balloons . . . Jane started walking back to the cabin.

## Chapter 8

# Good Morning, Heartache

*I*t was almost one o'clock when Jane awoke. The cabin was empty, and the air felt hot and close from the afternoon sun pouring through the bare window. The room had the look of abandoned places at the wrong times of the day—the way your bedroom looks on a school day, when you're sick and have to stay home, Jane thought. Or the way school would look on a Saturday. It was strange how the feeling of places was so specific to what you did in them, and when. And strange when you realized their existence outside of you—that they were there, not even waiting, really, when you were not. . . . Jane's thoughts drifted, and she lay in her loneliness, doing battle with the one thought that, finally, moved relentlessly to the surface.

She quickly got out of bed to get dressed and to find Robin. It felt like she hadn't talked to her best friend in days.

Robin was walking toward the cabin as Jane was pulling on her boots on the front porch. They flew into each other's arms.

"I'm so glad you're up!" Robin gasped. "I've been waiting all day!"

Jane looked down at her friend's sneaker-clad feet and spick-and-span khaki shorts.

"Didn't you ride today?" she asked.

"No!" Robin looked at her with disbelief. "I've been here, waiting for you to wake up, crazy. Besides, I *finally* got to the middle of *Watership Down*." Jane would've smiled if she could remember how.

"C'mon," Robin continued, "let's get some lunch. I just checked—everybody's gone down to the pond, so we can have the kitchen to ourselves."

Jane realized she was famished and started from the porch, then looked down in dismay at her boots. "I don't know why I'm wearing these. . . ."

"Because they're your summer uniform," Robin said briskly, tugging at her hand. "If you went and put on sandals I'd know you'd finally completely lost it."

The kitchen was cool and inviting after the sweltering gray glare of the farm at high afternoon, with two ceiling fans stirring the red-and-white-checked oilcloths that covered the long wooden tables where the campers ate. The dining area was actually a roomy screened-in porch just off the kitchen, but everyone simply called it "the kitchen."

Jane and Robin went up to the counter that halfway divided the porch from the industrial-sized stove, dishwasher, and sink, where Maria was up to her elbows in suds.

She smiled at them. "So, you are awake! *¿Tienes hambre?*"

"*Sí!*" said Robin, who was taking Spanish. Jane (who took Latin because she loved the ancient mythologies, though she'd found out that she did not love the ancient verb tenses) hazarded a nod of agreement.

Maria smiled. "I heard about your big night, you must be! Do you want to eat camper or Reyes?"

"Reyes!" Jane and Robin said in unison. Maria had to cook for two groups—the campers, whom she fed traditional American fare, and her own family, for whom she conjured a variety of thick bean stews, fresh vegetables, and homemade tortillas. Sometimes at lunch, when she had to prepare one right after the other, she'd offer the campers some of her family's food for a change. Jane and Robin and a few others always accepted, though many turned up their noses. Once Jane had even heard Emily loud-whisper to Alyssa, "No Taco Bell for me." She'd hoped that Maria hadn't overheard.

Their plates laden with a warm, spicy-smelling dish plentifully garnished with slices of tomato and onion, Jane and Robin went automatically to their usual table, though they had the whole porch to choose from. Jane felt Robin looking at her, but she found it hard to meet her friend's eyes. The lightening of her spirits from finally being in Robin's comforting presence had now subsided, and she felt yesterday's misery crawling back to her like the song from the Billie Holiday record that her parents sometimes played in the evenings. "*Good morning, heartache...*" She decided to plunge in, so she could at least talk about the thing that wasn't painful first, before Robin started asking questions she didn't want to think about yet, and for which she had no answers.

As she related the events of the previous night, which now had a cast of unreality, a too-bright and dreamlike quality, from the shadowless world of the illuminated barn at three A.M. to the fragmented, drifting, yet comfortable conversations with Ben, she and Robin began to piece together the chronology of the day before. Jane said that she was surprised that no one had mentioned Emily's departure that afternoon, and Robin reminded her that they had had their own crises to deal with. "And besides, even if Alyssa and Jennifer hadn't been hiding out—" She paused and gave Jane a look.

"We'd be the last ones to find out anything anyway," Jane finished.

"Exactly. After you'd gone to bed, I saw that Emily's stuff wasn't on her bunk, and I asked Liz where she was, but all she told me was that she'd decided to go on vacation with her family and didn't say good-bye to anybody. Then today, after Susan explained where you were—"

"Wait a sec, what did she say?" Jane asked, curious.

Robin shrugged. "Well, she just said that you'd been up all night helping Jose with Lancelot, and then she went off on how we all have to take responsibility for our horses. It was weird, she didn't say anything directly about Emily, but of course it was completely obvious. It was almost like she didn't want anybody talking about Emily or asking any questions. Then Jessica told me, well, she told Jennifer, and I was just sort of there, that Emily's mom and dad had been coming by the farm to drop off some more clothes and stuff for her, and when they got here she told them to wait, and she packed up and left with them. She said that Emily's mom and dad talked to Susan for a while, and then they just took off. . . ."

"Go West, young idiot," Jane said, and she smiled sardonically, thinking of the trouble Emily had left in her wake. But she couldn't hold the smile, grim though it was, for very long. It was as if there was a heavy wave just beneath her, and when she managed to get her head above the water for a moment, it returned, tugging at her, bringing her down once again.

"So what's Ben like?" Robin asked. Jane blushed, and Robin broke into a tentative grin, her eyes sparkling.

"No!" Jane protested. "This isn't a real *blush* blush, it's just that, you know, it's kind of weird thinking about it. You know sometimes I blush for no reason."

"Mm-hmm . . ." Robin nodded, unconvinced.

"He's nice," Jane said hastily. "He's . . . I don't know, a really easy person to be around. You'll like him a lot when you hang out with him more. That's it."

"Okay, sure," Robin said, but she still had a mischievous look that made Jane very much want to change the subject.

So, finally, there was nowhere else to go. They sat in silence for a while.

"I don't want to hear about the birthday," Jane said quietly.

Robin nodded. "Well, can I tell you about my plan?"

Jane looked up from her plate, where she'd been stirring her mostly uneaten food around in circles. She wasn't very hungry anymore.

"What plan?"

Robin took a deep breath. "I think you should ride Bess. Our lessons are never at the same time, and I think Bess could do the advanced stuff. You've ridden her before, and—"

But Jane stopped her. "No way, Robin. She'd get totally worn out. It's not fair to her." It came out sounding harsher than she'd meant.

Robin's eyes grew bright with tears. "I just want to help," she whispered.

Forcing back the lump in her throat, Jane leaned across the table and pulled her friend close to her. "You're the best friend ever," she told her. "It's the nicest idea ever."

But Robin was really crying now. "I just hate how *unfair* it all is," she choked out. "I hate it that you might . . . that you might have to *leave!*"

"Who said anything about leaving?" Jane shook Robin's shoulders, then grabbed her a napkin. Leaving was exactly what she had planned on doing; it had been in her mind all last night and greeted her when she woke up. But suddenly, hearing Robin say it aloud, seeing her friend's sorrow, she felt a surge of defiance charge through her veins like a current of electricity.

"Listen," she said quickly, before the feeling passed, "I'm going to figure something out. I'll talk to Susan. I can ride in your class, on one of the school horses. Maybe the new one. It'll be fine."

"Really?" Robin looked at her with mingled skepticism and relief. "You really feel that way?"

"Absolutely," Jane said stoutly. But even as she said it, doubts stole in, sapping her strength. Who knew how good Beau's replacement would be . . . Leaving Advanced I now, after she'd been so proud to get in . . . Not riding Beau . . .

She managed a smile. "C'mon. Let's go see how Big Red is doing."

"Who?" Robin asked.

"Oh, that's what Jose calls Lancelot." They bussed their trays and waved good-bye to Maria.

"Well, I guess it's a better nickname than the Nutty Knight."


*But Lancelot's stall* was empty and looked as if it had been recently cleaned. Jane glanced at the brass nameplate affixed to the door: LANCELOT/OWNER: EMILY LONGSTREET. She wondered if Beau's stall now bore a similarly smug declaration of property, but she stopped herself before she was tempted to turn and look. "C'mon," she said to Robin, "let's check the paddock." She felt a pinprick of worry.

What if Red had gotten worse? What if Doc Hallman had taken him away? But surely Maria would have said something, or Robin would have heard. . . .

Still, it was a relief to find the big gelding in the shady paddock, tearing out what mouthfuls of grass he could find by the roots and stamping impatiently at the fat, lazy flies that seemed like genies of the afternoon heat. He threw his head back as they approached and took one long sideways step, his nostrils dilating as he sniffed the air. The whites of his eyes shone as he snorted again and gave his head a few furious shakes, gracefully sidestepping again with a dressagelike precision.

"There's just something *fierce* about him, isn't there?" Robin whispered as they leaned against the fence.

"Something amazing," Jane replied. "You can't stop looking at him." It was true: There was an air about Lancelot, beyond the obvious beauty and breeding manifest in the sleek coat that looked poured over his rippling musculature like molten copper, in the proud, delicately chiseled head, that commanded attention. There was arrogance, certainly, but there was feeling as well. Robin sneezed and Lancelot spooked, giving a half rear as he spun around and cantered to the far side of the paddock.

"Crazy," Jane whispered after him. "What happened to you, anyway?"

"I wonder if we'll ever know," Robin mused.

"We got along pretty well last night," Jane said. "But he was sick. I wonder . . ." And suddenly she swung her leg over the fence, hopping to the other side with the ease of long habit. She reached back through the rail and grabbed a handful of clover and long grass.

"What are you doing?" Robin asked warily.

"Just an experiment," Jane called over her shoulder as she headed toward the red horse, who had stopped grazing and was attentively watching her approach. Jane whistled low and tunelessly, walking as nonchalantly as possible, not meeting Red's glare but pretending she was looking at something interesting just over his withers. He didn't move.

"Hey, nutty horse, hey, nutty Red," she sang, holding the grass out in the cup of her right hand. "Hey, you big palooka who kept me out of bed!" His ears flickered toward her, and he took a half-step backward. Jane continued to sing as she ambled up to him, then her hand was on his neck and he was eating the clover from her other hand, before he'd had time to startle, or she'd had time to think better of the whole idea. She stroked his glorious coat, still brittle in spots with dried sweat, as he chewed the grass, staring off into space. He sighed. "You're really all right, you know, Red," Jane told him.

"Jane, think you could get a halter on him?" Susan had joined Robin at the fence, looking tired and harassed.

"I'll try," Jane called. Lancelot turned and looked at her. "You want to go for a walk, buddy?" she asked. He blinked at her. *It's worth a shot*, Jane thought, and she grabbed a handful of his mane, as she used to do with Beau. She started walking forward, not looking at Lancelot, holding firm to his mane. To her great surprise, he moved with her. "Good boy," Jane said, and gave him a pat with her free hand. They walked side by side to the fence, where Susan and Robin were standing, slack-jawed.

"Well," Susan said, and her face relaxed into a smile. She handed Jane a new, stiff leather halter, which Jane slipped over Lancelot's ears, standing on tiptoe and staggering a little to reach as far as she could to his poll.

"What did Doc Hallman say? Is he okay?" Jane asked as she fastened the buckle below yet another small, shining nameplate fixed to the cheek piece: LANCELOT.

"He's fine," Susan said crisply, her smile fading. "But if Jose and Ben—and you—hadn't been there, it might have been worse. When will you girls learn to take responsibility for your horses . . . and Jose is not getting any younger. . . ." She stopped, the muscle in her cheek working furiously as she stared stonily at Lancelot, as if he were culpable for the campers' carelessness toward his caretaker.

"Well, not you," she said gruffly, giving Robin a sharp look that actually made her start. "You're a good owner to Bess, Robin."

"Thank you," Robin said in a small voice. They stood in silence as Susan scuffed her boot on the grass, still staring at Lancelot, who ignored her. Jane could tell that he was getting restless standing still so she began walking him around in a small circle while she waited for Susan to continue. She wasn't entirely sure what had put Susan in such a foul mood, but she very much hoped that she wasn't a part of it. *Well, what have I done? Is she just mad that*

I might have to take up another one of the school horses? She felt a sudden wave of resentment toward her grim-faced trainer. *If I'm such a problem, maybe I should just leave and get off her hands.*

"Susan, did you want me to do something with Lancelot, or can I let him go?" she asked brusquely. Lancelot was now shaking his head, and Jane was being dragged unceremoniously beside him as he tried to break into a trot. Suddenly Susan's stormy face broke into a new smile, with more than a hint of calculation in it, and her eyes danced as they flitted back and forth between Jane and Lancelot and Robin. She let out a great bark of a laugh, and Lancelot shied. "Oh, *really!*" Jane said in exasperation as she tugged on his halter. Another surprise: He immediately stood still again.

"Look at this!" Susan crowed. "I'm such an idiot!" Jane and Robin and Lancelot all stared at her in silence.

"Yes, Jane," she said merrily. "There is something I want you to do with my new horse. I want you to ride him."

## Chapter 9

# Susan's Big Idea

"Your new horse?"

"*Ride him?*"

Susan, still chuckling, answered Robin's question first. "Yep. I was so pis—ah, *angry* when Emily's parents told me she was leaving, and that she wanted me to train Lancelot for her this summer, that like a madwoman I offered to buy him." She paused, running a hand through her hair and tugging on it till the crown stood up in a small explosion.

"And they agreed?" Jane asked bewilderedly.

"Yeah, they called my bluff. Mrs. Longstreet has her shorts in knots that Emily's going to get hurt, and her dad seemed to want to wash his hands of everything. It was . . . odd, the whole situation. Especially how little Mr. Longstreet asked . . . ." Susan reached down to pluck a blade of onion grass and stuck it in the side of her mouth, and when she straightened, Jane could see that her expression had clouded.

"What did Emily say?" Robin whispered.

"They didn't even tell her." Susan grinned, and the cloud blew through, leaving a wicked sparkle behind. "Glad I won't be in that car when they do."

Jane doubted that Emily would care. She left her horse untended to get colic, whipped him when he defied her, and complained about him constantly. She couldn't imagine an owner who liked her horse less. But she was anxious to find out what Susan had meant by the other part of her amazing statement—*ride him?*

"Go ahead and bring Lancelot in," Susan said, reaching to open the paddock gate, and before Jane could say anything, her trainer had walked away, slapping her boot with her crop. Then she called over her shoulder, "Robin, you better come and tack up Bess for the afternoon lesson, too." The girls stared at each other.

"Ours not to reason why . . ." Jane finally said, quoting her father, who had the habit of reciting the ominous lines from "The Charge of the Light Brigade" when he had to make a difficult left turn onto a busy road, as an army of headlights streamed toward them. "Though hopefully this won't involve doing and dying," she added, and walked

Susan's fidgeting horse through the gate and toward the barn.

"No, Mum, really, it's okay," Jane repeated into the phone. This was a new experience, comforting her mother, but she didn't know what else to do. She was close to tears, which she now accepted as a kind of permanent state, but she was afraid that if she told her mother how she really felt that Mrs. Ryan, in a fit of maternal solicitude, would come flying out to the farm to comfort her. If that happened, Jane couldn't trust herself not to give in to her tumultuous feelings and leave with her. And she'd promised Susan. Steeling herself, she said, "And now you don't have to pay for the rest of camp. Mrs. Jeffrys said."

"Oh, honey, that's not what's important. I just know how much you love Beau . . . and I wish your father and I . . . Oh, here's Lily, I'll put her on now."

"No, Mum, please! I have to go! Tell Lily that I can't talk right now, that I have to go to a . . . on a hayride," she lied. She knew that whatever composure she could muster for her mother would crumble the instant that she heard Lily's voice. "I love you, Mum, and Dad and Lily. Bye." She hung up before her mother could protest and slumped against the smoke-stained wall of the kitchen, exhausted. Maria bustled over to her, holding a fresh ice pack wrapped in a washcloth. In return, she took a watery, melted sack from Jane.

"Keep it on the eye!" she scolded, and Jane gingerly raised her hand to her head again.

"Is this the big reward she gets?" Maria muttered furiously to Jose, who was sitting at the kitchen table drinking lemonade and rolling a cigarette. "She saves that monster and then he tries to kill her? And Susan lets this happen? They give another girl Jane's horse and make her ride the crazy one? Is everyone on this *farm* crazy? You tell me!" she hissed at her husband, whacking his arm with her rolled-up dish towel, as if he were to blame for the situation.

"I don't think he actually wanted to kill me, Maria," Jane said, slowly moving to a chair next to Jose and easing herself down. "He really wanted to run into a tree and kill himself, and I just happened to be on board. . . ."

Maria scowled, and her dish-towel hand twitched threateningly at Jose, then her face softened as she saw that Jane was smiling, though only from one side of her mouth, as any movement of her left facial muscles sent a dart of pain to her throbbing eye.

A scant few hours earlier, as Jane and Robin had listened to Susan's plan, Jane had found that she could easily understand why their trainer was in such a temper. Not only had she impulsively bought a troubled horse, she had to continue working with him or risk him growing more isolated, unresponsive, and rebellious. She also told Jane how proud she'd been of her the day before, both for her cross-country course and for her help with Lancelot—Jane blushed—and she was worried about losing a good horse,

Beau, and having to settle in the new school horse that the Jeffrys had bought to replace him.

"So," Susan had finished, latching her eyes on Jane's, "will you ride Lancelot for me?"

Jane hadn't answered immediately. She'd thought about Beau, about the camp competition that they had been training for, about the awesome, scared joy she'd felt as they sailed over the hedge. She'd thought about how the farm itself could never quite be the same again, no matter what horse she rode, now that Beau belonged to another girl. She realized that some kind of era had ended, but ended unexpectedly, in a way she never could have prepared for. You usually think of things changing at certain times, she'd thought. Like Lily going to college in the fall. Like graduating from trotting poles to cross-rails to the coop. Like changing schools. These things could be hard, but you knew they were coming. Now, she felt lost, unscripted, and fumbling her way toward what she was supposed to do, and to be. Could she help Susan, who had helped her so much? And this of course gave her the answer.

"Sure," Jane had said, and that was all she really needed to say. And as Susan had smiled with relief and thanked her, she'd felt some of her summer happiness, the kind of happiness that only came at Sunny Acres, and that smelled of sawdust and Murphy's Oil and fly spray, fade. But in its place there seemed to come a feeling that she couldn't define. The nearest word she found for it was stubbornness, and that, at least, was better than tears.

But her first ride on Lancelot had not gone well, to

put it mildly. Susan had told her to join Advanced II's afternoon class, and as soon as Jane had swung her leg over the enormous red horse, marveling at his size and how very far up she felt, she looked around and saw a horsefly settle on his hindquarters. Without thinking, she raised her hand to brush it away, as she had countless times with other horses, and Lancelot had bolted. She hadn't even gathered her reins yet and was caught in an awkward, backward lean. By the time she'd gotten herself straightened out and was making a grab for her right rein, which had shot through her fingers, he'd run under the low hanging branches of the big oak at the arena's far side, one of which connected with Jane's face, sending her flying backward off the still-charging horse, and landing hard on her butt on the twisted roots.

By the time Susan reached her, she'd already determined that nothing was broken and had managed to get to her feet. They caught Lancelot, and Jane was checking his girth before she remounted when Susan touched her arm. "Jane, you really can't ride right now," she said with an odd, tight expression. Jane glanced up, saw the look on Robin's face, and realized that something must be more wrong than she'd thought. Sure enough, when Susan had ushered her into the bathroom off the kitchen and she'd seen her face, rusty with blood from a gash over her left eyebrow, and her eye turning a vile shade of purple, she let out an involuntary gasp.

Susan summoned Mrs. Jeffrys, and together with Jose and Maria they determined that the cut wasn't deep enough to require stitches. Maria cleaned her up, and after the lesson ended Susan and Mrs. Jeffrys had a talk about Jane's new situation with Lancelot. Jane thought that her black eye and taped-up forehead might have helped Mrs. Jeffrys make the decision to return half of Jane's camp tuition to her parents.

Not, of course, that she'd told them about her fall.

Jose sighed, letting out a stream of smoke through his nostrils. "It does seem as if this summer is a test for our *bonita*," he said. "You maybe aren't having as much fun at camp as usual?" He winked at her, and she tried to raise her eyebrow, then winced.

The screen door banged open, and Jane saw Robin, then, with a little jolt, Ben, illuminated by the kitchen's soft yellow light. Robin placed a bundle on the table and gave Jane a fragile, one-armed hug. "I brought our p.j.'s and stuff," she said, and Jose graciously pulled out a chair for her to join them. Mrs. Jeffrys had invited Jane to spend the night in the guest room of the main house, in case she needed anything, and had invited "her particular friend" to join her. Jane could no more imagine waking Mrs. Jeffrys in the middle of the night to ask for aspirin than she could imagine chewing her own foot off, and she was grateful that Robin would be with her, for the house, and its mistress, had a formal grandeur that she'd always found somewhat intimidating. Mrs. Jeffrys was kind, but she was "Old Louisville," as her mother, a North Dakotan by birth, put it, and Jane had always semiconsciously felt that she was a Taylor person, and not a Ryan person.

She heard a familiar low whistle and turned to find Ben inspecting her bandaged brow from across the table. *So glad that half the times he's seen me I've been crying or beat up. He must think I'm a total basket case*, she thought, and fervently hoped that at least the bruises would hide the flush that she could feel staining her face.

"You look like you ran into a tree," he said.

"Funny, because that's exactly what I did," Jane replied, and he and Robin laughed.

"It's only a flesh wound," she said, in accent, to Robin, who looked over at Ben uncertainly before whispering back to Jane, "It's nought but a scratch really, my deah."

He looked at them with bright, questioning eyes. "Is that supposed to be, like, Russian?"

The girls giggled self-consciously, and Robin said, "Oh, dear, I never knew we were *that* bad—it's supposed to be British."

"Then, yeah, it's terrible," he scoffed smilingly.

The screen door banged open again, and Jane was startled to see Jessica saunter in, wearing boxer shorts and a tank top and flip-flops, her hair twirled up in a perfect messy bun. She punched Ben's shoulder lightly as she passed him, saying, "Hey, everybody," and casually tossed a CD over to Jane. "It's the new Love Suicides album," she said. "I thought it would be good get-well music. You can borrow it till whenever. Damn, you look terrible." She perched herself on a stool by the stove, cocking her head at Jane and studying her impersonally.

"Oh, awesome," Jane said, looking at the CD case, which seemed to depict Japanese warriors with Mohawks doing some sort of dance in outer space. "I love them," she lied. She'd never heard of them. She ignored Robin's kick under the table.

"Well, you're not missing anything in the outside world," Jessica drawled, waving her hand as if shooing away Jane's thanks. "Although I've got five missed calls from Emily, so it's possible that the family vacation is off to a rocky start. And Megan's freaking out over Beau. She had to be dragged out of his stall tonight to go to bed."

Jane's stomach plummeted and the hand holding the ice bag gave an involuntary jerk. She looked down at the CD as if something on it had suddenly caught her attention.

"So, um, who are the Love Suicides?" Robin blurted, and Jane loved her for it, especially since it made her sound so hopelessly out of it. She pretended to adjust the ice bag so she could dash away the tears that had inevitably begun to burn her eyes. It was as if Jessica had walked in and delivered a series of well-timed blows: from her strange, distant tone to this callous reference to Beau. Jane felt as winded as if Jessica *had* actually hit her, and not in the extremely friendly way she had just lightly punched Ben . . . .

"A band," Jessica said in a bored voice. Then— unexpectedly: "Ben, walk me back to the cabin. I can't see in the dark."

"So how'd you get over here?" The sharp words, and

their tone, were out of Jane's mouth before she could edit herself, and she realized with a sinking sensation that this was exactly how Jessica had intended her to feel.

Jessica smiled broadly. "By smell," she said, arching an eyebrow at Jane.

Ben laughed, but it seemed to Jane that he was uncomfortable, or embarrassed. He gave his grandmother a quick, abashed kiss and waved to his grandfather.

Jessica eased herself to the floor and waggled her fingers at Jane. "Sweet dreams," she said, and with a nonchalance that Jane could only marvel at, linked her arm through Ben's.

"That was really nice of you to bring her that CD," Jane heard Ben say as the screen door closed behind them. "Track five is awesome . . . you know the one . . ." And the sound of Jessica's voice singing the chorus, which sounded something like "Anodyne, end of time, you are mine," then Ben's tenor joining in, drifting back on the still July air to the quiet group gathered in the kitchen, where the only sound was the suddenly loud ticking of the old clock above the stove.


*"How are you feeling?"* Robin whispered, her voice small and close next to Jane's shoulder. "I'm okay," Jane muttered. She wondered at how many times today, and yesterday, and all of her life, that she had said those two words when they were patently untrue. She wondered why those two words were so essential, were her own lie

that she needed. *My lie,* she thought as she stared up and out to the dim, unfamiliar room. Light from the porch outside filtered through the long, narrow windows framed with heavy blue damask draperies that matched the wallpaper's flowers and curlicues that seemed to Jane's tired, throbbing eyes to be shifting and sliding along the walls. The house was cool and hushed. Jane was glad for the quiet, for the removal from the cabin and from the other girls, but the strange room also added to the isolation that threatened to cast her adrift.

Her forehead pulsed with a dull, grinding pain. Beau was gone. Advanced I and the competition were gone. Half of camp was gone, and when it went, Lily would be going. She was seized with the sudden strong desire to leave Sunny Acres, to spend the rest of the summer with her sister, with her parents, who had, after all, wished that they could have bought Beau ... her mother had almost said it. They did understand, at least a little. And she had lied to them. And Ben ... Her eyes swimming, she looked over at the CD that she'd tossed on the plump chintz tuft that stood before the grand marble-and-mahogany dresser. Even if she owned a portable CD player, which she didn't, she knew she'd never, ever listen to the Love Suicides.

"She must really like him," Robin whispered, making Jane jump.

"What do you mean?" she whispered back.

"The way Jessica was acting," Robin said slowly. "You stayed up all night with him in the barn, and she really hasn't talked to you at all today. ... No, don't interrupt!

115

She saw Ben come with me to the house, and she followed us and treated you like . . ."

"It doesn't matter," Jane said, turning toward Robin and burying her face in her friend's shoulder. Her face burned every time she pictured doing her stupid accent in front of Ben, her stupid accent along with her swollen, grotesque eye, and her babyish tears, just to have Jessica walk in looking so unconcernedly and perfectly cool. "And besides," she finished, "it looks like he likes her back." And when this last part of all of the things that were hurting was said aloud, Jane finally fell asleep.

## Chapter 10

# The Royal Ukrainian Cavalry

*T*he damp grass and clover flowers shushed past Jane's boots as she walked slowly out to the big field, jingling the chain of the lead shank in her right hand. She heard Robin's voice some ways ahead of her, calling to Bess, who Jane saw was in the valley to the left of the main group of horses quietly standing by the far copse of trees. Jane and Robin had been the first ones to the barn. They'd had a brief moment of hilarity earlier, trying to decide how to make up the enormous bed with its frills and flounces and multiple pillows of odd shapes (egg, log, triangle), before they escaped the silent, chilly house, running out into the warmth of the morning sunshine, gasping with laughter until Jane had clutched her throbbing head.

The restored ease she felt with her friend made the morning seem that much brighter after the dark night.

Now, as she reached the group of school horses, her hands went automatically to a familiar brown mane, and she slid her arm around the sturdy neck, leaning her cheek against the cheek that bent down to hers. She breathed in the hay and sun and clover smell from the saddle-colored coat and smiled. "Hey, Beau," she said.

She was only pretending, she knew, but Jane let herself pretend for a minute more.

She ran her hands over the soft muzzle that nibbled at her palm, looking for the carrot that she pulled from her pocket. She finger-combed the forelock that grazed his short eyelashes and gently brushed away a fly that had settled in the corner of his eye. Mostly she just looked at him, ordinary Beau on an ordinary morning, in a parallel universe in which the past two days hadn't happened yet, or perhaps would never happen. He bent his head and rubbed his forehead on her arm, and the familiar gesture made her eyes fill. She scratched his poll and he whickered contentedly.

As she gazed at him, Jane remembered the first time she'd ridden Beau, the combination of discovery and familiarity that she'd felt as she'd gotten used to his big stride, then later his eagerness to jump that sometimes made him rush at fences, the canter that could be controlled to a beautiful, collected gait, once she'd figured out how to keep him on the bit (with much encouragement and close contact with his mouth). She remembered sneaking into the barn at night to bring him carrots, and to escape from the confusing pressures and insecurities she felt with the girls at camp. Once she'd fallen asleep in a pile of hay in the corner of his stall and woken at midnight to find him lying on his side with his neck pressed against her back. She wrapped her arms around that strong neck now as she braced herself to say good-bye.

Beau was her harbor, she thought, as Lily and Robin were also her harbors. With a surge of resentment and longing, she thought that if she could just have him still be her horse for the rest of the summer, she could face, or ignore, Alyssa and Jennifer and . . . Jessica. She could hide out with him as she'd always hidden out with him, safe on his back, safe taking care of him. Then another image flickered through her mind, making a path through the thicket of sadness and memories, an image of the horse that had also been her companion during a hard night. A horse that had needed her.

Jane gave Beau one final stroke down his broad, plain face and turned away from him. As she walked slowly from the field, she could hear his hoofbeats following her, and she forced herself to walk faster. And as she approached the gate, she saw a small, slim figure walking swiftly and eagerly toward her, face aglow, new halter swinging from her shoulder. The girl didn't appear to see her; her sparkling eyes were fixed on something behind Jane, and she seemed barely able to contain the spring-heeled joy that animated her stride and the grin that pulled at her mouth.

Jane quickly veered to the right and managed to duck under the fence and around the big oak tree before she met Megan, now running to bring in her new horse.

Jane didn't look behind her as she made her way to the paddock, but kept her eyes fixed straight ahead on the red horse that was staring right back at her.

*Jane found* that her previous day's adventures had made her a figure of considerable interest around the farm. While she tried with increasing exasperation to get Lancelot's bit between his teeth as he arched his head back as high and far away from her as he could, she was also barraged with questions from Shannon and Liz and some of the younger campers. Overnight, her eye had turned a rotted plum color, streaked with yellow, and after the bandage refused to stay affixed to her sweating forehead, she had finally removed it, revealing a large, angry red gash just above her eyebrow.

"So you stayed up *all night* and made him better?" one of the midgets asked in an awestruck voice.

"Well, he's still nuts, but yeah, other than that he's all right," Jane sighed, temporarily giving up the fight with the bridle.

"What was staying at the house like?" Liz wanted to know.

"Scary," Jane said unthinkingly. Then, seeing the blank looks on Liz's and Shannon's faces, she amended: "It's haunted." In the next stall, Robin snorted. The other girls squealed and looked up at Jane with more eager attention than they'd ever shown her before. Scouring her mind for some creepy details from one of the nineteenth-century novels she loved, Jane tried to conjure Lily's dramatic sense of storytelling as she slowly said, "Well, there used to be this woman kept locked up in one of the bedrooms on the third floor...." Robin coughed conspicuously. "This was a long time ago, but the real estate agent had to tell the Jeffrys about it before they bought the house, because weird things kept happening up there...."

"Like what?" Shannon whispered, agog.

"Anyone who sleeps in that bedroom is attacked by hundreds of tiny pillows," Robin called out loudly, and despite her momentary pang of disappointment in losing her audience, Jane laughed.

The questions kept coming, and not just to her. The barn was abuzz with whispered conversations, and small groups gathered and broke apart like flocks of grackles descending on tree branches. As Jane walked to the tack room to find the martingale that she'd forgotten to attach to Lancelot's bridle, now thankfully on his head, she could hear murmurs coming from various stalls, like walking by houses with the windows open and overhearing snatches of the radio: "Jessica says that Emily's so mad about Lancelot that she's never coming back to ride here again...." *Good riddance*, Jane thought. Two stalls down: "Do you really think that *Jane* can ride him? Did you see her *face*?" *Watch me*, she muttered, and winced from the dart of pain that shot up as her eyes narrowed into a scowl. Her natural competitiveness had suddenly hardened into a kind of defiance.

"So where's *Benjah-meen* this morning?" There was an outburst of giggling, then a hush. Jane wilted, but couldn't help herself from slowing down to hear Jessica's reply to Alyssa's insinuating question. "We-e-ell, I would imagine he's with his cousins," she said casually, but with an unmistakable lilt in her voice. "He told me last night that they were going to be really busy today." She paused, then continued in a lower voice: "Which is why he can't meet me until after dinner . . ." A chorus of "Oooooh"s rang out, and Jane couldn't listen to any more. She stepped quickly into the tack room, grabbed the martingale, and fled back to Lancelot's stall, where Susan was waiting for her.

Her trainer scrutinized her face and tilted Jane's chin with one finger to get a good look at her eye. "So, I take it you feel up to riding?" She gestured to the tacked-up horse inside the stall.

"Yeah, I think so," Jane said. *If I don't throw up.*

"Well, why don't you and Lancelot just have an easy day today? I'm thinking you could do a trail ride around the farm, just walking and trotting. We've got to build this horse's confidence back up. Sound good?"

"Sure," Jane said, but she had a twinge of unease. She didn't want to say it to Susan, but she felt wary of being alone on Lancelot in the open fields, with so much room to run if he bolted. . . .

"I'll ask Ben to tack up Professor. He'll ride with you," Susan said, and then she turned and called out,

"All Advanced II riders need to be in the ring in five minutes! Advanced I, I want you to work on your own in the dressage arena, practicing the routine I gave you yesterday. Take turns, and try scoring one another. Okay?"

As Susan headed out of the barn, Jane quickly asked, "Um, Susan? Can't Robin ride with me?" She realized as she said them that the words sounded panicky, but she *felt* panicky . . . about being alone with Lancelot, about being alone with Ben.

Susan frowned. "She'll miss her lesson, but I suppose . . ." She gave Jane a quick, penetrating look.

"Yeah, no, okay . . . that's all right," Jane said. "I just didn't want Ben to, to have to, if Jose needs him, you know . . ." She stopped.

"It's fine, Ricky and Gabriel are back now." Susan patted her arm. "Hey, Shannon, what happened to saying 'Heads up' when you bring a horse out of the stall, please?" She turned back to Jane. "Remember, just walk and trot. Get used to each other. Who knows, maybe you guys'll even have fun!"

*The reins bit* into her hands as Jane was jounced and jostled in the fastest trot she'd ever tried to ride. She had to admire the royal curve of Lancelot's neck, but it was difficult to appreciate the powerful engine beneath her when she was desperately trying to slow it down. "Easy, easy boy, easy, easy now," she chanted, to little avail. Lancelot was breathing hard, fighting the bit, his chin tucked practically to his chest as Jane's arms achingly pulled him in again and again. *No, Susan,* she thought as Lancelot bumped unceremoniously against Professor, making the old Thoroughbred stumble, *I definitely wouldn't call this fun.*

She and Ben had hardly spoken since the ride began, and Jane felt almost grateful that Lancelot's antics made it impossible to carry on a conversation. Ben looked comfortable on Professor, a graying Thoroughbred that Susan had bought off the track years before and trained as a hunter-jumper. Professor's jumping days, as well as his racing days, were long behind him, but he was a trusty trail horse whose bright eyes and willing spirit belied the age that slowed his once considerable speed. He seemed not to mind his boisterous companion—probably, Jane thought, because he had experienced far worse jostling and tantrums from other horses on the track. She was thankful for Professor's comforting presence, even if she was distinctly uncomfortable with the way his rider kept darting concerned looks at her.

"You okay there?" Ben would ask.

"Yeah," she'd reply through clenched teeth. And that exchange, and variations on it, was all they'd said for the fifteen minutes they'd been in the field. Ben had suggested following the gentle slope toward the creek, retracing the route of the cross-country course Jane and Beau had ridden. But what with Lancelot's sudden surges and shies, they had wound up taking a meandering route to the farthest line of trees that marked the northern boundary of the farm. To their left, the opposite side of where Jane and Beau had entered, was the paddock and the shed where Ben had watched them only days before.

"You were great, you know, over that jump," he said now. Apparently he'd been thinking along the same lines.

"Oh, thanks," Jane said, blushing even as she redoubled her grip on the reins. "Can we just try stopping here for a second? My arms are tired." Ben immediately slowed Professor, and to Jane's relief, Lancelot seemed inclined to follow him. He finally came to a halt, throwing back his head and blowing loudly. Jane took a deep breath and relaxed the reins. Lancelot gradually stilled. She reached down and stroked his neck, marveling at the silken fineness of his coat, and glanced over at Ben, who was holding his reins loosely in one hand, looking out over the paddock. He wore his stirrups quite long, she noticed, and his legs were stretched out in a more relaxed manner than was usual in English riding. He must be used to riding Western, she realized.

"I thought Susan was a little crazy, having you guys jump that thing," Ben said, breaking the silence. Jane felt a rush of defensiveness—and prickly pride.

"Well, I think Susan knew what she was doing. We're in the Advanced class now, and the shru—the hedge isn't really any bigger than the jumps we'll be doing in the ring later on. I mean, I guess it was a kind of test. Anyway, you were there, right? If anything went wrong?" And to her great surprise, Ben flushed and said nothing.

Jane felt the unease grow palpable between them.

She'd spoken quickly, not really thinking about her words. Had she unwittingly said something dumb, something clueless? Was it even, *oh god*, her face, how gruesome she looked? She ducked her head down and fiddled with her stirrup leather, embarrassment coursing through her like a fever. Still, he said nothing.

Lancelot began to grow restless, tossing his head and giving a few shimmying steps away from Professor. Jane seized the chance to break the lengthening silence.

"Well . . ." she said, turning Lancelot around and glancing back at Ben.

"Yeah," he said, and pulled Professor behind the bouncing red horse eagerly heading toward the trees.

*Gradually*, Lancelot quieted down. Jane could feel his furious pull on the bit lessen and sense the coiled tension of his stride easing, and with this slow relaxation his gait seemed to liquefy.

"You know, Red," Jane said, "you could be a really great horse to ride if you weren't so busy trying to run full speed into large objects." She let an inch of rein slide through her fingers, ready to grab it back if Lancelot made another surge forward, but he maintained his—fast—walk, and she noticed that his ears flickered back as she spoke.

Jane heard a chuckle behind her. "There you go, talking to the animals again." Ben was laughing. "I think when I met you you were having a conversation with Rocky, right?" Happily, he couldn't see her blush, or the smile that split her face at his words, light and teasing in a way that reminded her of their night in the barn.

"Just call me Jane Doolittle," she managed.

"So does that mean that Red's telling you all his problems?" Ben had now brought Professor alongside Lancelot so they were riding stirrup to stirrup.

"He's trying," Jane said seriously. "But his accent's so thick, it's hard to make out. I think he's Ukrainian. And he, um"—she was beginning to crack up at the images that floated across her mind's eye—"really misses eating borscht." To her horror, she snorted as she really started giggling, but Ben was coughing—it sounded like he'd swallowed the wrong way.

"He was brought over here as a spy for the Royal Ukrainian Cavalry, and being undercover's pretty stressful. . . ."

"So *that's* why he's got that transistor radio buried in his stall," Ben said thoughtfully, and Jane dissolved again.

"You know," he continued, after they'd recovered, "it's weird, but he does seem to calm down when we're, like, talking and laughing and stuff. Remember in the barn? We were goofing around, and he sort of settled down—"

"He was sick then," Jane objected—then wished she hadn't as the implications, or possibilities, of what he had said hit her. "But maybe . . ." she quickly amended, hoping hard that he would say more. He did.

"Maybe he's telling us we should be friends?"

Jane dared to look at Ben full in the face. His expression was open and friendly. He was smiling, and his smile was a little crooked, which was perfect, and his eyes crinkled up a bit like Jose's, which was also perfect, and the sun shone in his messy black hair, and he was looking at her like there was absolutely nothing in the world worrying him. He looked at her with frank enjoyment. He looked at her like he looked at his family.

And so Jane knew. And so she said, "I think he definitely is."

Her smile felt like a slipping mask. "Let's try trotting again, okay?" As she let Lancelot bound forward she let her face fall apart. And she focused on the horse beneath her.

By *the time* they returned to the barn, Jane had managed to hold Lancelot in a controlled and even trot, trying half-halts, a few circles, and many changes back to walking. He'd attempted a final charge when they approached the gate, but Jane was ready for it and gave a low, but sharp, reprimand—*Whoa!*—willing herself not to tense up or clutch at the reins. It sort of worked—at least he didn't run into the fence—and she wished Susan could have seen it.

Ben had. "Nice!" he said as he reached down to unfasten the gate. And that was just about as good.

Jane swung her leg over Lancelot's back and hit the ground hard; in her tiredness, she'd forgotten how tall he was. Her arms felt stretched and rubbery, and her head was pounding. She threw Lancelot's reins over his head and looked at him, while gingerly removing her helmet and touching her aching forehead. He was obviously completely fresh—his bold eye surveyed the horses filing from the ring as the Advanced II class broke up. Jane ran her hand over his dry coat and stroked his neck, telling him he was good, really good, and he was going to be just fine, and everything really was going to be okay.

Ben dismounted and led Professor over to her. "How's your head?" he asked.

"Hurts." Jane smiled faintly. "Um, thanks a lot for coming with me." She felt as if she were testing an unknown material, like putting out a hand in the dark to find the dimensions of a room. *I need to know how to be your friend,* she told him silently. But as they walked the horses toward the barn, chatting about the ride, Jane realized she sort of knew it would be like this. And she would feel one way about it, and he would feel another. And, she vowed to herself as she saw Susan jogging over, no one, except for Robin, would ever, ever know how she felt, especially Ben. It felt good to make that promise—she felt protected. Protected but alone, with one more thing not to think about, one more thing to put away. *The story of this summer,* she thought.

"So?" Susan asked briskly when she reached them.

"It was okay," Jane said. "He was good."

"*Jane* was good," Ben corrected.

"That's great!" Susan beamed at them. "Now, I've got time before the next lesson. Why don't we go down to the dressage ring and—"

There was a loud grunt of disapproval, and Jane

turned to see Jose standing in the doorway of the barn, holding Brownie. Susan paused, openmouthed.

"I think, Susan, that Jane is tired and does not feel very good," Jose said sternly, and Jane was amazed to see her trainer suddenly look abashed. "And I think you should thank her for riding your horse so well, and then send her to Maria to check her eye and give her some aspirin."

"I'm okay," Jane muttered, torn and uncomfortable. She snuck a look at Ben, but he was looking at his grandfather, then gave him a short nod, of thanks, it seemed. It came over Jane, though she was uncertain as to how it had happened, that Ben had signaled to him.

"No, Jose's right," Susan said quietly. "I'm sorry, Jane." Jane hated to see Susan looking so unhappy, and she began a rush of words to fill the space that yawned between them, but Susan cut her off.

"Get Lancelot untacked, then go see Maria," she said shortly, and walked away.

*Feeling more unmoored* than ever from camp routine, Jane skipped lunch and lay in her bunk bed, reading *The Woman in White* and resting her eyes whenever her head gave a particularly nasty twinge, until Robin found her and suggested that they go down to the lake. As they sat on the dock with their feet dangling down into the cool green water, Jane told her about the ride, then listened as Robin described the morning class; she had a lot to tell—in fact, Jane hadn't seen Robin this happy about a lesson in a long time, and she told her as much.

"I'm not nervous," Robin said bluntly. "And that feels really good. And I don't . . . I don't know, have to worry about screwing up in front of Alyssa and Jennifer and . . ."

"And me," Jane finished.

Robin glanced away and took a deep breath. "I just don't want you to think that I'm some sort of a coward. But Jane, I'm not as good a rider as you, and I sort of don't want to pretend that I am anymore."

Jane stared at her, marveling.

"Why are you looking at me like that?" Robin asked anxiously. "Are you mad?"

Jane smiled. "No, I just think you're the bravest person I know, that's all." Jane put an arm around her. "Let's always ride together, and let's never compete, okay?"

Robin put her head on Jane's shoulder and gave a shaky sigh. "Okay," she whispered. "You're my best friend, Jane."

"So you hate feeling like you can't tell me something," Jane said, and felt the head on her shoulder nod. "Trust me, I know exactly how you feel."

It wasn't often that Jane felt lucky that summer, but sitting on the dock with Robin that afternoon, she knew that at least in one way—one very important way—she was.

Chapter 11

# High Fences-
## and Tempers

In the days that followed, Jane gradually fell into a new rhythm at Sunny Acres, one almost entirely focused around the big red horse who had become her project, her worry, and, increasingly, her pride. There was no doubt that Lancelot was difficult. She was gaining an awareness of Red, a sense of his ferocious personality, his willful spirit, and what made him act up. If she was tense, he was tense. If she was unfocused, he was unfocused. She began to realize that Susan was right—that despite his power, Lancelot had lost his confidence and trust in the world around him. She didn't spend much time wondering why anymore; instead, she simply spent time with him.

He made the other horses nervous, except for Professor

and, now, Bess. Bess was a lovely, quiet mare, much like her owner in her grace and patience, and she didn't pin her ears back or spook at Lancelot's plunging, snorting presence in the ring. And Professor had taken a positive liking to his boisterous trail ride companion. Jane started turning Lancelot out to the big field at night, instead of isolating him in the paddock, and in the morning she usually would find Professor and Lancelot standing together, swishing flies or grazing side by side. When she brought Lancelot in, Professor followed them to the gate, and if Lancelot saw Professor in the ring being ridden by one of the midgets, he would trumpet to his friend and receive a lower, more dignified whinny in return. Susan decided to put them in adjoining stalls during the day, and Jane fastened back the barred window between them. Afterward she told Ben how much the two horses reminded her of the girls in the cabin at night—always popping their heads in and out of the common room and bunk room, seeing what was going on.

It was Jose who remembered that high-strung racehorses were often calmed and comforted by other animal friends. They tried introducing Rocky to Lancelot, which resulted in Rocky bolting from the stall inches away from a flying hoof. They had more success with one of the many barn cats, who happily took up semipermanent residency in a cozy bundle of worn-out saddle blankets that Ben arranged in the corner of Red's stall. He suggested naming her "Cannon Fodder," but Jane and Robin laughingly objected, so they settled on "Florence Tabbygale" instead, after the heroic nurse. Ben gazed solemnly at the mangy, cross-eyed tabby washing her ears unconcernedly as Lancelot stamped around the stall, occasionally sniffing her, and intoned, "You are a brave creature, Nurse Flo."

Meanwhile, Jane observed that the Advanced I lessons were heating up, and Alyssa, Jennifer, and Jessica were now as drained and exhausted as Jane by the time they reached the cabins at night, though most evenings Jessica disappeared again after taking a quick shower and changing into regular clothes. Jane willed herself to close her eyes and ears to these comings and goings, which was made easier by the fact that Jessica was now openly ignoring her. She wouldn't dignify Jane's presence by avoiding her, but the sporadic fellowship they had once shared had disappeared. Now there was an even stronger sense of privilege and separateness about her group, reduced to three close friends. Jane and Robin sometimes watched their lessons, and Jane burned inwardly as she saw the kinds of new challenges that Susan was giving them, which Jane ached to try herself, from the extended gaits in dressage to steadily upward-climbing fences in the ring. Soon they would be jumping four feet and higher.

"I bet Beau could do that combination even better than Quixotic," she growled to Robin.

"I bet *you* and Beau could," Robin said loyally. "How is he?" Robin knew that Jane had been sneaking visits to Beau when she could. She didn't want Megan to find her lurking around his stall, and Megan was generally always with her new horse, so it was difficult—and painful—to see him. Mostly she managed surreptitious pats and covert carrots in the field when she was bringing in Lancelot.

"He's fine," Jane said quietly. "He looks happy." She almost wished she could see visible signs of him pining for her, but the truth was that he seemed exactly the same as ever and, she had to admit, Megan took extremely good care of him.

"I'm sure he misses you, Jane," Robin said reassuringly. "But it's not like you never get to see him, and you've got Lancelot to take care of now. He needs you."

"Yeah, I bet Beau thinks I've left him for a good-looking lunatic and feels sorry for me."

"He hasn't been such a lunatic lately. . . . Yesterday you guys did really great," Robin objected mildly. Yesterday's lesson *had* gone well, Jane knew. She'd had Lancelot on the bit for the entire lesson, and he'd only shied twice, both times when she'd been near Shannon, who carried a long crop. But it was tiring riding him; she felt each time she mounted that she had to be absolutely there for him, confident and reassuring and never nervous or impatient. It was as wearing mentally as it was physically.

Over the course of the week, they had become wary friends. He was accustomed to her everyday presence and, except in the ring, he now behaved in a gentlemanly fashion when she was grooming, tacking, or walking him on a long lead around the farm. She spent hours each day doing these things, because she promised Susan, because it gave her a distraction from everything else, and because she was growing to enjoy his company, different though he was from Beau. She could never completely relax around him, but she admired him. Then one morning when he whinnied as he saw her approaching in the field, and she threw him a spontaneous wave and called, "Hey, Red!" she realized that they were glad to see each other, and she smiled.

That day also brought letters from her parents and from Lily. They sometimes sent packages, though not as often as other parents, Jane noticed, slightly envying the large parcels wrapped in brown paper that disgorged candy, sparkling pastel bottles of bath gels and moisturizers, even new clothes. Robin passed her the bag of gourmet biscotti her parents had sent, and they pretended that they were having tea on an English lawn as they lounged under their favorite tree. But Jane soon was absorbed in her sister's letter. Lily had just picked her classes for freshman year—all except the most important, the prestigious first-year acting seminar taught by a legendary coach who had trained Broadway and Hollywood stars. For that, she would have to audition. "*What if I don't make it?*" Lily worried in her letter, caught between high anxiety and anticipation. "*And what if I do??*" Jane had no doubt whatsoever that Lily would be the first chosen and would quickly rise to stardom in all of the freshman productions. She had prodigious faith in her sister's abilities and was baffled by her periodic bouts of self-doubt. She pulled out her stationery packet and began writing a letter of reassurance and encouragement. The sisters had long experience in cheering each other up.

"Aren't you going to read your other letter?" Robin asked, and Jane paused mid-sentence. The envelope was in her father's handwriting, and if he was the main author of her parents' joint letter, then he was sure to be writing about her school choice. Sighing, she tore it open to read the inevitable, entirely reasonable, perfectly logical exhortation for her to make up her mind now or she wouldn't get a place in any school. In that case, Mr. Ryan went on, they'd have to sell the house and drive across the country searching for a school that would take Jane in—probably an unheated one-room schoolhouse in the wilds of Alaska, where Jane's mother might very well be eaten by bears and Mr. Ryan would undoubtedly get lost on a Native American spirit quest, leaving Lily and Jane orphans, and did she really want to be responsible for that tragic chain of events? Or, he suggested, perhaps they would home-school Jane, building a curriculum around such subjects as macroeconomic theory, weightlifting, and calculus. Jane laughed despite herself, and read the letter aloud to Robin, who loved the Ryans but was mystified that parents could be as goofy as their children.

"You haven't made up your mind yet, have you?" Robin asked.

"Not exactly," Jane began. "Wait a sec, I'm just going to put in a PS here to tell Lily to tell Mum and Dad that I'll have decided by the time they pick me up from camp." She scribbled in a note and sealed her letter.

"But you've been thinking about it?" Robin prodded.

Jane had. During her rambles with Lancelot, and late

at night in the cabin, she could feel her decision forming, like a place toward which she was slowly walking. In her mental journeys, less important considerations had been steadily falling by the wayside, and she felt ready now to try talking about it. She was not the sort of person who liked to discuss her problems before she knew what she herself thought of them. It made her uneasy to hash things out as girls often did together. She preferred knowing her own mind—at least most of it—first.

"I think I'm going to MLK," she said abruptly. She snuck a glance at her friend, but Robin's eyes were cast down to the clover that she was denuding of its leaves. There was a brief silence.

"I know I told you that I wouldn't get mad if you decided not to go to Collegiate," Robin finally said. "And I'm not—I'm totally not. But I guess I did get my hopes up a little. . . ."

"Oh, Rob . . . can you really imagine me there? With Alyssa and Jennifer and *Jessica*?"

"You'd have me," Robin said in a small voice.

"I know, but I have you now! We've never gone to the same school before, and we're best friends! Nothing's going to change, except . . . I'll be at a public school with a bunch of weirdos who don't care that I don't have the right kind of jeans! I just want a new place, where people don't know me. Plus it'll help my parents. . . ." She trailed off. She knew that if she were going to make this argument to them, she'd have to leave out the part about money.

"Anyway, do you think they're going to flip out? I mean, because I want to leave St. Anne's?"

Robin considered. "Yeah," she sighed, "I think they're definitely going to flip out."

"Me, too," Jane said. And they smiled ruefully, united again by the mutual dread of angry parents.

"Well, I'm not one hundred percent decided," Jane said.

"Yes, you are." Robin leaned over and squeezed her hand.


*Robin was right,* Jane realized, as she felt a weight come off her shoulders that day. Saying it aloud had solidified her feelings, and she found herself wondering for the first time what her first day of school would be like, instead of where it would be. Her decision would take her parents by surprise, she knew. They'd seen her infatuation with Collegiate and all it had stood for to Jane, and had helped her get the scholarship. They liked and trusted the program at St. Anne's. During her recent solitary walks, Jane realized she felt trapped in a choice between the private schools her parents were advocating. She felt trapped by her previous standards, all those old longings. But now . . . she was almost free from the person the clique had made her believe she was, from all she'd thought she wanted to be. This was, perhaps, her first truly free decision, made alone, and for herself.

Lily would be in a whole new world, and so would she! As she led Lancelot from the barn toward the ring, she felt a surge of happiness that she and her sister would be linked in this way, though miles apart. Somehow, she thought, it made it not quite so much like being left behind.

*Susan was adjusting* a straight rail that was part of the course Jane had watched the Advanced I riders work through that morning. Her trainer lowered it, then stood back with her hands on her hips, staring at the jump. She glanced over at Jane and Lancelot, who had just reached the middle of the ring, and abruptly undid her work, raising the rail to its original height.

"You want to try the course?" she called over. Jane stared at her. Susan had carved out this hour for an extra lesson, but she hadn't told Jane what they were going to be working on.

"He can do it. He *has* done it—courses like it—hundreds of times. I think it's time to remind him what he's capable of."

"Ah—okay," Jane said. She nodded to Susan, nodded to Lancelot.

"You had a solid ride yesterday. You can do this."

Jane continued nodding till she hit the back of her helmet on the top knob of her spine and winced. *I can do this? He can do this?* She caught herself looking toward the barn for Jose, remembering his firm, repressive voice as he'd told Susan to let Jane off her horse.

He was nowhere in sight, and she felt a stab of shame for seeking her protector. Susan was treating this casually. So would she. *Sure.* Her heart slammed against her ribs. She nodded again, to no one in particular, and jammed her foot into the stirrup and swung herself onto Lancelot's back.

"He's already worked today, right?" Susan asked, nudging a ground pole farther from the straight rail.

"I took him down to the dressage ring before lunch." Jane decided not to mention that he'd almost unseated her when he'd gotten spooked by Rocky, who'd bolted after a squirrel.

"Great. You can do a couple of laps at a posting, then sitting trot. Bring him back to a walk, then canter him twice around." Susan continued studying the jumps, and Jane squeezed her heels into Lancelot's sides.

The afternoon haze had settled into the trees and the fields, and the air felt almost too thick for breathing. Jane tried to quiet her heart as she quieted her horse. The farm was sleeping—everyone was down at the lake or inside the cabins' air-conditioned common rooms. Jane could hear the waves of cicada song rising and falling in the trees, almost in time with the hoofbeats and breaths that to her ears were the only other sounds. *Boom, boom, boom, boom* went the hooves and her seat as she absorbed her weight, sinking it into her heels. She slowed Lancelot to a walk. He was doing what Ben called his "parade horse routine"— grandly arching his neck and placing his hooves meticulously on the ground before him. Jane liked to think he was being the true Lancelot.

"He looks good. Let's go ahead and try him. You're going to canter the half-ring, then take this rail"—Susan pointed to the straight rail she'd been worrying. "Cut across to the double cross-rails"—these were at a left diagonal to the first jump—"then stay by the rail into the turn and take the oxer"—she pointed to the far end of the ring—"then cut to your left to the coop"—there was the green hulk in its place of glory in the middle of the ring—"make a tight circle to your right, cut across the center to the triple"—*the triple?* Jane stared at the three cross-rails so steeply raised that they looked like Vs—"then right again back to the rail to do the first jump again, from the opposite direction. Got it?" Jane hoarsely repeated the course back to her, and Susan nodded. "Don't worry about how high they are—I'm sure he's used to it," she finished.

*But I'm not,* Jane thought a little desperately. Surely she should warm up more, do a few trotting poles, try a cross-rail or two, before attempting the highest jumps she'd had to tackle, on a horse she couldn't trust? Or could she?

As she signaled Lancelot to canter, Jane forced herself to focus. She thanked the heavens that there was no one watching except for Susan. Lancelot was going well, his beautiful stride even and controlled. But who knew what was about to happen? He hadn't jumped since Emily's disastrous last ride. . . .

And suddenly Lily popped into her mind again. When she had starred as Helen Keller in her high school's production of *The Miracle Worker,* Jane had asked her how she had the nerve to get up on stage and assume the role of this utterly foreign character, in front of so many staring eyes. And Lily had said, "Well, I suppose I just fake it . . . till I feel it."

"Okay, Red," Jane muttered as they finished the circle and headed toward the first jump, "we're going to pretend that you're a normal championship horse, and not a crazy championship horse. We're going to pretend we can do this. We're going to fake it because I sure as heck don't think I'm going to feel it." And then there were only three strides more before the jump and suddenly Lancelot's knees were neatly tucked beneath his chest and he was sailing over, landing lightly, and returning to his rocking-horse, collected canter. *Focus, focus, focus,* Jane breathed, *confidence, confidence, confidence* . . . and that was the double cross-rail. The next jump, the oxer, was huge, but Jane refused to look at it. She steadied her hands and allowed Lancelot to pick up a bit more steam. The height took her breath away—Jane felt as if she were floating above the saddle, unanchored, as if she as well as Lancelot were hurtling over it. They landed hard and for a numbing second Jane desperately fought for her stirrup, shoving her heel down and scrambling to shorten her reins, dimly aware of Susan shouting, then actually closing her eyes as they pounded to the coop in six strides that tore the grass beneath Lancelot's scissoring hooves. A softer landing, and Jane sank deep in her seat and guided her horse with her legs and the rhythm of her body as they made the sharp turn right, briefly back at the rail, then pointed arrow-straight at the triple. Lancelot threw his head back and sped up. Jane held firm and he steadied. She knew from the feeling of weightlessness, followed by the lurching, and, finally, the jarring of her stomach when they landed on the other side of the last of the combination that she'd never jumped a triple anywhere near that size before. Her breath and her heart seemed caught in her throat—*is this almost over?* And then she reached up into two-point again as they soared over the first jump for the last time. She felt like she might be sick.

Sound came rushing in. Jane realized that she hadn't heard a thing Susan had said during the entire course.

Her trainer was whooping. She was jumping up and down and whooping, her gray braid waving behind her head like a flag.

And there were other voices whooping—Jane looked up to see Jose and Ben at the fence, hollering and pounding their hands together. She was barely aware of the horse beneath her. Because she didn't have to be. Because she knew that he was fine. Suddenly, she stopped him and leaned down and threw her arms around his neck. She stayed like that for some time, her arms rising and falling with his deep breathing.

"*Here*, let me do that." Ben reached over to take the girth from Jane's badly shaking hands. He quickly loosened the buckle and lifted the saddle from Lancelot's back, revealing a saddle-shaped pattern of sweat. Jane sank back against the stall, letting Ben take over, struggling against the light-headedness that made her limbs feel leaden and weak.

"Are you okay?" he asked for the third or fourth time.

Jane nodded. "I'm just a little sick to my stomach," she whispered.

"I bet it's like some kind of delayed reaction. . . . I mean, you were perfect when you were doing the course, then it kind of hit you once it was over?"

That was exactly what it felt like, and Jane felt a surge of warmth toward Ben, so strong that she actually made an abbreviated movement toward him, catching herself before she took a step forward . . . and then the question came bursting out:

"Was it really okay?"

Ben eyed her incredulously. "Jane, you're totally the best rider here. I mean . . ." He shook his head and sighed. "I don't know what to—" But he was cut off.

"Irresponsible? You think I'm *irresponsible*?" Susan's voice, coming from somewhere down the barn's corridor, was a cold, outraged hiss. Jane raised her finger to her lips, and Ben froze, his mouth half-open.

"What do you want to call it? Fine, you put Jane on a crazy horse. Fine, you let her get almost killed when he runs her into the tree—" Jose's barking, angry reply was interrupted by Susan's protests.

"Let me finish!" he shouted. "But then—not warning her, not telling her, oh, no—to out of the blue say, 'Okay, here are all of these high jumps. I know you've never jumped this crazy horse before, but why don't you please make him go over all of these?' Eh? Does that sound *responsible* to you, Susan?"

Jane and Ben stared at each other. He slowly put Lancelot's saddle on the ground, then together they tiptoed to the stall door to peek through the bars. Jane could see Jose's back; he was standing, as if braced against a wind, with his legs set sturdily apart and his arms folded across his chest. She couldn't see her trainer—but she could hear her.

"I have been Jane's instructor for years! I know what she can handle! You saw her—if I'm not mistaken, you were cheering her on, not trying to stop her! She's been riding one average horse for a long time, and I knew she had a hell of a lot more ability than she could show on Beau! I'm trying to give her a chance to be the great rider I know she is! And yes, I throw her into things—because she's proven again and again that she can handle it! There's no one riding at this barn who works harder!"

Jane flushed crimson—first from anger at Susan's scandalous assessment of Beau, then with embarrassment and wonder at her assessment of Jane herself. Ben glanced at her with an I-told-you-so smirk playing at the corner of his mouth.

"So you're doing all of this *for Jane,* is that it?" Jose answered with pointed sarcasm.

"Of course!" For the first time, Susan sounded confused. "What are you trying to say?"

"It's your horse she's riding, isn't it?"

"What does that have to do with anything?" Susan demanded fiercely.

Jose's voice took on a conversational tone. "Just this. Jane trains your new horse for you. Fun for Jane, especially when she runs into trees. Then you get a champion horse—very nice for you. And what happens to Jane?" His voice rose to a shout: "*She gets to have another horse taken away from her, that's what!* Back she goes to the school horses, with another broken heart!"

And with that, Jose turned on his heel and stalked from the barn, leaving Jane and Ben just enough time to duck out of view as Susan strode after him.

"Well, what are you suggesting I *do*?" she shouted. "Should I send Jane home? Put her on Brownie? *What*?"

"Maybe you should start thinking about what's *best* for her!" Jose roared back.

The only sound was Lancelot's restless movements around the stall. He looked to Jane as unnerved as she felt, pawing at the sawdust and pacing. She felt the beginning of tears—of anger, confusion, and shock—prick her lids. Ben reached out for her. The moment she felt his warm hand on her arm, it was whisked away, and she looked up to see Jessica glaring at them through the bars of the stall.

## Chapter 12

# Jane's Big Idea

Jessica's voice was dangerously sweet, especially when paired with the ice in her blue eyes:

"Oh, am I *interrupting*?" she chirped. "I was about to go swimming. . . ." And with her usual languid grace, she pulled her T-shirt over her head, revealing a skimpy red bikini top that she filled in a way Jane doubted she ever would. Jane was transfixed, like a mouse caught in an owl's lantern gaze, as her brain made rapid-fire comparisons between her own sweaty, dirt-streaked, bruised face, grubby T-shirt, and horse-spit-flecked jods and Jessica's golden tan arms with stacked coral bracelets, her shining hair skimming her shoulders, the huge sunglasses perched saucily on top of her head. Jane quickly surrendered, not bothering to look at Ben, guessing his jaw was hanging a few inches from the ground.

"Nope, just leaving," she said, picking up Lancelot's tack and ducking through the stall door. She waited in the tack room until she couldn't hear their voices, then retraced her steps to her horse—to Susan's horse—to cool him out.

Oddly enough, with all she had to ponder and sort through, Jane found herself thinking mainly about Jessica as she ran a damp sponge over Lancelot's chest and squeezed water over his withers. She thought of the high, fake tone of her voice, like shiny plastic. She was so different from the unreliable but *real* girl who had used to be her on-again, off-again friend. It was, of course, because of Ben. But why? Surely Jessica didn't see her as a threat. Could the mere fact of their friendship really cause such a drastic change? Or, almost worse, did Jessica change because she was, Jane had to admit it, sort of going with Ben? What if Robin started dating someone next year and changed, too? As she picked up the scraper and began sloughing the excess water from Lancelot's back, a new, ugly vision of freshman year appeared before her: a minefield of phony people just like the worst of the girls at Sunny Acres. . . . Jane shivered. She admitted to herself that she didn't have a lot of experience with these things. She'd watched Lily's loose, buoyant group of friends go through high school together like a single organism—loyal and inseparable. But they were *theater* people, almost a different category of teenagers altogether. Still, Jane wondered . . .

Checking to make sure that Lancelot was cool and relatively dry, Jane hastily put him in the pasture and ran to the main house to use the phone.

*Luckily, there was* no one in the kitchen, and Jane had the room to herself. She dialed, hoping upon hope that Lily would pick up first.

"'Allo?" said a voice in a thick Russian accent almost as bad as Jane's British accent, and Jane breathed a sigh of relief.

"Oh, Phyllis, I'm so glad it's you!"

"Oh, eet ees the young person. Vat do you vhant? I was vaiting for my sailor to come. . . ." Phyllis was a character that Lily had invented years before to amuse Jane and Robin. She liked "Russian sailors, who bring me calculators," and she came from "ze old country."

"Phyllis, I need to talk to Lily. It's kind of important. . . ."

Lily dropped the accent at once. "Are you okay, Janoo?"

The whole story came pouring out. It was like a tap had been released in Jane's throat, and all of the things that had happened at camp were spilling from her heart into Lily's listening ear. Their mother had already told her about Beau, and Lily now angrily exclaimed against the Jeffrys. She was horrified by Jane's fall. And she listened in sympathetic silence about Ben and Jessica.

"I guess I'm just wondering if this is what it's going to be like," Jane finished slowly. "I mean, next year. Is this what girls are going to turn into, when, I don't know, they start hanging out with boys like that?" Jane knew she wasn't saying it well, but Lily seemed to get her meaning.

"Well, it can certainly happen," she sighed. "Don't you remember Courtney?"

Jane did, though Courtney had been Lily's best friend in middle school, when Jane was very young. She and Lily had been joined at the hip, always inventing skits that they performed in the living room for the Ryans and talking on the phone from the minute they each woke up. But when they started high school together, the friendship had faded.

"Courtney and I didn't just grow apart," Lily explained now. "She started dating older guys and stopped talking about anything else. Even worse, the guys she dated were jerks, so our entire friendship became me listening to her first bragging about them, then complaining about them. And I had to be there to cheer her up when they did something awful, but then she just went back for more. It was miserable."

"I bet," Jane said. It occurred to her that a lot of people relied on Lily for comforting. "But did she also act fake?"

"Oh, boy!" Lily chuckled. "When she had a crush on someone, she was a totally different person. The giggling, the games . . . she would even pretend to fall down all the time so they'd pick her up."

"Huh?" Jane asked, confused.

Lily laughed again. "It was sort of her way of flirting.

She'd trip and fall, and then everybody would make a fuss over her. So dumb. But it worked. Guys totally fell for the helpless act."

"Wow," was all Jane could think of to say.

"I know. I always came across as the boring, adult one. It got really old. The only time she acted like herself was when she needed me to talk to, when her boyfriend was being mean to her or ignoring her. Then finally, she started getting suspicious that her boyfriends really liked me and not her. That was when I called it quits. So yes, I know exactly what you're talking about."

"Ugh," Jane said. "I don't think I want to go to high school anymore."

"Oh, it's not that bad," Lily said reassuringly. "Only some girls are like that, and it's sad, but you just don't have to be around them. You'll find your own group, with people who are smart and funny and brave like you are. People who write and paint and talk about things besides themselves. Trust me, it's possible. High school is hard, but it's a lot better than middle school."

"Thank goodness," Jane said fervently, and they both laughed.

"Speaking of which, Dad's about to have a hernia, you know. This morning he was threatening to drive up to Sunny Acres."

"Will you tell him I'm going to MLK?" Jane said.

Lily shrieked. "That's perfect! Jane, that's *perfect*! Why didn't I think of that? Of *course* you should go there! The arts program, and all the interesting people, and being downtown, so close to home . . ." Lily was in raptures in the way that only Lily could be.

"So you'll tell him for me? I'm just worried that they're going to be mad I don't want to stay at St. Anne's."

"Don't worry about a thing. I'll tell them. I'll convince them! They're going to be over the moon, I promise!" Jane was skeptical, but she appreciated Lily's enthusiasm and willingness to go to bat for her.

"But Jane," Lily interrupted herself, growing serious again. "What are you going to do about Susan and that new horse you're riding?"

And Jane told Lily her plan, formed almost unconsciously in the aftermath of her tumultuous day, and still only partly thought through.

Lily was worried. "I don't know if that's safe, Jane. I mean, he sounds like a really unpredictable horse. And you don't know what sorts of things—"

Jane cut her off gently. "I'll be okay, Lily. I need to do this. And you'll be there to watch me, remember?"

"If I don't keep my eyes closed," Lily groaned.

"You better not," Jane told her. "Lancelot and I are going to surprise everybody, and I want you to see it. After all, it was thinking about you in *The Miracle Worker* that got me through my last ride."


*That evening,* after dinner, Jane grabbed her sketchpad and pencils and headed to the fields for a solitary walk. The farm glowed in the early dusk, its shadows deepening to soft charcoal and its undulating grassy acres shading to emerald. It was past eight, but the sun held to the lip of the horizon, just bright enough to gild the tops of the tallest oaks with a mellow gold. Jane could hear the tumbled-together voices of the younger campers preparing for a campfire and gave a silent thanks that the older girls were now spared this weekly ritual of sharing feelings and singing songs ranging from the stupid to the unutterably sad. She remembered all too well the churning anxiety of being asked to "share" with the group what she had experienced and learned during that week of camp. Jane snorted as she imagined what would have happened if she'd ever been honest during one of those painful sessions: *This week I learned that Alyssa told Jessica and Jennifer that she thinks I'm hopelessly boring and weird. I learned that my jeans are too high and that no one wears tennis shoes like mine anymore, if they ever did.* She usually had avoided being called on, not all that difficult, since the counselors had an uncanny knack for absorbing the campers' social structure and favoring the popular girls, or she would make up something about an arts-and-crafts project she would say she enjoyed, when really all she wanted to do was live in the barn. And then heaven help her if they sang "Cat's in the Cradle" or "Corner of the Sky"!

"Phooey," she said aloud now. She thought for one moment of joining this campfire and telling the younger girls that this week she'd learned that she no longer gave a flying fig about working her way into the clique, because they were mean, possibly racist, and definitely cheats.

That even the seemingly savviest girl can become a total nightmare if she liked a boy. That her trainer and the barn manager were fighting over her, and that she'd decided to go to public school. That she was maybe the best rider in the barn. That she was determined to prove that she was.

Jane threw her leg over the fence rail and swung herself to the other side. Just ahead, she saw Beau grazing, and her heart gave a painful squeeze. "Hey, buddy," she whispered, and he raised his head and whickered, taking a few steps toward her. She met him halfway and put her arms around his neck. His coat felt very soft and his mane was impeccably combed. "I'm glad you're getting taken such good care of," she told him. And then out of the corner of her eye, she saw a seated figure near the willow tree slowly stand up, hesitant, and she turned around. It was Megan.

"Oh, hi," Jane said awkwardly. "I'm sorry, I was just . . ." Her voice trailed off. But Megan was smiling shyly at her. She joined her at Beau's side and stroked her horse's muzzle. She was the one who broke the strained silence.

"Um, Jane? He really knows you? He came right up to you?" She had the ten-year-old way of turning everything into a question. Jane was forcibly reminded of how young she was, and something painful and knotted in her seemed to come undone.

"Oh, he knows you, too. He was just telling me how well you're taking care of him."

"Really?" Megan's eyes shone up to her. "He's the best horse in the whole world," she said in a breathless rush.

"He's so pretty and so good, you know? And he can be so funny! And he's just the best at going over trotting poles, and he has the best canter ever, and I just think . . ." Jane smiled as Megan launched into a detailed depiction of her horse's perfections. This was love, she knew. Beau's new owner loved him more than anything else in the world.

". . . and you know, I told Susan that, like, you can ride him anytime you want?" Megan finished, and Jane looked up, surprised.

"That's really, really nice of you, Megan," she said slowly. "I might take you up on that sometime. Keep taking good care of him, okay?" Megan nodded furiously. Jane fished a carrot out of her pocket and handed it to Megan to give to Beau. She left them standing together in the gathering dusk, Megan carrying on some urgent conversation with Beau's patiently listening, kind, and homely face. She felt a pang of longing toward her horse, toward Megan's horse, but she was also smiling. Megan waved to her, and she waved back and continued down the sloping knoll to look for Lancelot. And Jane smiled again as she realized that Megan was skipping the campfire.

*Someone was calling* her name, and Jane paused, deciphering Robin's voice hailing her near the cabin. It was too dark for sketching, she realized, and despite her lonely mood, she did need to talk to her friend. "I'm in the field!" she hollered back. "Looking for Nutty!" She heard Robin laugh, then heard her jogging footsteps approach. "Ben just told me—*why* didn't you tell me?—about"—*gasp*—"your ride! Omigosh, Jane! I can't *believe*—" Robin was in a tizzy, flushed and out of breath. She threw her arms around Jane, knocking her off balance, and they collapsed ungracefully to the ground, laughing and throwing handfuls of grass at each other.

"I'm sorry, I'm *sorry!*" Jane cried, fending off Robin's attack. "I just didn't want to talk about it with everybody there at dinner!"

"So when *were* you going to tell me?" Robin rubbed a handful of grass in Jane's hair, hard, and Jane shrieked in protest.

"This is unbecoming behavior, young lady!" she yelled in accent.

Robin gave up, flopped on her back, and sighed. "No more secrets, remember?" She eyed Jane with mock grumpiness. "Even if you do have to wander alone in the fields like some *woman of mystery* . . ."

Jane cracked up. "But I am the woman of mystery." She chuckled. "Doomed to haunt the fields of Sunny Acres, searching for my own horse . . . who never comes . . . until the full moon . . ."

Robin made a ghostly *whoo-ooh-hoo* sound and they threw some more grass around.

"Did Ben tell you about the fight?" Jane finally asked, brushing herself off. Robin nodded.

"You don't think Jose's right, do you?"

"I'm not sure," Robin said thoughtfully. "It's hard to believe that Susan would put you in any danger."

"Right," Jane agreed, though the image of the enormous triple, the towering straight rail, surfaced vividly in her mind. But with a surge of pride, she also remembered sailing over them.

Robin seemed to be following the same train of thought. "She *does* ask you to do really hard things, but you always do them! I mean, remember the shrubbery?"

"How could I forget?" Jane muttered. She still wondered why Ben had seemed so uncomfortable that day, on their trail ride. Had he, like Jose, felt that Susan had gone too far?

"And it's not like I think of Red as being *my* horse," she added. "He's not like Beau. Actually, he's *nothing* like Beau." She laughed a little sadly. "But here's the thing . . ." She assumed a more matter-of-fact tone than she actually felt. "I'm not going to get my own horse. At least, not anytime soon. Beau belongs to Megan now. Even if she did say I could ride him." She related her encounter with Megan, and Robin agreed that it was strange that Susan had yet to mention Megan's offer to Jane. "Anyway," Jane continued, "I've got to do the best I can with the horse I'm riding for now, even if I never get to ride him again after this summer. . . ." She trailed off as the familiar feeling of loss stole over her, despite her assertion that she didn't feel possessive about Lancelot.

Then a soft brushing, munching sound broke the quiet, and Jane and Robin turned to see the tall silhouette of a horse tearing at the leaves of the hedge lining the part of the fence that faced the side of their cabin. "Speak of the devil."

Jane raised an eyebrow to Robin, then winced. The gash there was still sore. "Hey, Red," she called in a low voice, and the big horse broke away from his landscaping and loped over. He startled back a bit when Jane stood up, but stayed still as she pulled another carrot from her pocket. He took it neatly and allowed Jane to reach her arm under his neck to lightly scratch his far cheek. The moon had risen, and Jane saw it shine in his liquid brown-blue eye. She blew gently in his nostrils, and he snorted softly back.

She cleared her throat and forced herself to finish: "I'm going to ride Lancelot in the show, at the end of camp, and I'm going to try to win."

Robin frowned. "Well, yeah," she said. "Of course you are. . . ." She stopped, confused.

"Not the Advanced II show," Jane told her. Robin's eyes widened in comprehension.

"You mean . . ."

"The Advanced I show."

"But Jane," Robin protested, "that's in . . ."

"Less than three weeks. I know." She looked again at the moon in the deceptively calm horse's eyes and moved her hand to his neck. He startled, jerking his head away. They watched as he turned abruptly on his heels and bolted down the slope toward the pond, the moonlight flashing on his flying shoes.

"We've got a lot of work to do," Jane said.

## Chapter 13

# A Spy and a Special Delivery

*U*nlike Jane, Robin was excellent at making lists, schedules, and plans. She was also becoming a fairly accomplished spy. At one time, it now seemed a long time ago, Jane wouldn't have hesitated to ask Jessica for Susan's plans for the Advanced I competition, but now there was no one in that group she could approach, unless . . .

"Operation Kiss-Up, under way," Robin whispered to Jane two nights later as they shared the bathroom sink, Jane examining the remnants of grayish-yellow streaking the inner corner of her eye and Robin vigorously brushing her long wheat-colored hair. She then called out, in a higher falsetto, "Hey, Jennifer? I'm totally out of toner, could I borrow some of yours? I'll trade you for some

Godiva my parents sent me. . . ." They guessed from the ensuing squeal that Jennifer was agreeable, and Robin gave Jane a conspiratorial wink as she left the bathroom to bond with her new "friend." Jane tried to wink back but succeeded only in giving herself a headache. As she dampened a cotton ball with antiseptic for her forehead, she grinned as she heard Robin blurt an entirely unconvincing (at least to Jane) "Omigah! This is *so much* better than mine!"

But perhaps predictably, after two days of this Robin had had enough. As they led Lancelot and Bess to the ring for their morning lesson, Robin confessed ruefully that if she had to have one more conversation about boys from school she couldn't stand, mixers she hadn't gone to, and clothing labels she'd never heard of, she would scream.

"How is it possible to have *nothing* else to talk about?" She grimaced. "I mean, we don't even talk about riding, unless Jennifer's being patronizing about our class. I finally just asked her if Susan had told them anything about the event, and she said no. But Jane, I don't think I can keep this up to find out when she finally does."

She glanced at Jane apologetically, but Jane actually felt a bit relieved. She didn't think she could take much more of Robin's absence, either, or the gruesome, though remote, possibility that she would actually click with Jennifer and her group. She gladly let her friend off the hook, but still asked, "So you didn't find out anything new last night?" Jennifer and Robin had joined Alyssa for a late-night visit to the kitchen to raid the fridge.

"Just that Emily's having a great time at the beach and met some boy, or says she did. Alyssa's convinced she's making it up. God, they have the *worst* opinions of each other. It's like they don't even really like one another. And, well . . ." She hesitated.

"What?" Jane pressed her. She stopped Lancelot in the center of the ring. Robin checked over her shoulder, but Liz and Shannon were just emerging from the barn. "Well, um, they don't like it that Jessica's hanging out with Ben."

Jane's stomach gave an abbreviated heave. "What did they say?" Her knuckles blanched over Lancelot's reins.

"I think it's part of their whole weird jealousy, competitive thing . . . the way Alyssa was so snotty about Lancelot before he threw Emily, the way they talk about each other. . . ."

"Robin, tell me what they said!"

Robin blushed. "Alyssa said that Jessica was just . . . slumming."

Jane gave the reins an involuntary jerk and Lancelot flattened his ears at her. "Sorry, Red," she apologized, and rubbed the question mark on his forehead in a gentle circle till they both felt calmer. She lengthened her stirrup and mounted, her lips pressed together in a grim line, and added another reason to her mental list of why in just over two weeks she wanted to beat all three of them.


*Lancelot was improving* every day, but Jane worried that they weren't doing the kind of work that would prepare them for the Advanced I event. She was supposed to be schooling Lancelot on her own, as she needed to, during Advanced I's lesson, and during her and Robin's lesson, Jessica, Alyssa, and Jennifer were practicing parts of dressage routines that she knew would be her biggest challenge. Sitting under their tree, devouring ham and pimento sandwiches from Maria, Robin suggested that they bite the bullet and ask Susan directly.

"She'll just say no," Jane said flatly. "Especially if she thinks we're asking because I'm doing, well, what I'm doing."

"What if I just ask her, like, out of curiosity?" Robin suggested. Jane was doubtful, and sure enough, when Robin cornered their trainer in the tack room later that day, Susan merely chuckled and said, "Oh, you'll see."

"She probably thinks I'll tell them, as if!" Robin protested to Jane in frustration. It was now two weeks before the end of camp.

She sighed, pulling off her boot-stained socks and flopping onto Jane's bunk. "We're just thinking about this the wrong way. Susan's probably not going to tell them what the courses are until the day before they do them."

"Or maybe even the day of," Jane said gloomily. "But it won't matter to them, because they'll have practiced—" She was cut off by the noisy entry of Alyssa and Jennifer, their arms laden with plastic-draped bundles.

"You got blue? How sweet!" Alyssa crowed to her friend. "Of course, in real eventing you couldn't wear blue, but . . . so *cute*! Really *cute*."

Jennifer stared at her, flushing with anger. "Well, what did *you* get?"

"Black," Alyssa announced, and with a flourish, tore the protective bag from a long, elegant riding jacket, splendidly new, beautifully cut, suspended from a silken padded hanger. Jane glanced over at Jennifer's smaller, slightly less dramatically cut jacket, a dark midnight blue. She thought they were both beautiful, but as Alyssa slipped into the formfitting, inky black coat and turned to admire herself in the mirror on the back of the door, Jane had to admit that the effect was good. Alyssa's silky, layered bob just grazed her collar, and her highlights were thrown into relief by the matte black below. Alyssa frowned at herself in the mirror. "I still wish we'd had time to custom-order one from that tailor in London that Emily uses. But this'll do for now."

Jane rolled her eyes at Robin.

"What are those for?" Liz asked, coming in to see what the fuss was about.

"For the event," Jennifer said. "Robin, you want to try my jacket on? We're the same size."

"Uh, no thanks, I don't want to mess it up, but it's a really pretty color, Jennifer," Robin the retired spy said kindly, and Jane was amused to see Jennifer stick her tongue out in a very unsophisticated way at Alyssa's elegant back.

"What event?" Shannon asked over Liz's shoulder, her mouth an O of admiration and unapologetic envy.

"Um, like the one at the end of camp? *That* one?"

Alyssa said sharply. Jane was relieved that Shannon was asking her questions for her. She wouldn't have braved Alyssa's tongue, she knew, and felt a surge of annoyance with herself. Now that she didn't have Jessica to occasionally laugh at her jokes or take her side, she rarely entered into a general conversation. At least, she told herself, she was no longer smiling sycophantically, pretending to be with it.

"You mean Susan made you get those?" Shannon blundered on.

Alyssa sighed in exasperation. "I'm sure it won't be necessary for *your* show, Shannon, but our competition is going to be like a real event."

"But there's only three of you," Shannon protested. "How is that a real event?"

This time Jennifer answered, her pride evidently pricked. "It's *quality*, not quantity," she snapped.

Alyssa threw her an appreciative glance and slapped her five. "I like that," she said merrily, "*quality*, not quantity. That should be, like, our slogan. We'll have to tell Jess."

This time it was Liz who rolled her eyes, jammed in her earphones, and sheepdogged Shannon out of the room. Jane wondered suddenly if the two girls would continue riding. . . . Maybe they'd stay on another year or two, but they were growing more and more distracted in the ring, and both were spending a lot of time on their cell phones with other friends away from Sunny Acres. The split in the group had created a divide, she realized, and it burned her again that she was stuck with the less ambitious riders

(*Except for Robin*, she added mentally, with a twinge of guilt). She watched Alyssa's face in the mirror, eyes narrowed and lips curled in a half-smile. To Jane, she was clearly imagining a multicolored ribbon fluttering from Ariel's bridle. Suddenly Jane wondered, though really it was the least of her worries, what in the world she was going to wear.

*Jane was* in the kitchen mopping up the last of her pancakes, thinking about what she would do with Lancelot that morning, when she looked up and was startled to see Mrs. Jeffrys approaching her table.

"Special delivery, Jane," Mrs. Jeffrys said with a bemused smile. "This must be very important indeed, to bring the express delivery truck all the way out here," and she handed Jane a heavy package stamped OVERNIGHT in several places. Jane thanked her and stared bewilderedly at the large, rather battered lump.

"What on earth?" Robin said, leaning over for a better look, as did Liz, Shannon, and Jennifer.

"Did you order something, Jane?" Shannon asked.

Jane couldn't help laughing. She'd never ordered anything in her life. "It must be my custom-made jacket from England." Somehow the words popped out, *aloud*, into the kitchen, leaving a heavy silence in their wake.

Then Liz and Robin started laughing, and Jane continued recklessly, "I'm so glad Emily's tailor could fit me in. Of course, the queen told him that I'd inherited Emily's charming horse, and I'm sure he wanted to see me killed in style." She glanced over at the adjoining table, and even Alyssa was smiling reluctantly.

"Come, Robin," Jane said in British, the first time she'd done so in front of the clique, "let us admire my finery in private."

"But of course," Robin chortled, and they bussed their trays and made a dash for their tree, Robin shrieking, "I can't believe you said that!" as they ran.

*Neither can I,* Jane thought.

They tore open the package to reveal—books. A stack of faded, worse-for-wear books, with a note written on the back of a bookmark in Lily's elaborate cursive: *I don't know if these are right, but maybe some of them will be helpful. Good luck! Love, Lily.* "What in the world?" Jane wondered, slipping the rubber band off the pile. "*Techniques of Western Showmanship?*" She stared at the battered ex-library book in wonderment. "*Saddleseat for Beginners?*" She started laughing as she reached *Expert Calf Roping.* "Oh, Lily, you wonderful weirdo! She must have thought these would help with the event!"

"And she was right!" Robin said excitedly. "Jane, look! Here's *The Art of Dressage!*"

Encouraged, Jane reached for the last volume and was thrilled to discover *Listening to Your Horse,* a book Jane had asked for for her birthday (her confused parents had instead given her *Chicken Soup for the Horse Lover's Soul,* which she had hastily donated to her school library). As she surveyed the motley collection, Jane felt a rush of appreciation for her marvel of a sister. She recognized the bookmark from the used bookstore where Lily's friend Harold worked and pictured them scouring the badly organized shelves and tottering piles of paperbacks for horsey material.

Robin was already deep into *The Art of Dressage*. "There are practice courses, Jane! Just look!" But Jane's mind, for the moment, was in the dusty bookstore with her sister, who was turning the pages of a book saying, "Well, I don't really remember there being *cows* at the barn, or Jane using a rope, but maybe that's what they work up to. . . ." She grinned and took the book that Robin was shoving in her lap.

*Armed with The* Art of Dressage, Jane and Robin headed down to the large oval ring near the lake an hour later. "I wonder how much Lancelot was able to do before . . . I mean, when he was showing," Jane said as she glanced up at the towering horse beside her. He seemed in a good mood this morning, despite the temperature that was crawling steadily upward past ninety degrees. Robin had taken the precaution of putting Rocky in the house, and Lancelot had seemed inordinately pleased by the big dog's whimpers as Rocky scratched plaintively at the porch door behind them.

"Well, let's think about what you know instead," Robin said sensibly.

"Right," Jane sighed. "Well, I've done basic flat work with Beau. Collected trot, medium trot . . . except he could never really manage that . . . he usually just sped up . . . and a collected and medium canter . . . ditto. . . . Let's see, ah, half-halts, and backing up, and bending. He was really good at all that. But it's weird, I mean, I know how Beau does all these things, but I haven't figured all this stuff out with Red. It's not the gaits, it's the actual *dressage* part I'm worried about—"

"'The harmonious development of the physique and ability of the horse'? 'Achieving perfect understanding with his rider'?" Robin quoted from the book. "You mean that?"

"Yeah," Jane sighed, "I mean that."

"Well, think of it this way, then. We don't know what Lancelot knows. But we're not training a green horse. This isn't new to him, or new to you, right?"

This time Jane quoted: "'We've got to remind this horse what he's capable of.'"

"Exactly." Robin nodded.

"I just hope I don't screw him up," Jane muttered.

Twenty minutes later, she feared she was doing just that. Lancelot was bounding around the ring in a very un-harmonious and misunderstanding way. "Hey, Robin," Jane called out through gritted teeth as she gamely held on to her plunging horse, "can we maybe not *start* with flying lead changes?" But just as the words left her mouth, Lancelot, as if to make a point, changed leads with a cheer-ful swish of his tail. "Oh, brother," Jane said as Robin crowed with delight. Jane gave Lancelot a pat and slowed him to a working walk. She felt foolish for pushing him so fast, yet humbled by his ability, sporadically though he chose to show it. It was clear that while Lancelot could morph in the jumping arena, a more gradual approach was needed on the flat. And if she couldn't control him in the dressage ring, how could she hope to in the fields of the cross-country course?

"I'm just going to try some leg work—walking," Jane called over, and eased Lancelot to a halt. He wasn't on the bit, didn't seem to be listening to her at all. Instead, his eyes were focused on the rolling hills that framed the farm, and his ears were pricked straight forward, at attention to something far beyond his rider. When she asked him to move ahead, he picked up a fast, bobbing walk, head high. She gently played with the tension in her reins and one of his ears flickered back to her. Maintaining steady pressure at the girth, Jane tried to keep his forward momentum while bringing his head down, and after a few sweltering rounds she had him on the bit and listening.

"That looks great!" Robin stage-whispered as Jane rode past her.

"Why are you whispering?" Jane whispered back, but she had already moved out of earshot of whatever Robin murmured back. She asked Lancelot to trot, mentally crossing her fingers that his concentration wouldn't break. She tried to be as quiet and connected with him as she could, and without really thinking about it, slid her feet from her stirrups and let her legs reach even longer down his sides, absorbing his trot deep in her seat. Lancelot surged forward gracefully, with a stride so long and smooth that it took Jane's breath away. But not her horse's: Lancelot snorted noisily once, twice, then a final blast that made Jane snort herself, with laughter.

"Classy," Robin giggled in her normal tone of voice.

An hour later, Jane slid wearily out of the saddle, her legs shaking with exhaustion. They had practiced serpentines, circles, halt to trot, trot to halt, and everything in between, but no cantering. Jane was drained, mentally and physically, and even Lancelot showed signs of tiredness. But she was elated, and slightly stunned, by their progress. She rubbed the question mark on his forehead over and over, praising him while he stood quietly, his head near hers. She stroked his neck and loosened his girth.

Robin's eyes were sparkling and she looked ready to throw her arms around both of them.

"Jane, what have you done to that horse?" Susan yelled at her hours later, during their afternoon lesson. Jane was incorporating some dressage techniques while they were hacking, sneaking in as much practice as possible. "And why don't you have your feet in your stirrups?"

"Ah, I don't know. It just feels better?" Jane panted, concentrating hard on supporting Lancelot's hindquarters as she encouraged him to bend into the tight circles they were drawing at the near end of the ring.

"Well, he looks great, even if he is noisy," Susan barked.

Lancelot snorted loudly in reply.

*Chapter 14*

## What Jessica Didn't Say

Yowch," Jane exclaimed, bending down and blinking her streaming eyes, trying to dislodge the hay dust that had come down along with the cobwebs she was sweeping from the corners of Lancelot's stall. Then, as she stepped back straight into a large pile of manure, "Argh!"

"Is this some sort of new dance move?" In a blurry squint, Jane made out the features of Ben peering into the stall, laughing down at her.

"No," she said grumpily—*why, oh why, did he always see her looking her worst?*—"I just got something in my eye, then stepped in a big pile of . . . Hey!"

"Um, that doesn't look like hay you stepped in there, Jane."

"No, I know, it's . . . never mind." She mopped her face with a relatively clean edge of her T-shirt. She wanted to ask Ben something, but though they were definitely friends now, it could still be difficult to form the right words around him.

"What were you going to say?" Ben persisted.

"Well, I was just thinking about taking Red out to the big field again. . . ." Amazingly, she didn't have to finish.

"I'll tack Professor up as soon as I get Lady Blue ready for the farrier," he said easily.

"Shouldn't Liz be doing that?" Jane felt renewed annoyance at the other girls' sloughing off of the care of their horses to Jose and his family.

"She's swimming," Ben said neutrally. Jane rolled her eyes, and he smiled. "I don't mind. I like Robbie and Doc." Robbie was the farrier, a lanky, raw-boned man with a shocked brush of curly hair and a curling mustache, and Doc was his wiry terrier mix who lived for chewing hoof trimmings. "There's his truck," Ben said, and Jane could hear the rumble of the engine as the battered Chevy pulled into the curve of the drive near the barn.

"I'll help," she offered, and, scraping off as much of the muck from her boot as she could, Jane tossed the last of the dirty sawdust into the wheelbarrow and pushed it from the stall to the compost pile outside the barn, waving to Robbie, who was laying out his tools on the tailgate of his truck. He was a virtuosic whistler and was now piping "My Bonnie Lies Over the Ocean." He reminded her a bit of an Irish sailor, with his weather-worn face and his sparkling blue eyes, made lighter and bluer by his deep tan. She hadn't seen him since the previous summer, and he called to her that he wouldn't have recognized her, she had grown so tall, except for the filthy clothes.

"Thanks," she said sarcastically as she joined him and Ben and Lady Blue.

"A compliment to hard work," Robbie said, doffing an imaginary cap to her.

"Or to slovenly personal habits," Ben remarked. Jane raised her eyebrows pointedly at his own grubby jeans.

"Yeah, but you actually pay to do this," Ben said, and Jane, childishly, tried to kick his shin. He avoided the blow gracefully.

Lady Blue stood quietly as Robbie inspected her hoof and Jane and Ben sparred amicably. Luckily, Liz's horse only had a loose nail, and Robbie mended it quickly, apologizing to Doc that there wouldn't be any hoof treats today.

After saying good-bye to Robbie and petting Doc, Ben and Jane returned Lady Blue to her stall, and Jane fetched Lancelot from the paddock. Ten minutes later, she met Ben, already astride Professor and waiting for her. "Which way do you want to go?" he asked.

"We can just go through the fields again, like last time," she said, and blushed. The idea had struck her suddenly in the stall, taking Lancelot out to the site of the cross-country course to look around, but now she remembered their earlier ride, with its uncomfortable silences and Jane's unwelcome acknowledgment that Ben thought of her as a friend, and only a friend.

But Ben seemed unperturbed, as he had, for the most part, then. They swung the horses out toward the gate, and Lancelot bounced happily next to Professor. He was full of pent-up energy, as Jane had had to skip the morning lesson to teach a class of midgets whose counselor had a bad cold.

They followed the familiar route down the gentle slope, and Jane took a reading of her horse. He was lively, but he seemed to be listening to her, and moved easily between a trot and a walk, not fighting her as he had before. "I'm going to try a few of the jumps that are out here," she announced.

Ben looked at her with surprise. "They're not all out here anymore," he said. "I mean, some are, like the old log, but Granddad and I are building new ones. I don't think you want to try those."

Jane looked at him stupidly. *New jumps. Why didn't I think of that?*

"For the course, of course . . ." Ben grinned at her, and she smiled back, though she felt a sinking disappointment. She'd wanted to try Lancelot out here, in the fields, but practicing the new jumps before the others did was cheating. Wasn't it?

"Has Advanced I done any of them yet?" she asked hopefully, but Ben shook his head.

"Nope. Just like in real eventing. They'll get to walk the course, of course, beforehand, but it'll be the first time for their horses. Want to see some of them? There's a real doozy we've made out of barrels."

"Darn!" Jane burst out in frustration.

Ben stopped Professor. "What's wrong?"

Jane fought several internal battles at once. Did it really matter if she got a head start? After all, she already faced very long odds at winning as it was. It dawned on her that Ben could actually help her, if she dared to ask him, and to trust him. And if he didn't think she was crazy.

"Can you keep a secret?" she asked, feeling her cheeks heat up.

"Sure." He looked at her curiously, shoving his black hair behind his ears.

"Even from . . . from Jessica?" She could barely keep from gritting her teeth while saying it.

It was Ben's turn to blush. "From Jess?" *Jess?* Jane silently gagged. "Sure, I mean it's not like we, like I tell her . . . you know, everything," he said lamely, stumbling over his words.

Jane wrestled her stew of jealousy, nausea, contradicting desires, and second thoughts into submission. She told him everything. (Or almost everything.)

When her words ground to a halt, and he still hadn't spoken, except for an initial startled exclamation, they'd reached the paddock and the shrubbery.

"So," she finished, feeling a wave of shyness, "I could really use your help, if you have time. . . ." As she spoke, she realized that he very well might not. "And if you don't mind not telling anybody . . ." Which he very well might.

She waited, distracting herself by making a show of petting Lancelot and not looking over at the boy next to her.

Suddenly, Ben laughed. "Like *National Velvet!*" he exclaimed.

"Well, it's hardly a steeplechase," Jane objected.

"No, but you're still doing something you're not supposed to be able to do, and you're enlisting the aid of a kindly stable boy to help you." His eyes were alight as he answered, teasing but not, so far, chastising her or shutting her down.

"I don't remember the stable boy," Jane said, thinking, "but then again, I'm probably one of the few horsey girls in the world who didn't really like that book."

"I only saw the movie, but Mickey Rooney was definitely some kind of stable hand," Ben argued.

"Now I can see the resemblance," Jane said seriously. "You're just about his height, too."

Ben made a face at her. "I don't know why I'd help such a brat, but basically you want me to spy on the other girls' lessons and tell you what they're doing? And not tell Susan or my grandfather or, well, anyone else?"

Jane nodded, glancing at him warily.

"I'll start tomorrow." He grinned, mischief crinkling his eyes up in the way that made Jane's heart do a trapeze flip in her chest.

"Thanks" was all she could think of to say.

"No problem. Now you want to see some of the new jumps?"

"That would be cheating." *Right?*

Ben paused. "Yeah, I guess it kinda would. But it wouldn't be much worse than me telling you guys about that." He pointed at the gloomy mass of hedge in front of them.

Jane looked at him, confused. "What are you talking about?"

"You know, at the beginning of camp. You haven't forgotten jumping that thing, have you?"

"Of course not, but what do you mean you told us about it?"

Now Ben was confused. "I told Jess how big it had grown and told her to warn you guys. I thought Susan was nuts having you jump it. And I thought Jess was going to kill me for telling on Alyssa and Jennifer for skipping it. Maybe I shouldn't have, but Susan asked how everyone had done, and . . . I guess I have that honest thing that you've got. And Jess didn't care, she thought it was funny . . . but now they hate me, and that kinda makes things weird."

The simple pieces of the puzzle snapped together. This was why Ben had been so embarrassed the last time they stood in this spot. And how Alyssa and Jennifer had planned together to avoid the enormous jump, and why Jessica was so sure they had. And perhaps how Jessica, prepared, had cleared it on her first attempt. But Jessica, again probably because she *thought it was funny,* didn't tell her two friends that Ben would be watching. And she hadn't told Jane anything, anything at all.

"Jane? Earth to Jane?" Ben waved his arm at her, snapping her from her thoughts.

"She didn't tell me," Jane said simply. "She told the others, but she didn't tell me." She looked him straight in the eye, then turned Lancelot away from the paddock.

"I'm just going to canter around the fields," she called over her shoulder, not caring if he followed, not caring about much of anything except for the horse beneath her, who didn't lie, who didn't pretend to be friendly when he wasn't, who was incapable of dishonesty, of plotting and conniving. She didn't hear any hoofbeats behind her. A wave of disgust, of outright horrified anger and hurt, flooded through her. Jessica's behavior wasn't new, she realized. She had never, it seemed, been on Jane's side. Jane suddenly remembered Jessica's mysterious comment, it felt like years before, that the others were intimidated by Jane. It was a game, wasn't it? For surely this proved that Jessica had always thought of her as beneath contempt, wanted actively to keep her at a disadvantage. *Well, maybe you're the one who's intimidated, "Jess,"* she thought fiercely. But how to square this with the Jessica on the porch that night, the Jessica who had actually seemed proud of Jane's ride? She urged her horse to greater speed as they ate up the ground beneath them.

They ran for a minute more, then Jane slowly pulled Lancelot back to a canter, watching for signs of fatigue that didn't appear. They kept an even pace up a gentle slope and down the steeper opposite side. Jane opened up her seat and let the reins slide through her fingers, allowing Lancelot to find his own balance and stride. Her thoughts flickered back to Ben; she hoped he knew she wasn't angry with him. But what must he think of her, that Jessica hadn't even thought she was worth warning?

She took Lancelot through the shallow part of the creek, then trotted him down and up the bank that had worried Beau. She reined him up and circled him back to do it again. Once, twice, three times Lancelot made the leap down and up, never hesitating.

He trusted her. And she didn't go looking for any of the new jumps.

*Jane spent* the rest of the afternoon with Lancelot, then, when he seemed impatient with her company, alone. She let him out in the pasture with Professor, and the two ambled down to a shady spot together to swish flies. Jane headed to the cabin and, ignoring the girls sprawled on the floor in the common room, playing cards, she grabbed *Listening to Your Horse* and her sketchpad and started for the lake.

Glancing automatically inside the barn as she walked by, Jane saw the person that her eyes always seemed to unconsciously seek out, but whom at that moment she wanted to avoid. He was there, leaning against the tack room door, his back to her, apparently deep in conversation with someone Jane couldn't see. She sped up, but then heard her name and looked back to see Robin, stepping in front of Ben, waving to her.

"Where have you been?" Robin asked. "Ben was just

telling me that you told him. I think it's great, as long as he doesn't get in trouble. I mean, he does work here."

It was like Robin to think of that first, and Jane felt a little ashamed of herself. She lingered by the barn door and didn't answer. Robin gave her a funny look.

Reluctantly, Jane glanced quickly at Ben. "I don't want you to get into trouble," she managed. "Don't do anything you shouldn't."

"I could say the same thing to you . . . if I was totally lame," he replied, and despite herself, Jane smiled.

"No one has to find out I did anything," he continued. "And besides . . ." he stopped, his voice cracking a little. He cleared his throat and finished determinedly: "I really want to see you win."

Jane stood rooted to the spot. The words, and the emphasis he put on the words, filled her with a liquid warmth.

Robin saved her from a complete sentimental breakdown. "We've got a week," she said, matter-of-factly.

"Yeah," Ben said.

"Yeah," Jane echoed.

# Chapter 15

## Stormy Weather

A new mood seemed to sweep over the whole farm, not just Jane and her friends. Everyone was under pressure, and it showed. Susan stalked the farm like a guard dog, yelping at and shepherding and instructing everything that came in her path. Mrs. Jeffrys was constantly consulting with Jose and Maria about preparations for the incoming parents, and wondering out loud if these competitions weren't such a good idea and perhaps should be postponed for next year, comments that made Susan turn interesting hues of puce. Finally they seemed to sort out their main scheduling hassles: The Intermediate riders, whose "event" was a written exam, a stall and tack inspection, and a halter competition in which they'd lead their horses around the arena and be judged by the horses' appearance and grooming, would take place on Friday, before the parents arrived. Advanced II's show, hacking and jumping, would take place on Saturday, after which their parents could take them home, or they could stay on for Advanced I's event on Sunday, and "get a ride home however you can." Mrs. Jeffrys threw up her hands. "And now I've got to call all the parents *again,* and figure out where the judges are going to stay!"

"The judges?" Shannon almost spat out her cereal. It was Tuesday morning, and all of the campers were having breakfast and listening to Mrs. Jeffrys's harassed explanation of the schedule.

"Yes, dear. For your shows. You remember—Susan invited Jill Grabel from Long Run and Tom Cumbler from Windsor Farm to help judge, but where they're going to stay is beyond me at the moment. . . . Maria, do we have a plan for the *food* yet?" And with that, she rushed from the kitchen.

Jane looked around at the other girls at her table. All of them wore the same uncomfortable look. It was obvious that everyone, Jane included, had forgotten what Susan had indeed told them nearly six weeks before.

"Well, I'm sure they won't have to be here to grade our exams or to judge our hoof-picking," a girl in the Intermediate class muttered crossly. Many of the younger campers were disgruntled that they weren't going to get to ride in a "real" show.

"Grooming and barn management are *very* important,"

Alyssa said in patronizing tones. "When you're a more advanced rider, you'll do more advanced activities." The girl nodded, but when Alyssa turned back to her cereal, she stuck her tongue out at her.

*Alyssa seems to get that a lot.* Jane smiled to herself. *And she's one to talk about "barn management," considering that she leaves hers to Ricky and Gabriel.* She'd noticed that Megan didn't seem to be complaining about their test; in fact, the day before, she'd asked Jane to teach her how to braid Beau's tail, and Jane had happily complied, giving her the tip to use Vaseline to make the short hairs at the top stay smooth.

The events weren't the only scheduling problems the farm faced, however. It turned out that the ailing counselor had bronchitis, and Susan and Jane both had to fill in for her classes and reorganize the times, which had been rather free-floating and subject to the trainer's moods to begin with. Now, with the pressure of the impending shows, they were set firmly and allowed Susan barely a free minute throughout the coming days.

Poking her head into Lancelot's stall, she apologized to Jane that she wouldn't be able to work one-on-one with her anymore. "But you've done a great job with this horse, Jane. He's improved tremendously. I don't think you'll have any problem with the show, especially the jumping. You'll have to watch him during the flat, though."

Jane nodded. Lancelot still had problems working in the ring with the other horses, pinning his ears back and sometimes charging or attempting a nip if he were passed too close by anyone except Bess, or kicking if a horse came up behind him. Jane wasn't worried about it, because she'd decided not to ride in either of the Advanced II shows. But she wasn't ready to tell Susan that yet. It was actually quite convenient to have Susan so busy, even if she did lose out on valuable training with her. It gave Susan even less opportunity to notice the other training Jane was doing. No matter how hard her trainer liked pushing her, Jane didn't think she would've let her out on a cross-country course, and she probably would dismiss her intense dressage work as premature.

Ben, citing his and Jose's belief that Susan would encourage Jane to do anything difficult, asked her why she didn't just ask Susan directly if she could be in the Advanced I event. Jane considered it, but the risk that Susan would refuse her was too great. After all, she hadn't bumped her up to the top group despite Lancelot's progress. More important, she had something to prove to Susan, as much as to the other girls and to herself. It was difficult to put into words, this feeling, but it was bracing, burning steadily within her, despite her fears. Jose had said it weeks before: This summer was her test.

It was risky—all of it. Telling Ben, training away from everyone's eyes, betting that when she showed up for the dressage course on Sunday that Susan would even let her in the ring. She was counting on surprise, and the fact that Mrs. Jeffrys would do anything to avoid a scene in front of the parents and trainers from the other barns. She was probably putting her favorite people in a tough position, but after everything that had happened, she thought it was worth it . . . and she prayed they'd understand.

She devoured *Listening to Your Horse,* half-dreading that she'd discover that she'd been somehow mistreating Red without knowing it. It was strange taking instruction from a page instead of from Susan's familiar bellow, but as she read on, she grew a deeper appreciation for her tough mentor. It seemed that Jane, haphazardly, had done pretty well over the past weeks, at least according to the world-famous author, a healer of troubled horses and trainer of Olympic riders. He essentially advocated patience, spending a lot of time with the horse, never punishing, only asking. He probably wouldn't have approved of Jane and Lancelot's adventure over the stadium course, given his belief that a horse's confidence must never be endangered by presenting it with too-sudden challenges, but Jane thought that Susan had intuited rightly that Lancelot needed to be reminded of what he could do.

The chapter on horse health before an event had sent Jane flying to Jose for liniment and bandages, and she ran her hands obsessively over Lancelot's fine, sinewy legs, delicate looking but strong as steel. She minutely inspected his hooves for cracks and lavishly spread hoof conditioner on each night, though she suspected most of it smeared off on the pasture's grass. She went over her tack: Emily's sumptuous saddle, which she kept clean and polished within an inch of its life, was a dream, and while not entirely suitable for dressage, it had served them well so far. Lancelot had a martingale and a breastplate, and she could borrow Bess's leg wraps. She considered his grooming. She'd let his light, fox-colored mane grow out somewhat from its closely pulled brush (she'd never cared for the plucked, pulled, and shaved styles most of the campers favored for their horses; they seemed pointless and a whole lot of bother for something that didn't really do anyone any good). She decided on a single running braid, which suited him, even though she knew it would be frowned upon in a real event.

She read and reread the chapters on cross-country, mentally checking to see if the descriptions matched what she remembered feeling and doing in the saddle. For dressage, she had Robin there to watch and help her, and to quote arcane bits of advice from *The Art of Dressage*, which sometimes had a turn-of-the-century whiff about the prose. And now, on Tuesday afternoon, she was waiting impatiently to hear what Ben had learned from Advanced I's morning lesson, before going into her own. She dawdled while tacking up, hoping he'd find her before she had to leave the barn. She finally had to give up, hearing Susan hollering for her, and joined the others in the ring. For the next hour, they drilled over low jumps, practicing turns and judging exactly where their horses should take off for each obstacle, counting strides aloud. Like Beau, Lancelot had a tendency to rush jumps, even easy ones, and the exercise was good. Susan had her do a circle of ground poles at a trot to further stretch and contract his stride, and when concentrating, he handled them effortlessly.

"He should be a stunner at dressage one of these

days," Susan mused. "He can really move, and when he's focused he looks like a pro."

Jane gave a silent cheer and patted her horse.

Ben was waiting for them at the barn. Jane and Robin led their horses farther away from the others to sponge them off, and he followed them, glancing around, Jane imagined, for Jessica.

But while Jane had been lunging Lancelot in the paddock, Advanced I, like her class, had been jumping, and there wasn't much, Jane felt, that she needed inside information on there. But, grateful for Ben's efforts, she thanked him and was glad to learn that at least Susan had outlined the kind of jumps she'd be facing: verticals, triple bars, oxers, and combinations.

"Well, you've done all of those," Robin said reassuringly.

"Susan also said something about jumping an angle, but I didn't hear all of it."

"That's a new one," Jane said, pressing the sponge against Lancelot's chest. "But I think this horse would jump a truck." She stepped back for a moment to look at him. She'd spent so much time with him lately that she felt she hadn't actually *seen* him clearly for a while.

"Ahem, should we give you guys some privacy?" Ben said, and Robin giggled.

"What?" Jane asked, a flush rising to her cheeks.

"You're blushing again!" he mocked her.

"Stop! That always makes it worse!" Jane tossed her sponge at him.

"You two *did* look totally in love, Jane," Robin told her.

"Well, I mean, look at him! Who wouldn't be?" At that moment Lancelot, going for a fly, bonked her, hard, with his head, and she stumbled.

"It's a slightly abusive relationship, I'll admit. . . ." Jane sighed. "And I'll always love Beau first. But this horse can do anything. I can feel it."

*The sun was* just cresting the top of the hills as Jane half-sleepwalked through the pasture to collect Red the following morning. She'd decided to try to be clear of the barn before Susan and the other riders arrived, since today she wanted to practice more cross-country, where there was a greater chance of being seen. Yawning, she greeted Beau and allowed herself a minute of comfortable communion with her first favorite, so solid and dependable, from the way he delicately chose a carrot from her hand as if it were caviar to his utterly unflappable attitude toward his life at the farm. Unflappable, or simply happy even without her. *Well, good,* Jane thought. "You deserve it, friend," she told him. She was startled when she looked up to see that his ears cocked crankily backward, but she soon saw the source of his disgruntlement. Lancelot, as unpopular among the other horses as Jane felt she was among the campers, was idling toward them, ears pinned back, blowing in a surly fashion.

"Good morning, sunshine," Jane greeted him ironically, and went to get his halter on before he tried anything with Beau.

Since she had to avoid the horses in the pasture and the girls who would soon be collecting them, once Jane had quickly tacked Lancelot, she headed him toward the far boundary of the farm, out of eyesight. The dawn's freshness had lapsed into a sullen gray haze, and Jane had sweated through her T-shirt five minutes into her ride. It seemed unnaturally quiet, as if the birds were too hot to sing, and even the crickets were subdued. Still, the lowering sky brought out the fields' sweep of deep green, and the stillness, Jane realized, tasting the air, was the pregnancy of rain.

After fifteen minutes of warming up, and waking up, Jane decided to do another slow canter of the fields. She wanted to make sure that Lancelot was used to the uneven, changeable footing of the pasture, and being ridden over it at moderate speed. She gave him the signals, and he almost burst from her hands, worrying the bit and kicking out his forelegs like a charger. Jane eased him back, while trying to check her position, forward and slightly out of the saddle. She suddenly felt a rush of pure exuberance, astride this high-spirited horse who held her up so high. She let him gather a bit more speed, and they soared along the line of white fence.

A strange shape caught the corner of her eye, and she slowed her horse, doubling back in a wide curve. As they approached it, the thing revealed itself to be two squat wooden barrels on their sides, with a gathering of brush on top sticking up like a bad hairdo. The barrels were held in place by poles on either side, and Jane realized that she was looking at one of the new jumps. It wasn't terribly big, she noticed with relief, though it certainly did present an odd appearance. Lancelot eyed it casually, not particularly interested. Glancing around, though she wasn't sure for what, Jane thought, *Trying* one *jump wouldn't be so bad, would it?* She answered herself in the negative before she could change her mind and cantered Lancelot in a circle to square up to the mohawked barrels.

He hardly noticed it, and they were on the other side in one majestic, unconcerned leap. She had to laugh at how easy he made it look. She patted him as she slowed him to a trot and headed toward the creek, feeling guilty but very pleased.

The sky seemed to have bulked even closer to earth, and the air had taken on an electric glow, neon lighting the leaves of the trees. Jane knew that she had to go in, though she was reluctant to end their ride. Horses' metal shoes and lightning were a bad combination, and a storm was definitely brewing. She picked up a faster trot and decided to take a shortcut across a woody, overgrown part of the creek that she usually avoided. As she navigated Lancelot through the small, brushy trees, she felt a sharp branch catch her leg and she swept her hand down to unhitch it from the cloth of her jods. The branch, released, arced away from her but then came down with a hiss onto Lancelot's quarters.

She possibly could have held on for a rear, possibly could have maintained her seat for a fast bolt, but the sawing, bucking explosion under her came too quickly for

Jane to react. The reins tore through her hands as Lancelot scissored right, twisting his hindquarters in a catlike leap away from what he felt as the hated whip. This sent her over his left shoulder, frantically grabbing for her reins, then his mane, then anything at all as the earth rose up to meet her. She landed hard, skidding on the rock-and-pine-cone-studded dirt, then felt herself dragged like a rag doll—her left foot was caught in the stirrup. Jane couldn't think, couldn't breathe. Her helmet glanced off a tree trunk, and the ground ripped into her back, almost pulling her shirt over her head. With one panicked wrench, she kicked out as hard as she could, and then the crazed, earth-turning motion stopped, and she lay very still, listening to the dull tattoo of hoofbeats pounding away.

For a minute, Jane fought for her breath, heaving out in ragged bursts, then she was seized by a racking fit of coughing. As she coughed, she became aware of her body, feeling in particular a pinecone wedged under her back. Groaning, she managed to flop over and away from it, then lay on her stomach for a moment more, trying to find herself again. Her head was throbbing dully, and other parts of her hurt, but she was so dizzy and disoriented that she couldn't sort out everything that did. Then she heard a deep, throaty rumble and the two feet of woods that she could see around her dimmed. It began to rain.

Her arms were shaking so badly that it took her several attempts before she forced herself up on her knees. She grabbed a tree trunk next to her for support and made it to her feet. Her helmet felt like a vise, and she tore it off her head as she stumbled forward—her shoulder throbbed so painfully that she felt slightly faint. But Lancelot was running somewhere in the field, and it was starting to storm. She had to find him.

A crack of lightning in the distance spurred her on, and as she splashed across the creek and scrambled up the muddy slope of the far bank, the rain poured down in gusts and torrents, held off in some spots by the trees and flailing down in others. She limped as fast as she could from the woods, and finally made it free from the line of trees blocking her view. She saw the fields stretched before her, empty and sodden, blurred gray as a Monet in the streaks and shadows of water that flooded down. She saw no red horse, stirrups dangling, reins flying, anywhere.

Thunder rumbled again. Though she was far from the barn and the riding arena, Jane could make out, at least, that there seemed to be no one outside, probably all having fled to the shelter of the barns. No one would hear her call for help. She desperately tried to guess which part of the acres of pasture Lancelot would run to, if not the part close to the barn. The shed!

Jane had a long way to run to reach the far paddock, having to recross the creek and make it up the steep hill beyond. By the time she limped-ran through the gate, she had a stabbing stitch in her side that made her bend nearly double. But she soon felt a warm flood of relief as Lancelot whinnied to her, a high, frantic note in his voice, his head peering out from around the corner of the lean-to. Jane straightened up as best she could and hobbled toward him, throwing her right arm around his neck and leaning against him while she tried to calm her hammering heart. She realized that Lancelot was trembling beneath her hands.

When she felt a bit less shaky, she pried herself away from her horse and looked him over. The thorny branch had left a tiny nick on the side of his powerful, curved quarters, now splattered with mud and rain, but other than that he seemed fine. She gave a quick prayer of thanks that he hadn't stumbled over the reins or otherwise come to harm. He was breathing hard, obviously still upset, but he accepted her ministrations willingly enough. She spoke soothingly to him and rubbed the mark between his eyes until he seemed less anxious. Then Jane turned to examine the weather outside.

It was still pouring, and the occasional thunderburst rolled over the sky, but the sound seemed farther away. Still, Jane didn't relish the thought of leading Lancelot back to the barn, a good fifteen-minute walk through fields pooling with water and with an animal that was essentially a lightning rod. But Jane could see no break in the clouds, and they couldn't huddle in the shed forever. Susan would be looking for them, wondering what Jane was doing out here. . . .

The shoulder that she'd landed on twinged painfully again, and Jane realized that she hadn't checked the extent of her own damage. Her T-shirt was ripped through at the shoulder, and her left arm was scored with scratches, some bleeding, some just raised welts. Her left shoulder, bare through the torn fabric, was the worst; as she gingerly moved her arm back and forth, it seared with a strange, deep burning sensation. Her back hurt, too, and Jane gingerly felt under her shirt, which seemed to be torn in the back, too. Her fingers came away damp with blood, but not a great deal of it. She ached all over, as if she had, well, fallen off a really large horse and been dragged through the woods. "We'll live," she told Lancelot, and he snorted at her.

Jane decided there was nothing else for it. She knew she had to get back on after falling off, anyway. It was a psychological and practical necessity hammered into all the riders from their very first spills. Jane didn't trust her left leg to hold her as she remounted, so she led Lancelot out of the shed and into the downpour, sidling him next to an overturned water bucket. Shakily, she managed to throw a leg over and clamber aboard, her ankles wobbling in her stirrups and her fingers trembling over her reins. The big red horse was still nervous, circling and tossing his head, taking little sideways jumps that unnerved Jane herself. She fought for composure, knowing that he would not calm down unless she did. She petted him and found her seat, firmed up the reins, and relaxed her back. When she felt ready, she asked him for a trot, and they made their way through the fields back home as the rain poured down.

## Chapter 16

Secret Agent Man

W hat *happened* to you?"
"Oh. My. God."
"Are you all *right?*"

Jane hadn't had a choice except to bring Lancelot to the barn, but when they were hit with the glare of lights and the staring faces of half the campers, lounging on hay bales and folding chairs, cleaning tack, she stood, flummoxed, in the doorway, hoping for a second that she could hide, retreat. She didn't see Robin or Ben.

"I'm fine," she mumbled, and tugged Lancelot toward his stall. He rolled his eyes nervously at all the people crowding the aisle and dashed inside; Jane ducked after him, sliding the door firmly shut. Faces grouped around its bars.

"Jane, what happened?" asked Shannon, her eyes goggling.

"Nothing, I just fell."

"Should we call Susan? She's at the house," Megan piped up. Jane could only see the top of the girl's head and her two bright, worried eyes.

"I don't need Susan, I'm *fine*," she said tensely. She turned her back on them and started undoing Red's tack. She gritted her teeth as her shoulder throbbed. She could barely lift his saddle from his back and had to take his bridle off one-handed. "Darn it," she whispered as tears pricked her eyelids. Abruptly, she sat down in the corner of the stall and put her head in her hands.

"Jane?" she heard Robin's voice. "They just told me you—oh, Jane." Then Robin was beside her, gently tugging her hands from her face. She put her arm around Jane and helped her from the barn.

*Stinking of* a weird combination of floral bath gel and antiseptic ointment, Jane lay comfortably on her bunk, listening to the rain typing furiously on the cabin's tin roof. Robin was lying on the opposite end of the bed, her feet tucked under part of Jane's pillow, reading. Jane shifted the sling that crossed her chest to snuggle farther under her blanket. She felt oddly cheerful. Maria had made a fuss over her shoulder, but Jane was convinced that there was nothing really wrong with it. It hurt—it hurt a lot—but so had her head, and that had healed. Susan had told her that she shouldn't ride the next day, but Jane had just nodded absently at her. She'd told Susan essentially the truth about her fall, though she'd downgraded her activities in the field to a trail ride, and her trainer hadn't pressed her.

The best part of the day by far had been when Ben took her mud-encrusted, blood-spattered, shredded T-shirt and tacked it to Lancelot's stall door, adding a handwritten sign: BLOODY BUT UNBOWED. Jane couldn't speak when she saw it, and then he had hugged her for the first time, and not only couldn't she speak, she also couldn't breathe. Susan had made him take it down, scolding him that it would scare the other campers, but not before Robin had taken a picture of it. Ben reluctantly dismantled his work, but he hadn't given Jane the shirt back.

Now Jane, warm and relaxed from her bubble bath, propped securely in bed with her best friend nearby, luxuriated in a brief spell of cozy laziness. The rain and her scraped, bruised, and aching limbs kept her from the barn, and she felt a bit like she was on vacation. *A vacation from camp.* The thought made her smile, and she looked over to Robin, frowning with concentration over her book, her toes sporadically twitching, jiggling Jane's pillow.

"What is going on down there?" Jane asked, giggling.

Robin looked up, her face a picture of intense worry.

"You did *not* tell me that this was a scary bunny book," she said seriously, and Jane laughed.

"It's a traumatizing bunny book, actually," Jane agreed.

Robin closed *Watership Down* emphatically. "I think that's all I can take tonight. I'm going to have nightmares about cats and wire traps and farmers. . . ."

"Well, I'll be having nightmares about random twigs, so we'll be in about the same shape tomorrow morning." Tomorrow morning. Thursday. Jane yawned on purpose, trying to forcibly quell the jolt of anxiety she felt. She tentatively touched her shoulder and winced. Robin raised her eyebrows and was about to say something, but Jane cut her off.

"Don't," she said. "It's going to be fine."

The cabin door banged open, and Alyssa and Jennifer came in, wet and complaining about the weather. Jessica wandered in from the common room with an armload of laundry that she dumped on her bed.

"Why are you here?" Alyssa asked her. "I thought you were hanging out with Ben." Jane studiously examined a hangnail.

"It's raining, if you haven't noticed," Jessica said coolly.

"So?" Jennifer questioned insinuatingly. "It's not like you *have* to walk around in the rain." Jane snuck a look at Jessica. Her face was clouded over and she was folding socks with unnecessary violence.

"He had to do something with his family," she said shortly.

Jennifer and Alyssa exchanged a meaningful glance. They changed the subject back to the weather a little too airily, and Jane wondered with a stab of hope if Jessica and Ben had argued. . . . Part of her thought it would be wonderful if they had argued over her, over Jessica not having told her about the hedge, but a larger part of her wanted them to simply not like each other, and to leave her out of it altogether.

"So what do you think of the dressage test, Jess?" Alyssa asked.

"Oh, did you guys get it?" Robin asked, wiggling her toes vigorously.

Jennifer nodded. "It's pretty hard. . . . Take a look." She handed Robin a piece of paper inked with circles and dotted lines. Jane leaned forward eagerly and her shoulder throbbed.

"All King Edward's Horses Can Make Bad Fudge," Jennifer announced.

"Pardon?" said Robin.

"The letters around the ring—A, K, E, H, C, M, B, F, with X in the center."

"Oh, it's a mnemonic device," Jane said.

"*Oh, it's a mnemonic device!*" Jessica shrilled mockingly. Jane sat back, startled into silence. But nobody laughed.

"Jesus, Jess, chill," Alyssa said sharply.

*Alyssa, coming to my defense?* Jane's crimsoned hurt turned to astonishment.

"Whatever!" Jessica threw her pile of clean T-shirts onto her bunk and stomped from the room. They heard the cabin door slam behind her.

"She is being *such* a brat!" Jennifer exclaimed. But she

and Alyssa didn't extend their temporary support of Jane to actually addressing her again or including her in the conversation. Instead they disappeared into the common room for a whispered conference, and Jane, shoving away her questions for the moment, dove for her sketchpad and furiously started copying out the dressage test with Robin's help.

"*All King Edward's* horses can make bad fudge, all King Edward's horses . . ." Robin chanted under her breath as she and Jane headed for the barn the next morning.

"I keep picturing these big Percherons wearing crowns and standing with their hooves in mixing bowls, looking confused," Jane said.

"Well, they're terrible with the measuring spoons," Robin agreed.

"But great with cracking the eggs."

"Not so good with the whisking."

"No clue about oven temperature."

"And they always forget to wear aprons."

Laughing, they almost ran into Susan, barging around the corner of the barn. Her hair was sticking out in alarming tufts from her braid and she barked at them to watch where they were going. Then, more kindly, she asked Jane how her arm was.

It was still very sore, and Jane had struggled pulling her jods and boots on, but she just said, "Okay."

"Why don't you lunge him today?" Susan advised. "The ring's a mess but I think the paddock's not too bad. And get that arm back in a sling."

Jane agreed, and they spent a calm, rather dull morning in the paddock. She couldn't use a lunge whip with Lancelot, so she practiced body language techniques from *Listening to Your Horse* that worked fairly well, though she got dizzy from turning around and around in circles, trying to keep her shoulders at the proper angle to his body. The weather was still uncertain, sudden gusts of wind sending clouds whipping through the sky, bright shafts of sunlight occasionally breaking through and setting fire to the myriad puddles dotting the farm like a chain of silver medallions. Jane just hoped the ground would be dry by Sunday.

It was too wet to sit under their tree, so after lunch Jane and Robin headed for the cabin, the test tucked safely in Jane's pocket. But the cabin was full of people, so they decided to go down to the dressage ring, where they hoisted themselves on a fence rail. Jane pulled out the paper and unfolded it on her knee.

"I really hope we copied this down right," Robin worried as they stared for a minute at the arcane squiggles and dashes that confronted them.

"Me too," Jane said with a wry smile. "Okay, we've got King Edward's horses, but we've also got a D and a G in the middle, before and after the X."

"Daring Gopher?" Robin suggested.

"Demented Geese," Jane returned.

"Dreadful Goat!" squealed Robin.

"Dreadful Goat?"

"How is that weirder than 'Demented Geese'? Your 'mnemonic device' is fixed."

"Fine, but don't go around chanting it," Jane sighed. She focused on the page before her. *Enter at a working trot, halt and salute at X, proceed at a working trot to C, turn left....*

"This really looks like stuff you've done, Jane!" Robin said excitedly, after many minutes of mute absorption in the test.

"Except the circles are a lot tighter. I mean, half of our marks aren't King Edward at all, but points right between the King Edward letters. And do you think we're supposed to canter on the wrong lead here, or do a flying change?"

Robin shook her head. "It doesn't say. We'll get Ben to find out. Here, why don't you do the course on foot—I'll call it out to you and tell you how your circles are."

And so they spent the next hour walking, trotting, and cantering Jane around the ring, until she felt like she pretty much had the course by heart. Tired and wanting to take a break, she snorted in imitation of Lancelot to make Robin laugh, and then pretended to completely freak out, bolt, rear, then trample her rider.

"NOT funny!" Robin yelled at her.

As they walked slowly back to the cabins, Jane realized that she'd managed to spend an entire morning and half an afternoon without worrying, and she told herself that that must be the best medicine of all for her shoulder. Or so she hoped.

The day passed alarmingly quickly, and by dusk Jane's anxiety returned with the pain in her shoulder. She had to admit that it felt worse after her day's activities, which hadn't even included riding. But she refused to think that she might not be able to compete on Sunday. The thought was impossible. Her shoulder wasn't broken, so she could grit her teeth and bear it. *Right?*

She visited Lancelot in the barn after dinner and found Ben in his stall.

"I was just, uh, checking on him, since you're not feeling so hot," he said almost shyly, and Jane's stomach did a flip-flop that she tried to suppress. "I figured he should stay in the barn tonight, in case it rains again."

"Nurse Flo seems to be happy," Jane said, seeing the skinny tabby curled up tightly in her corner nest.

"Yeah, Red always looks like he's going to step right on her, but he just misses, and she doesn't seem to care."

"Meant for each other," Jane said. An awkward silence fell.

"Oh, hey, I can't believe I forgot this," Ben finally said, digging in the back pocket of his jeans. "Secret agent man delivers." He handed Jane two sheets of paper covered with Susan's familiar drawing style.

"The jumping course! And cross-country! How did you get these?" Jane eagerly ran her eyes over the pages.

"Well, it might make me sound less heroic, but it was really easy. Susan asked Ricky to go into town to copy the tests, and I got him to make a couple extra."

"You're brilliant. And heroic." Jane beamed at him. She was so relieved he hadn't gotten them from Jessica, she felt like doing a small jig.

"What has my grandson done that's so wonderful?" Jose asked, and Jane and Ben jumped. She felt his hand on her good shoulder and looked up to see him smiling with affection and curiosity at them.

"Mucked out Lancelot's stall for me, because of my shoulder," Jane lied hastily, shoving the papers into her pocket and trying not to blush, which never worked.

"Well, heroic maybe, but I don't know how brilliant that is," Jose said.

"Ah, but *Abuelito,* you haven't seen my new technique. You see, when I've got a really big pile of poop, I do this thing with the shovel. . . ."

Jose waved him off. "I don't want to know." He chuckled. "But don't tell your grandmama how you're using your brain to muck stalls better. She'll make you stay inside for the rest of the summer, reading your school-books."

Ben grinned ruefully at him. "I definitely won't," he promised.

Impatient to study the new courses, Jane told them good night, escaping from Jose's questions about her shoulder and his pointed glance toward her pocket. One usually comforting and now perilous thing about Jose was that he always and rather mysteriously knew everything that was going on at the farm. Jane hoped that he wouldn't guess their secret, and if he did, that he wouldn't try to stop her.

*Friday dawned* in a blurred red fireball blistering the newly washed sky, and by breakfast, the humidity had reached its usual August level of barely-less-than-unbearable, and the campers were for once longing for the lake over the barn. The beginners and their one healthy counselor headed for the canoe launch directly after breakfast; the advanced riders could join them if they wished, but everyone lingered in the kitchen with the intermediates, curious to see their exam, which they'd be given after they'd finished eating. Jane noticed that Megan looked slightly green, and her untouched bowl of cereal had turned to mush. It sounded like she was whispering the parts of a horse's leg over and over to herself.

Finally Susan came in, holding a sheaf of papers and accompanied by two strangers. Jane whispered to Robin that they must be the guest judges, and similar whispering rippled down the long picnic tables.

"Okay," Susan said, grinning and frowning simultaneously. "My advanced girls can clear out now. You've got a free day, as you know, but if you want to work your horses, go ahead. My intermediate riders will take your exam now, then go down to the barn to finish preparing your stalls and your horses. You need to bring your horses to the outdoor ring for the halter competition at noon, so if any of you advanced riders have set up jumps, please make sure they're out of the way then. And I should introduce our two guests who will be helping with the judging. This is Jill Grabel, a trainer at Long Run...." There was a murmur of hellos from the girls, and the surprisingly young trainer gave them a friendly wave that set her shiny brown ponytail bobbing. "And this is Tom Cumbler, from Windsor Farm." The stocky man in jeans and a Western-style shirt and cowboy hat nodded to them. His face was lined and expressionless, except for piercing hazel eyes that somehow managed to escape the shadow of his hat to cast a penetrating look around the kitchen.

"Okay, everybody out except my intermediates, let's go."

As Susan shooed them from the kitchen, Jane looked back over her shoulder and caught Megan's eye. She gave her an encouraging grin, and Megan sent a wan smile back. "You'll do great," Jane mouthed to her, and Megan's smile got a little stronger.

Jane mulled over her first impression of the judges, and Susan's funny speech: *my* intermediates, *my* advanced girls. *She's proud,* Jane thought. She's proud and showing off a bit, showing Jill Grabel and Tom Cumbler what sort of shop she runs around here. It made her smile, then made her start worrying again about Sunday. With a jolt, Jane remembered that Long Run was where Jessica had said Lancelot came from, and so Jill Grabel had probably trained him and his former owner—and they'd won championships! What if she embarrassed the whole farm in front of her, and in front of Tom Cumbler? Jane's vivid imagination provided her with a whispered conversation between the trainers: *Well, Lancelot used to be a great horse, but he had a great rider then....* Jane shuddered at the image, and at what Susan's reaction might be.

All of the Advanced I riders were going down to the dressage ring, so Jane and Robin decided to practice jumping instead, especially since this was the part of her show tomorrow that Robin was most worried about. Liz and Shannon, declaring it too hot to ride, headed for the lake, so they had the outdoor ring to themselves.

To Jane's mounting horror, she found her shoulder too sore for her to effectively ride Lancelot, who was in a cantankerous mood. Each time she had to firmly pull him in, her shoulder gave a sickening stab, and he soon was dragging them all over the arena. She was wordless and near tears by the time they had to clear away the jumps for the halter show. Robin was, for once, too absorbed in her own performance to quiz Jane on how she felt, so Jane was left to her own darkening thoughts as she rubbed down her horse.

All around her, the barn was frenetic with activity. Some intermediate riders were putting the final touches on their horses; others had hitched them outside to finish raking their stalls. The tack room was a blur of hair spray and boot polish. Jane decided to go ahead and put Lancelot in the field so he wouldn't be upset by all the clamor. As she threaded him through the other horses and frantic girls, she saw Ben, carrying a toolbox, pass by the barn and hailed him.

"Secret agent, I need your help again," she said. In any other circumstances the cocky salute and warm smile he returned would have melted her, but Jane felt a little desperate.

"I've got to get something for my shoulder. Anything that will help me ride on Sunday. I've looked through the first-aid kit, but I don't think a Band-Aid's going to help much."

"I can see what we've got at home, and maybe raid the main house," he said immediately. "But, not to go Granddad on you—do you really think it's okay for you to ride?"

She just looked at him.

"All right. I'll bring you everything I can find. But don't hurt yourself, Jane."

"Okay, Granddad." She smiled. "And thanks."

"Let me put this away," Ben said, waving the toolbox, "and we can go watch the show."

As they walked over to join the other girls—the whole camp had turned up and was lounging around the outside of the ring—Jane saw Jessica staring stonily at them. She averted her gaze when Jane caught her eye, but apparently Ben had noticed as well. "Um, let's go stand over there." He indicated a spot far from where Jessica and Alyssa and Jennifer were standing. Jane, already heartened by Ben's medical mission, felt her spirits bounce further upward.

The judges completed their inspection of the stalls and walked toward the ring, followed by a line of girls leading their horses out from the barn. Jane searched the procession for Beau, and when she spotted him she gave Ben's arm an unplanned, hard squeeze. "Look at Beau!" she gasped.

He was magnificent. As he strode through the gate, the sun shone from his gleaming coat, polished to a glassy shine Jane doubted she had ever produced in her years of grooming him. It brought out unexpected red highlights on the curve of his hindquarters, behind which a blue-ribboned and perfectly braided tail swished saucily. He carried his head high, obviously aware of his splendor, and the row of neat braids, shot through with the same deep blue and, Jane saw with amazement, tiny white daisies that she recognized from the flower beds around the barns, lay perfectly against the crest of his neck.

Megan, standing stiffly beside him, barely reaching the top of his shoulder, hadn't fared quite as well, Jane noticed. Her boots were impeccably polished and her shirt neatly tucked in, but her jods had a telltale swipe of horse slobber streaking her thigh, and her face was bright red from her exertions. Several of the other girls seemed to have spent more time on their own grooming than on their horses—some were wearing sundresses, some had French braided their hair—and Megan definitely looked worse for wear compared to them. She was even wearing her riding helmet, which none of the other intermediates were. But she stood as tall as she could beside Beau, and when the girls were asked to walk their horses, she strode forward confidently, her horse bouncing beside her with a spring in his step.

And when, twenty minutes later, Susan pinned a blue ribbon on Beau's halter, and Megan threw her arms around his neck, Jane got a hard lump in her throat.

"She loves that horse," she whispered.

Ben took her hand and gave it a brief squeeze, and then they started to clap, as loud and as hard as they could.

## Chapter 17

❧⚘U⚘☙

# Robin's Ride

An air of festive confusion, which reminded Jane of eighth-grade graduation in its tumult and nervous anticipation, gripped the farm. Mrs. Jeffrys had taken it into her head that all the campers—including the advanced riders—should sing for the parents when they arrived, and Alyssa and Jennifer discussed a boycott, of which Jane heartily approved, even if she wasn't invited. But it was almost worth it to get to experience Susan playing temporary counselor, banging through their cabin door at eleven o'clock on Friday night, kicking them out of bed, hurling sheet music at them, and leading them in a sleepy, confused, very off-key version of "My Old Kentucky Home." Luckily, most of the girls already knew the words.

"Beautiful," Susan barked. "Go to bed." And she banged back out again.

When Jane rose early on Saturday morning, Robin's bed was empty, her sleeping bag neatly zipped with her ancient stuffed rabbit peering cockeyed from the coverlet. Alyssa and Jennifer were still asleep, but Jessica's bunk was missing its inhabitant as well.

Jane yawned her way to the barn. She wanted to get in a morning ride before the parents showed up for lunch and the Advanced II show. The parents. She stopped in her tracks, stunned. Her parents. Mrs. Jeffrys saying, *I've got to call all the parents again.* Her parents would be coming today, for a show she wasn't riding in. She started running for the main house.

She called Lily's cell phone, which was usually jammed under her pillow, since she also used it as an alarm clock. Her sister was going to kill her for waking her up at this hour, but Jane hoped she'd forgive her before sending a missile from the house to the farm.

The phone rang and rang. Finally, "*Mmph?*" and deep breathing.

"Lily? Lily? It's Jane. Wake up, Lil."

"Gah."

"Lily, are Mum and Dad planning to come to the farm today? Did Mrs. Jeffrys call them?"

"Whah tize it?"

"Lily, wake up for just a second. *Please!*"

She heard more breathing, then silence.

"LILY! WAKE UP!"

A scrabbling sound, then: "I answered the phone when Mrs. Jeffrys called. I told her we had other plans today and would pick you up tomorrow. To tell you we were sorry we were going to miss your show. She probably thinks we're horrible people, but it was the best I could do. I didn't say anything to Mum and Dad." Her sister had the cross, clear, overly articulated voice of someone talking in their sleep.

Jane exhaled a sigh of relief. "You're the best, Lily, you really—"

"GOOD NIGHT." And the phone went dead.

Jane replaced the receiver, limp with relief and gratitude for her sister. She grabbed an apple from the bowl in the kitchen, hunted around for a granola bar since she was planning to skip breakfast, and was interrupted by Mrs. Jeffrys, perfectly dressed and lipsticked at seven in the morning. Jane wondered if she'd slept in her clothes.

"Oh, Jane dear. Here, come here, my dear. I'm so sorry. I should tell you . . . your parents . . . Would you like to sit with me for a bit of breakfast?" She was obviously torn between her role as farm owner and den mother, frantic with the day's preparations, but wanting to break the news that Jane knew was coming gently.

"I'll just take a granola bar, if there are any, thanks," Jane said firmly and, she hoped, cheerfully. "And don't worry, I just talked to my parents. I don't feel good enough to ride in the show, anyway, so it's actually great that they're not coming today."

"Oh, your poor shoulder. Such a brave dear. So glad

it's not worse than it is. Here's a granola bar," and with that, Mrs. Jeffrys was out the door.

Jane gave her poor shoulder a few shrugs as she jogged back to the barn and swore. She hoped Ben came up with some first aid soon. The ice packs she'd been using three times a day for the past two days, on Maria's instructions, seemed to have helped some, but they were messy and required sitting still for longer periods than she had patience for. Her scrapes and cuts were healed, though sensitive, particularly the pinecone bite on her back, but her upper arm and shoulder still hurt.

The barn was silent when she entered, but she headed for Bess's stall in case Robin had already brought her in. Sure enough, there was Bess, who looked at Jane calmly with her great doe eyes, but her owner was nowhere to be seen. Jane decided to check the tack room, and as she reached the door, which was slightly ajar, she heard voices. She paused, trying to figure out who they belonged to, and if she wanted to talk to them or just go straight to the field to collect Lancelot. As she stood indecisively, she heard another noise—a faint scratching sound, like a mouse. It seemed to be coming from the stall that abutted the tack room, and Jane walked over to investigate. She jumped when she saw Robin crouched down on the sawdust, her ear pressed against the conjoining wall between the stall and tack room. Jane opened her mouth, but Robin hastily put a finger to her lips, so Jane slipped through the open stall door and joined her friend's unusual eavesdropping.

The voices on the other side of the wall rose, and Jane realized that there was really no need to press her ear against the dirty stall: Ben's and Jessica's voices came through perfectly clearly now.

"I think it's obvious," snarled Jessica.

"*What's* obvious?" Ben replied. He sounded defensive.

"Why you do all this stuff for Jane."

Jane and Robin huddled closer together.

"I'm not *doing* anything for Jane. My grandmother told me to give her this for her shoulder."

Now Ben got a taste of Jessica's mimicry: "*My grand-mother told me to*," she said mockingly.

Apparently Ben had had enough, because Jessica quickly added, "You better not leave before you tell me what's been going on."

"There's nothing going on!" Ben practically shouted. "I told you that I thought what you did was crappy, because it was. And yeah, Jane's my friend. She was my first friend here, before you, before you and me ..."

"Before you and me *what?*"

Silence. Then Jessica continued, "I didn't tell Jane because Jane doesn't need my help."

"Yeah right. But Alyssa and Jennifer do? If you're saying that she's a better rider than they are, then you're right. But I don't think that's why you left her out."

"Oh, then why did I *leave her out?*" Jessica asked icily.

"Because you wanted her to mess up. Or get scared. Because you're jealous of her, obviously."

"I am *not* jealous! How could I be jealous of *Jane*?"

"Then why are you grilling me?" Ben yelled.

And now it was Jane who had had enough. She strode out of the stall and banged her fist on the tack room door. "If you're done talking about me, can I please come in and get my halter?" she asked loudly. She heard Robin come up behind her. The tack room fell into silence.

She pushed open the door and looked straight at Jessica, whose face was beet red.

"For your information, there is nothing 'going on.' After all, how could you possibly be jealous of *me*?" she said softly. "Now please get out of my way."

Jessica opened her mouth, shut it, and stormed through the door that Jane held open for her.

Jane looked at Ben. "Sorry," she said.

"It's okay," he muttered. He handed her a plastic bag. "Here's some stuff for your shoulder." And he walked out.

"He's not mad at you," Robin said urgently. "He's mad at Jessica. He's just upset."

But Jane felt hollow inside as she went to get Lancelot from the fields.


*Working trot to K, change diagonals at X* . . . Jane gritted her teeth, fighting to keep her hands steady. She hadn't had the heart to go through Ben's supplies yet, but at least she didn't have to go into two-point in dressage. Pushing her arms before her over jumps was definitely going to be the most painful part of tomorrow's riding, unless of course Lancelot bolted and tore her shoulders from their sockets altogether. She remembered imitating him the day before and suddenly felt more nervous than amused.

But he was going well, recovered from yesterday's mood, and she took him through the dressage test several times before heading in. She still wasn't sure about the counter-canter vs. flying change, but figured she'd watch what the other girls did the next day. She didn't lie to herself about today's ride: It was mediocre; she was stiff, and Red was only half-attentive. But they made it through the motions, and she'd make them do better tomorrow. She'd make herself focus completely tomorrow. Her shoulder *would* be better tomorrow.

When Jane returned to the barn, she realized that she'd made a miscalculation.

"Jane, what are you doing on that horse? Mrs. Jeffrys told me you weren't feeling well enough to ride!" Susan blindsided her as she slipped from Lancelot's back. Jane froze, unable to think what to say. "Ah, I was just . . ."

"Put your arm back in that sling," Susan harrumphed at her. "You'll be able to ride Lancelot again when you're feeling one hundred percent." She turned on her heel and headed for the outdoor ring, where Jose and Ben were beginning to set up Advanced II's jumping course.

"Whew," Jane said to Red.

She passed by Jill Grabel as she led Lancelot to his stall and thought the Long Run trainer might recognize him and say something. She did give Jane a brief smile, but that was all, and Jane was too shy to start a conversation with one of the judges.

As soon as Lancelot was settled in, Jane grabbed Ben's bag and went to find Robin. She knew she must be nervous about the show, and her parents would be arriving soon. She found her in the cabin, changing into clean jods and a lavender button-down shirt that looked freshly ironed. She had pulled her hair back into a sleek ponytail and put on a bit of lip gloss. "You look great," Jane told her.

"Ugh," Robin said. "I just want this to be over and done with. Jane, I really don't think I like having shows at camp."

"Don't you want to start showing Bess this fall?" Jane had always assumed that this was a next step for Robin; indeed, she'd already entered and done well in some smaller shows last winter.

"Honestly?" Robin looked at her with large, worried eyes. "No, I really don't. And my mom keeps telling me I have to. Like, What's the point in having a horse if you don't show?"

"You've never told me that before," Jane said wonderingly, though it fit with what Robin had told her at the lake.

"Well, I knew how much you *did* want to show, and I guess I just felt stupid. And it hasn't come up again until now, really. My mom called me this morning to tell me how excited she was." Robin's mother had been a horsewoman, too, before arthritis had forced her to stop riding. When they were younger, she'd even come out to Sunny Acres with them, taking lessons with Susan after trail riding with the girls. It had always seemed wonderful to Jane to have a mother who understood about horses, though she found Mrs. Zimmerman remote and intimidating out of the saddle. But now she understood that Robin felt pressured. She'd even felt pressured by Jane, before their lakeside conversation. She just wanted to enjoy horses, to enjoy Bess, and riding, and camp, without it being about winning and losing. Given her own emotional roller coaster over the past several weeks, Jane thought Robin might, after all, be much, much smarter than her.

And yet . . . Jane knew she was made differently. What she enjoyed was the work of it all, was getting better, and, yes, being better. Did that make her a worse person than Robin? She suspected it might. Or maybe, as long as she didn't cheat or act badly toward others, she could make it a good thing. Or was she selfish?

She turned her thoughts back to her friend, now sitting on the edge of her bunk looking gloomy.

"Listen," Jane said, sitting down next to her and taking her hand. "You absolutely don't have to show Bess if you don't want to. You happen to be a really good rider, and you'd win, just as I'm sure you're going to win today, but if you don't like it, then that's that. No one will think anything about it. And I could always get Mum to give a speech about the importance of showing, which to her is zilch." Jane smiled and squeezed Robin's hand, wanting to physically push encouragement and support into her friend.

Robin smiled back, then gave her a hug.

"Thanks, Jane," she whispered.

*The driveway was* beginning to fill with cars when Jane and Robin emerged from the cabin, and adults in sun hats and khakis and sandals were milling on the lawn behind the house, while younger children hung around their parents or ran shrieking to the cabins to find their siblings.

Jane saw Shannon's parents, comically mismatched in height, and Liz's, who she'd always thought were nice, then a crowd of strangers who must belong to the midgets, most of whom were leaving today. Jane realized with a jolt that she'd been too preoccupied to notice that these weren't the same midgets as the beginning of camp, then reasoned that of course they must have switched halfway through. She commented on this to Robin, who looked at her strangely.

"This is actually the third batch of midgets, Jane. They usually only stay for two weeks. Haven't you noticed?"

Jane shook her head. "They all look the same—short," she said, and Robin shoved her gently, then spotted her parents' car pulling up in the driveway and ran to greet them. Jane lingered behind, not particularly eager to join in the lunch, which was spread out on picnic tables under the lawn's shady trees. And when she saw Mrs. Jeffrys waving to the campers to form a group in front of the buffet, she turned to make an exit. She had a feeling that they were about to sing.

"Not so fast, young lady." She was stopped by Susan's glare. "Singing won't hurt your shoulder," she said with a chuckle. "Back you go."

And, Jane had to admit, when they reached the final, tender verse, "Then my old Kentucky home, good night," and she looked around at the green splendor of the farm, the majestic oaks and glossy magnolias, and the rolling fields of bluegrass dotted with horses, it was a pretty nice song.

*She was starting* to get nervous for Robin as she helped tack up Bess. The parents and the other riders were now grouped around the fence of the outdoor arena, and the three judges were in the center, carrying notepads and looking very official indeed.

"Just imagine it's another lesson, except there are a bunch of idjits wandering about," Jane advised in her British accent.

"How many points do we get off for throwing up on our mount?" Robin Britished back.

"None, as long as you don't hit a judge," Ben chimed in from outside the stall.

"Was that a silly accent, or do my ears deceive me?" Robin asked giddily. She sounded a little punch-drunk from nerves.

"'Tis no worse than *yours*, my lady," Ben retorted, and Robin blew an unladylike raspberry at him.

Jane had shut up when she heard Ben's voice and occupied herself with Bess's girth.

"Madam Ryan, after we witness the triumphant victory of Madam Zimmerman, might I advise you on how to bind your pathetic wound?"

Jane looked up reluctantly from the buckle. But Ben's cheerful smile and crinkled-up eyes seemed to be radioing assurance through the bars of the stall. And his British accent was almost as bad as hers.

"It's already injured, no need to insult it," she said faux-crossly.

"Well, it is pathetic."

"Is not."

"Is too."

"Really! Enough!" said Madam Zimmerman, and they moved aside to let her lead Bess to the ring.

"Good luck!" Jane and Ben said together as they followed her out.


*But Robin didn't* need their luck. Though she might not like shows, she loved to ride and it was obvious, from her graceful seat during equitation to the nearly flawless jumping course she completed. Jane pounded her hands together until they ached when Susan pinned the blue ribbon on Bess's bridle, and Robin flashed her a happy, abashed grin.

Jane ran to her as the girls filed out of the ring—Shannon with a red second-place ribbon and Liz with a yellow third—and joined Robin's parents around her stirrup. Her mother was adjusting Bess's ribbon and saying to Robin, "Well, I hope this has convinced you to show this fall." Robin and Jane exchanged looks.

"Um, Rob, didn't you say something to me about wanting to put the money you spent on shows into your college fund instead?" Jane blurted. Robin stared at her.

Mrs. Zimmerman gave a little laugh. "Dear, you don't need to worry about your *college* fund, for goodness' sakes!" She looked perplexedly at her daughter, who fiddled with her reins.

"Why, I think that's a mighty good idea," Mr. Zimmerman broke in, as Jane had been counting he would. "With the market these days, you never know what shape you're going to be in a few years down the road. I think that's very smart, honey." He patted her boot and beamed up at his daughter.

"Thanks, Daddy," Robin managed, then burst into a sudden fit of coughing that didn't fool Jane one bit.


*Later,* as they pinned her ribbon in a place of honor on their bunk, Robin asked Jane how in the world she'd come up with that idea.

"It was Ben, actually," Jane told her. She'd filled him in a bit on Robin's parents as the show started, and he'd hit on the notion of the college fund—it was a ploy he had

used on his parents when they'd wanted him to take pi-
ano lessons.

"Ben's brilliant," Robin said appreciatively.

"His accent is atrocious," Jane replied, blushing.

"How's the stuff he got for your shoulder?" Robin
asked, peering into the bag that now lay on Jane's bunk.

"I guess we'll find out," Jane said, pulling out a heating pad and Ace bandages. "He said to keep doing the ice
bags, then the heating pad at night. Then tomorrow I'm
going to put this hot-cold ointment on my shoulder and
wrap it up in this bandage. And until then, I'd better keep
wearing the sling." She saw the anxious look on Robin's
face. "Seriously, it's going to work. What's the worst thing
that could happen?" And in a flash she remembered the
terrible feeling of being dragged through the woods. . . .

"Okay, forget I asked that," Jane muttered, and went
to get some ice from the house.

Chapter 18

# Sunday, Part One

The green numerals of Jessica's clock spelled 4:46, then 5:10, then 5:28, and Jane gave up trying to sleep. Her mind ached with mixed-up courses and directions, spinning from the creek's banks to a tight turn to confront the oxer in the stadium course, to a flying change (counter canter?) in the dressage ring. She had a feeling she was going to forget the courses entirely by the time she had to face them.

She pushed aside the heating pad, now uncomfortably warm in the stuffy cabin, and gave her shoulder a few slow, circular rotations. Sore, but not as sore. Certainly not as sore. She squeezed it and nearly yelped aloud. *Note to self: Do not squeeze,* she thought, employing a Lilyism.

Jane dressed quietly, rummaged in her bag until she located her sketchpad and pencils, and tiptoed from the cabin. The sun hadn't risen yet, though the midnight blue of the sky had paled around the edges, and the birds were making a merry racket in anticipation of dawn. In a few hours, Jane thought, her parents and Lily would be here. She remembered how homesick she had gotten the first time she'd come to Sunny Acres for overnight camp, and just as Lily had done, she'd called her sister and they'd stayed on the phone until they both were too sleepy to speak. But now it had been six weeks since she'd seen her family, and so much had happened. She wondered if they'd sense a difference in her, if there *was* a difference in her. Did she feel changed? As Jane headed to the still-dark field to find Lancelot, she considered it.

She'd lost Beau, that was the biggest change. But though her heart still hurt when she thought of him, she also knew for a certainty that he had a good owner who loved him. She hoped he missed her, but she also saw that he was content and, loving him, she couldn't really wish for anything else.

She'd also discovered new things about Robin and had seen her friend grow less shy toward everything around her, including Jane. She hoped that her decision not to go to Collegiate wouldn't cut off their new closeness . . . and she hoped that MLK was the right choice. She felt deep down that it was, that it was the sort of place that matched her . . . what, difference? Weirdness? For that was the other big change of this summer—no longer wanting to be like the clique. Of course, she'd never managed to be like them in the first place, but she'd always wanted to, desperately, it now struck her. She felt sorrow for her loss of Jessica, despite everything, but then she'd never really "had" her to begin with. And then there was Ben.

From the lightening shadows around the trees, Jane saw a reddish form emerge. She hailed Lancelot and paused for a moment at his side, looking up at the first bits of sunlight reflecting in his large, bright eyes. He snuffled at her sketchpad, moistening a page with his breath, and she pulled it away from him. "If I don't fall asleep, I'll make you a portrait," she told him. Sketching always calmed her, and she thought it might be a good idea to force herself not to think about what lay before her today.

An hour later, she was putting the finishing touches on her drawing of Lancelot's head and neck, crosshatching his coat and adjusting the shading around his ears, when she heard voices outside and peered from the stall to see Susan and Jose entering the barn.

"Who turned the lights on already?" Susan was asking, and Jane called, "Me," and waved to them.

"And what are you doing here so early, *bonita*?" Jose asked her. He looked very dapper in clean jeans and a neat Western shirt with roses on the shoulders. Jane held her drawing up for him to see and he nodded, smiling. "Very nice," he told her. Susan was looking distractedly around the barn, as if formulating a plan of attack. She, too, was more dressed up than usual. At least, her hair was combed and braided tightly, her field boots were clean, and her CLUB SODA, NOT SEALS T-shirt looked freshly washed.

"Susan, can I talk to you for a second?" Jane asked suddenly.

"I'll start bringing in the school horses," Jose said, and as he turned he winked at her. Jane again had the slightly uncomfortable feeling that Jose had an inkling of what she wanted to talk to her trainer about.

"What is it, Jane?" Susan asked, now looking over the clipboard she'd pulled down from its nail by the tack room door.

Jane swallowed hard. "I'm going to ride in the event today." It came out as a croak.

"Mm-hm," Susan said, flipping pages and frowning.

"I was going to just go out with the others, but now I . . . I guess I figured I should tell you first."

Her trainer looked up. "Tell me what first?" she asked. She obviously hadn't been paying any attention.

"That I'm going to ride in today's event."

Susan looked at her blankly. "You can't. Your shoulder," she said automatically.

"It's fine," Jane lied.

Something seemed to finally sink in through her trainer's abstraction.

"You're telling me you want to ride in *today's* event?" she asked incredulously. "Jane, you haven't been doing any of the training. You don't know the dressage course; you've never done cross-country on that horse. . . . It's impossible!"

"I know the dressage course, and I've been training Lancelot for a while now," Jane continued doggedly.

"What do you mean, 'training him for a while'?" Susan barked.

Jane felt herself becoming flustered. "I mean I've been practicing for this. I've done a bunch of dressage, I know he can jump, and we've gone out in the field—"

"And got dragged through it!" Susan exclaimed, with a look of dawning comprehension.

"That was only because a stupid branch hit him," Jane protested. "Before that he did really well."

"Forget it, Jane," Susan said brusquely. "I haven't seen you train, and I have no idea if you're up to this." Was it Jane's imagination, or did Susan not look as dismissive as she was trying to sound?

She decided to press on. "You said that I was, well, that I was a good rider. You told Jose"—Jane knew she was taking a risk in reminding Susan of that argument and revealing that she had overheard it—"and I just want a chance to prove it!" Jane's hands were becoming clammy. Susan *had* to understand. . . .

"Why not let her try?" asked a calm voice. Jane and Susan turned to see Jose standing at the entrance to the barn, holding Brownie. He was smiling gently and looking at Susan.

"But *you're* the one who said I pushed her too hard," Susan spluttered in disbelief. "And now you're saying . . ."

"I'm saying that you should give her a chance to live

up to your faith in her," he said with a bit of mischief in his voice. "It's true that she's been practicing for this, and doing very well from what I hear. I have also heard the opinion"—he winked at Jane—"that maybe I am . . . a little protective of my *bonita*."

Now it was Jane's turn to gape at him. *So Jose did know, and from the sound of it, had known for a while,* she thought. And he'd called her *my* bonita.

Susan seemed to be deflating. "Why didn't you tell me earlier, Jane? Or"—she flared up again—"was this a secret between you two?"

"I didn't know Jose—"

"Jane didn't know that I—" they said simultaneously.

"You haven't answered my question," Susan grumbled.

"I guess I wanted to . . ." Jane didn't quite know how to finish the sentence. "Prove something," said aloud, sounded too arrogant, or too desperate. "Surprise you" sounded dumb. She let her voice trail off. She knew she wouldn't be able to explain how all of this had come about.

Susan sighed. "And you really think you can do this?" She looked at Jane sharply. "You know the courses? You can ride with that shoulder? There are a lot of factors that make me think this is a bad idea, Jane."

Jane's heart pounded as she said, in the steadiest, most convincing voice she could manage: "I can do this." She waited, in a silence that grew more oppressive with every passing moment, her eyes averted from her trainer's embarrassing glare.

"Fine," Susan growled. Jane's eyes flew back up. Incredibly, Susan was wearing her familiar smile-frown. "I'm going to trust you. And I'm going to trust my instinct. Which is that, yes, you'll be able to do this."

Jane felt giddy with relief. She looked happily at Jose, who winked at her again. "Thanks, Susan," she said with some difficulty. "Thanks so much!"

"Don't prove me wrong, Jane," Susan said, with a fierce look, but as her trainer bent again to examine her notepad, Jane thought she saw the ghost of a twinkle in her eye.

*The morning hours* passed with alarming speed. Immediately after her conversation with Susan, Jane had gone to walk the cross-country course before the other girls were in the fields. She didn't know if they'd already done this or not, and she didn't want to run into Alyssa or Jessica at the hairy barrels. Plus, this way she got to see the ground conditions exactly as they would be while riding, unless they were hit with another rainstorm.

There didn't seem much chance of that—the sun was now scorching the sky and the fields were mostly dry. Jane hastily made her way up the hill to the far paddock, where she would again be jumping the shrubbery. It looked brambly and menacing as she examined it, and she felt a wave of nerves crash over her. She quickly moved on.

There were sixteen jumps in all, some in combination, and by the time Jane returned to the barn she was very sweaty and feeling more than a little ill. She hadn't been expecting the narrowness of some of the jumps, and she remembered with a sinking feeling Lancelot's run-outs while jumping with Emily. And the fences into and out of the edge of the pond! Lancelot hadn't shown any fear of water, but then she hadn't galloped him through large stretches of it. . . .

At breakfast, she told Robin about her conversation with Susan—but Robin had already heard about it from Ben, who'd heard from his grandfather.

"I wonder if everybody knows," Jane whispered. It wasn't a comfortable thought. She looked around at the other tables—Jessica, Jennifer, Liz, and Alyssa were grouped at one, not eating much either, except for Liz, who was plowing through her huevos rancheros with enthusiasm. Shannon had gone home yesterday, but Jane was surprised to see Megan and two of her friends at another table.

"I don't think so," Robin told her. "I was in the barn early, looking for you, and ran into Ben. I definitely don't think Susan's made any kind of general—"

"Listen up, everybody!" Susan strode through the actual kitchen and onto the porch, propping one boot on the bench of an empty picnic table and slapping her leg with her clipboard.

". . . announcement," Robin finished lamely.

"The dressage test will begin in one hour and a half. You'll continue immediately to the cross-country course. We'll take a half-hour break, then the jumping test. The scoring will work as follows. You'll get a score for your dressage test and carry that score with you to the cross-country. We are *not* timing the cross-country, so you will only get points off if you do the course incorrectly or if your horse refuses a jump. You'll get points off for each refusal, and if your horse refuses the same jump three times, you'll be disqualified. In the jumping course, you'll again get points deducted if you go the wrong way and for refusals. Three refusals means disqualification. Also, you'll get points deducted if you knock down any rails. This is similar to real eventing scoring, though we've made some adjustments to make it a little simpler. If riders end up in a tie at the end, we'll have a jump-off. Any questions?"

"What are the penalty points?" Jennifer asked.

"Three points for a knock-down, and five points for each refusal or course mistake," Susan explained. "And by the way, Jane's competing with you." She grinned broadly at the campers. "No more questions? Great. See you at the dressage ring in an hour and a half." She marched from the porch, banging the screen door behind her and leaving a loaded silence in her wake.

"Right," Jane muttered to Robin. "That's my signal to leave." She swung her leg over the bench and grabbed her tray, trying to ignore the staring faces around her. Suddenly, she heard fake-sounding laughter behind her and turned to face it.

"Well, well, well," Alyssa said archly, her arms folded across her chest and an awful look of smug amusement on her face. But Jane noticed that Jennifer did not look like she found it quite as funny as her best friend did, and Jessica looked positively furious.

"Yes?" Jane said, trying to sound unconcerned.

"It's sad, really," Jessica said in a high, unnatural voice, staring daggers at Jane. "How you've always tried to get in with our group any way you can. Really *sad*." Alyssa gave a contemptuous snort of agreement.

Jane's face burned. It was too close to being true, and now that it wasn't true anymore it was horrible to be falsely accused. She turned to the door and said as coolly as possible over her shoulder, "I don't want to join you, Jessica. I just want to beat you." And she walked out.

*"Ow," Jane said* through gritted teeth as Jose pulled the bandage tightly under her armpit. Ben shot her a concerned look, and she managed a smile. "It's okay," she told them, "just pinches a bit." Jose fastened the bandage with a metal clip, and Jane gave a tentative stretch. She didn't want to tell them, despite the ointment and the wrap, how much it still hurt, so she just gave a false, bright smile: "Much better!" Jose patted her knee, and Jane rolled down the sleeve of the olive-green button-down Robin had lent her to make up for her lack of jacket and stock-collared riding shirt the other girls would be wearing. Robin had also bravely braided Lancelot's mane, though the enormous horse still made her nervous, and now she was working on Jane's hair, pulling it back with a barrette to keep it out of her face.

"Hey, that looks nice!" Ben said, giving her a critical stare.

"What?" Jane asked, getting antsy under Robin's ministrations.

"Whatever Robin's doing. That hair thing," he said. "It looks good."

Jane blushed and jumped up. "Okay! Enough!" she said. "Next you're going to be putting makeup on me!" She turned and saw Robin's outstretched hand, proffering a tube of lip gloss, and they cracked up. "No way," Jane said. "Lancelot would think I'm Emily and try to ditch me."

Sounds of slamming car doors and voices filtered into the barn, and the riders paused in their various stages of preparation to dash outside to look for their families. Giving Lancelot one more swipe with the soft rag, Jane followed Robin and Ben outside to see who had arrived. There were the Taylors, leaning against their massive black Land Rover with a broad-shouldered boy with golden blond hair talking to Alyssa—her brother, Clay, looking as full of himself as ever in his dark sunglasses and loose-fitting, pale blue polo shirt. They were joined by Jennifer's parents, who could have been the Taylors' twins in style, and Jennifer's younger sister, who was talking excitedly about coming to Sunny Acres next year. Jennifer rolled her eyes at Alyssa.

More cars pulled up and Jane saw Jessica's brother, Dalton, tall and good-looking with swept-back hair, longer in the front, stroll over to knock knuckles with Clay. She didn't see Jessica's mother or father. Her parents were divorced, and it was usually her mom who came to riding-related events. Then, finally, Jane heard the familiar rattle of the Ryans' dirty-white Volvo making its way up the drive to come to a lurching halt under a tree. Her first instinct was to go running to them, but conscious of Ben at her side, she remained where she was, giving what she hoped was a casual enough wave toward her folks, now climbing out of the car.

But Lily was having none of this nonchalance. Her sister hurtled across the lawn, and Jane couldn't help herself—she ran to meet her halfway, and they rocked back and forth in a tight embrace before Lily released her and held her at arm's length to get a good look at Jane with her sparkling, violet-blue eyes.

"You look wonderful, Janoo! You should always wear your hair like that," she said delightedly. "And you're so tan! And old! You're anciently old! You should be going to college, not me!" And they hugged again for another long moment.

"Where's Robin?" Lily demanded. "And this wonder horse of yours? And your whole life—I want to see all of it! Mum and Dad are saying hello to Mrs. Jeffrys—show me first!" Jane grinned. There was nothing in the world more enthusiastic than Lily enthusiastic. Her sister grabbed her hand tightly and they headed toward the barn.

Lily's entrance had caused a bit of a stir. Indeed, her sister was pretty much an event in herself. She looked beautiful, Jane thought, with her dark wavy hair pulled up in a loose knot with tendrils coming down around her face, her long, dangly earrings, and a vintage wrap dress offset by big, brown men's shoes. Lily never looked like anyone else, but she always looked marvelous, and Jane noticed Clay and Dalton casting very interested glances in their direction.

Lily hugged Robin hello, and Jane introduced her to Ben, who looked a little awestruck. "Hi," he said, his voice squeaking a bit, and Lily smiled warmly at him. Jane was about to take Lily to see Lancelot when she heard her parents calling her. "Where's my daughter?" her father was saying in a mock-ferocious voice, and Jane blushed.

"Has Jane told you how weird our parents are?" Lily stage-whispered to Ben. "It's a miracle we're so well adjusted." She crossed her eyes as she spoke, looking totally nuts, and Ben and Robin cracked up.

And then Jane was hugging her mother and father, with a rush of released missing that she'd bottled up over the past weeks. It felt so good to have their arms around her, she had to force herself to step away so she didn't look like a total baby. Her mother's face, surrounded by a cloud of dark curls that Lily had inherited, was wreathed in smiles, and her father stooped down to kiss the top of her head. Just as Lily didn't look like other people, the Ryans certainly didn't look like other parents. Jane fondly took in all their familiar, beloved details: her mother's face, tanned from gardening, with blazingly blue eyes, her faded denim skirt, and her one piece of jewelry, a thin silver chain with a locket that Jane's father had given her long ago. And her father, tall and knobby-kneed in his old shorts and sandals, his fair hair and beard towering over them all, his pipe tucked into the pocket of his wrinkled checkered shirt.

But before they could really talk, or Jane could show them Lancelot, Susan was waving her arms to get everyone's attention and telling the families to go down to the dressage ring, where they'd find seats from which to view the first test, and lemonade as well. Then, spotting the Ryans, she came over to say hello.

"Jane told you that this is a bit of a surprise . . . ?" Susan looked enquiringly at Jane's mother. "Riding in today's event?"

"Jane's always surprising," her father commented.

"Well, Lily told us that Jane wanted to ride in the more challenging show, yes," Jane's mother said calmly, smiling at her daughter. "We think it's wonderful."

Susan's eyebrows shot up. She looked skeptically at Jane, who gave a slight shrug. There were benefits after all, she supposed, to having parents who understood nothing about horses.

"Well, okay, then," Susan said, clearly ready for more of a discussion and not finding one. "I've got to inspect the horses, so I'll see you all down at the ring."

Mrs. Ryan kissed Jane and wished her good luck, and her father squeezed her shoulder, making Jane flinch. "Break a leg," he told her.

"Dad, no! That's what you say to *me*, not Jane! Especially not when . . ." Lily paused, and Jane mentally finished her sentence for her: *Especially not when it could actually happen.*

"Well then, break a hoof, or what have you," Mr. Ryan continued cheerfully. "'Boot, saddle, to horse, and away!'"

Lily drew Jane aside, reaching into the pocket of her dress. "Here, Janoo, for luck. It's Saint Christopher, the patron saint of travelers. I thought he was the most appropriate." She lifted a delicate chain with a silver medallion over Jane's head and tucked it under her shirt. They grabbed each other's hands for a moment, then the Ryans headed down to the ring.

"Wow," Ben said, looking bemused, "your family is really . . ."

"Aren't they?" said Jane, and she smiled as she watched them go.

# Chapter 19

### ❧ ♘ ❧

# Sunday, Part Two

Susan made her way down the line of horses standing in a row before the barns. There was Thunder, rangy and gray, his mane and tail braided in a tight, complicated weave, with ribbons that matched Jennifer's midnight-blue coat. Quixotic seemed edgy, pawing and trying to circle away from Jessica's grip. "Cut it *out*, Quiz," Jessica muttered, and gave a sharp yank on the reins. Ariel, of course, stood calmly at Alyssa's side, looking immaculate and alert. Lancelot towered over the Arab mare—Jane hadn't realized just how much bigger he was than these horses, not having seen them this close together since the very beginning of camp. He made the others look curiously diminished, and Jane admired with pride his massive form, his gleaming, fire-red coat, his three white stockings (which had been green until Jane scrubbed the grass stains from them) flashing below his knees, and his sculpted head, held high and warily eyeing the horses beside him. The other girls looked smart in their jackets, and Jane felt underdressed in her shirt. But, she thought, at least she'd be cooler.

Finished with inspection, Susan gave each of the riders a leg up, wishing them luck and giving last-minute advice. "If you feel at any point that you don't want to continue, just tell me," she told Jane in a low voice. "No one will blame you."

*Yeah right,* Jane thought, picturing Alyssa's glee, Jessica's scornful triumph should she quit in the middle of the show. No matter what happened, she was going to see this through.

Susan, observing the expression on Jane's face, patted her boot. "Just take it easy, then," she sighed.

As they turned the horses toward the dressage ring, Alyssa "accidentally" waved her long dressage crop directly in front of Lancelot's face, and he spooked. He took five enormous, leaping strides forward and sideways before Jane stopped him, her shoulder blazing with pain.

"Oops, sorry," Alyssa said, and kicked Ariel into a trot, leaving Jane red-faced and furious, hands shaking, horse shaking, behind her. Jane took a few steadying breaths, petted Lancelot, and followed her, muttering every bad word she could think of at Alyssa's jaunty back.

*She felt like* swearing some more as she watched Alyssa complete a nearly perfect dressage course (it *was* a counter canter, Jane discovered) and smile proudly at her family as she and Ariel exited the ring. Jane noticed that Clay wasn't paying any attention to his sister; he was leaning back on his folding chair, balancing on its back legs, trying to catch Lily's eye without being obvious. Lily was wearing her serious face, intensely absorbed in everything except Clay's existence.

After a moment of consultation and comparing of sheets of paper, the judges, sitting at the far end of the ring, on the other side of the fence from "C," awarded Alyssa and Ariel forty-five points out of a possible fifty. The crowd applauded loudly.

Next was Jennifer, and Jane thought she looked nervous. She was sitting stiffly on Thunder, and when he didn't perform the counter canter, but stayed on the right lead, her face screwed up in obvious distress. She looked unhappy as she left the ring, and unhappier still when she heard her score of thirty-nine points.

As Jessica entered the ring, Jane looked around for Ben, finding him sitting next to his grandfather in a spot of shade somewhat away from the parents. He was watching Jessica, who gave the judges a cocky salute, but then his eyes met Jane's, as did Jose's. They winked at her simultaneously, and Jane managed a smile.

Jessica rode beautifully, though Quixotic only took two steps of the requisite five in the rein back, and Jane thought he wasn't bending into the turns as well as she knew Lancelot could. And then she was walking on a long rein from the ring to enthusiastic applause, her score of forty-two announced. It was Jane's turn next.

As she squeezed Lancelot's sides and he bounded forward, Jane distinctly heard her father say, "Good lord, that beast is enormous!" and Lily shushing him. She halted at the X, saluted, then for a brief, panic-stricken moment forgot everything that came next. She forced herself to shut out the sound of the audience, not to look at Susan or Ben or Lily or Robin or her parents, and to think. *Working trot to C, turn left, medium trot diagonally across the ring* . . . She let out her breath and began.

Lancelot had decided that today was a fine day for his parade horse routine. He transitioned to a medium trot fluidly and bent around and against her leg in the tight circle at A better than he ever had before. Jane felt herself relax. She guided him straight across the ring, easing to a working walk for a few strides across, then repeating the same actions crossing the ring from the opposite direction. From M to K, Lancelot bowed his head grandly in another working trot and snorted loudly. Back at A, she halted him, then took a deep breath for the rein back. He responded immediately, taking five relatively straight steps backward, snorting with satisfaction at his brilliance, then starting his canter from the halt with another snort and flick of his tail. She guided him quietly with her seat and legs in a circle at the lower third of the ring, relaxing even more into his molten stride at this gait. Jane then looked forward to the rail, where she'd ride till R, then turn left and loop back around in a diagonal on the counter canter. But just as she was almost to the rail, two explosions happened at once.

The first—Clay Taylor losing his balance on his chair and crashing backward into Dalton—Jane barely registered, though she heard his idiotic "My bad! My bad!" as she struggled to control the second explosion—Lancelot. He'd spooked so quickly, half-rearing then smashing her right leg into the fence, and Jane had reacted so fast to bring him under control, helped considerably by the close contact she already had, that it was over before the audience's gasps had died down. As were Jane's chances of winning the dressage competition.

"You *dummkopf!*" Lily hissed loudly as Clay clambered shamefacedly to his feet, and her sister's indignant voice gave Jane heart. Ignoring the renewed throbbing in her shoulder and the brand-new sharp pain in her calf, and not looking at the judges, dreading Susan's expression, she gave Lancelot's neck a few strokes, gathered her reins, and asked him again for a canter. There were a few beats of silence, then she heard a burst of applause.

Jane wasn't sure how she made it through the rest of the course, but she did, and she exited to enthusiastic clapping that didn't do much to assuage her fury and her disappointment. She knew that Lancelot had done better than any of the others and that were it not for that stupid, stupid Clay she'd be rivaling Alyssa for points. But, she reminded herself, having your horse not spook at loud noises was surely one of the most obvious prerequisites of dressage. Ariel probably wouldn't have batted an eye if a mushroom cloud had billowed over the farm. But still . . . it was maddening.

Robin tiptoed across the grass to join Jane to hear her score. The judges seemed to be taking an inordinately long time. Finally, Susan cleared her throat. "This has been a difficult one. All of us are in agreement that Jane Ryan and Lancelot rode the strongest course"—Jane heard Alyssa give an outraged "Pah!" behind her, and heard Lily give a loud wolf whistle, which inspired sycophantic laughter from Clay and Dalton. Robin wrapped her arm around Jane's boot, bouncing a little on her toes. "However"—Jane had a feeling that there was going to be a "however"— "because of the . . . unfortunate spook, we can't award her top marks. The score for Jane Ryan and Lancelot is forty." There was another smattering of slightly confused applause from the audience and a loud exclamation of "Unbelievable!" from Jennifer, who was now in last place.

Jane still felt angry and disappointed, but she knew the score was probably fair. She tried to give Robin—and her family—a reassuring smile and shrug. Her parents both looked much more anxious than they had at the barn when Susan asked them about Jane riding today. Now that they knew what that really meant, Jane hoped they wouldn't have a parental meltdown. "Will you go say something to Mom and Dad?" she asked Robin. "I don't want them getting worried about me."

"Sure thing," Robin said. "I'll see you at cross-country." And Jane turned Lancelot toward their next task.

*It took a while* for Mrs. Jeffrys to usher the parents to various points around the cross-country course from which they could see the action but be out of the way, and Lancelot was getting restless. Jane walked him in circles, going over and over the course in her head. Jose stopped her so he could wrap Lancelot's legs in Bess's green bandages, and the big horse made a bit of a fuss until Jose expertly calmed him. Jane knew she had to wait even longer, being last, and Lancelot's agitation was starting to rub off on her. She got an attack of the nervous yawns, and was sitting with her mouth ridiculously agape when Ben jogged up to wish her a quick good luck before heading to the field, where he'd take up a post of observer for the jumps into and out of the pond. Jose told her that Ricky and Gabriel were also monitoring various jumps, as were all of the judges, so if anything happened, someone would be there right away. This, Jane found, did not exactly calm her. She had a memory flash of hurtling over Lancelot's shoulder and gave another shuddering yawn.

Finally, there was a blast of a whistle, and Alyssa was cantering away. Jane saw her clear the first jump, a big log on a downhill slope, then just as neatly take the second, a corner jump that Jane hadn't liked the look of when she walked the course that morning. She decided not to try to watch anymore and took Lancelot into the ring to walk and trot their nerves out.

In seemingly no time at all, Alyssa was back. She hopped off Ariel and began to hot-walk her, ignoring her friends as well as Jane, and since there was no one else around to ask, Jane was left to try to read how her ride went from her expression, which didn't look quite as glowing as it had been after dressage. Another shrill whistle, and Jennifer was off. It seemed a slightly longer time before she returned, and she couldn't have hidden her reaction if she tried. She was crying noisily, and as she went to comfort her friend, Alyssa looked distinctly pleased. Jennifer's parents were coming in from the field as well, and Jane soon learned that Thunder had refused the shrubbery three times, disqualifying them.

*Shouldn't have skipped it before,* Jane thought with a rather savage delight, and watched with amusement as Jennifer threw a princess-sized tantrum to her parents before storming off to the barn with the sheepish Thunder in tow.

There was the whistle again, and Quixotic burst away. Jane and Lancelot resumed their restless pacing.

Jane didn't stop to examine Jessica's expression when she returned—she was aching to be off, anything to cut short the awful suspense and waiting. She trotted Lancelot briskly through the gate, almost colliding with the exiting Quixotic and earning a snarled "Watch the hell out, Jane" from his rider. Lancelot was dancing under her hands, and Jane firmed up her reins, almost ready to beg Jose to blast the whistle. And there it was—they were off.

It occurred to Jane after Lancelot sailed over the log and made a sharp left turn to the corner jump, a solid-looking wedge that required precision but proved to be as easy for the big horse as the barrels had been, that cross-country was, perhaps, her favorite kind of riding. It was the most like her dream of escape: of taking off with a horse on a journey through the world, free and filled with anticipation for what was over the next hillock, around the next bend. Filled with joy. These thoughts flashed through her more as feelings than anything else since she had to be so utterly in the moment, which was also exactly where she wanted to be.

The third jump was slightly uphill—a sawed-off picnic table that was fairly low but very wide; it felt strange to jump flatly, as one huge stride, rather than Lancelot's usual powerful leap. Jane gave him more rein to get up the hill, curving to the right to point him toward the far paddock. Here, she knew, Susan had set up a jump in the entrance itself, so they would be literally jumping into the paddock, making a circle around the shelter, then jumping out via the shrubbery. Lancelot hesitated, obviously put off by the idea of jumping what should be a barrier preventing him from entering, and Jane gave him a strong leg and firmly centered him straight before it. *Now it looks like a jump!* she could almost hear him thinking, and he tucked himself over it with a catlike grace that seemed to even take into account the slower speed he had to drop to while barreling around the shed.

Jill Grabel and a group of parents were standing in the shelter, applauding and whistling as Jane and Lancelot came around the corner. For a second Jane felt pleased, then Lancelot threw up his head and took a leftward bound that almost unseated her. "Please, no clapping, sorry, just... hush!" Jane gasped.

*Oh gosh, that sounded rude,* she thought guiltily as Lancelot surged over the shrubbery, eager to be away from the crowd, then, *Oh gosh, was that the shrubbery?*

And then Jane really started having fun.

Lancelot soared beneath her, his enormous stride devouring the ground, and Jane felt not one with him, but that they were two matched halves—partners. She could never forget who Lancelot was; he was too unique, too strong, too completely individual and proud to think of as an extension of herself. She respected him too much to think of him as something that could be *hers*. He was, simply and grandly, himself, and she was herself while riding him. But he trusted her—and she trusted him. And, she realized, loved him completely.

Jane thought none of this during her ride—it came to her much later—but it was all decided then and felt in her very bones.

She forgot her shoulder, forgot the soreness in her leg as they cleared the Mohawk barrels, wove between two copses of trees, and leapt an angled, brushy monstrosity whose height took Jane's breath away. Around more trees to the bounce: two striped verticals that must have been imported from the outdoor ring. Then Jane eased Lancelot up a bit, preparing for the woodsy trail that led into the creek, and they plunged into the dim, forested glade. Jane started chanting: "Branches away, branches away, branches away." She kept up the mantra until she spotted another group of people watching their approach, and trying for a bit more politeness this time, called out, "Please don't clap or anything! Thanks!" then braced herself for the downward plunge into the creek. Her words did no good, but they were through the flying water and leaping the far log in a tremendous bound when the applause began, and then it didn't matter because they were gone, flying toward what struck Jane as a ridiculously narrow cord of wood. Lancelot flickered his ears back as if to say, *Do you really want me to jump this silly thing? It would make much more sense to go around it.* She assured him that she meant him to take it, and he did, though he popped it, adding a chipped stride directly before he jumped, and Jane was ungracefully thrown up onto his neck.

She recovered, pointing him right and to the ditch. Lancelot didn't like the look of it, though to Jane it appeared completely harmless, and he zigzagged toward the jump so unwillingly that she decided to circle back and square him up again before he could refuse. She didn't give him much room to think about it, and he took a huge leap, as if crossing a crater in the Grand Canyon. When they'd landed with a jarring thud of hooves on the other side, she gave him a quick pat and reminded him that his nickname used to be "Nutty." Now to the left and could it already be the pond? It was, and they were in, rainbowed water spraying everywhere, temporarily blinding Jane, and she gave a whoop of sheer exuberance as they galloped through, mud churning, water drops glistening on Lancelot's pale fire mane. Another leap out and they faced their last fence, but not before Jane remembered that Ben was supposed to be watching the water obstacles—she slowed Lancelot and cast a glance over her shoulder.

She spotted him, right by the trees at the edge of the pond, then she heard him: "And the home of the brave, Jane!" he yelled, and threw his arms over his head, waving both hands to her.

And with that image resting first in her eyes, then tucked away in a place deep down, where she kept things like Lily's notes, the smell of her father's pipe, the sound of her mother's voice laughing on the telephone with her sisters, the way a new sketchpad and pencils feel in your hands, and the perfect form of a horse, she and Lancelot sailed over the final jump and cantered back home.

## Chapter 20

Sunday, Part Three

*I*t was Susan who brought the news: Jane, with no points deducted from her score, was now tied with Alyssa for first place. Ariel had refused once, at the entrance to the paddock, and Quixotic once, bringing their scores to forty, forty, and thirty-seven respectively. When Jane heard from Robin that Quixotic had balked at the jump down into the creek, she felt a pang of remembrance of the day they first jumped in the water, how Jessica had sung "The Star-Spangled Banner" after Quiz had bolted down the creek, how Jane had borrowed the song for her own courage. It seemed appropriate that Ben shared in the joke, and that he'd remembered. *She used to be that person,* Jane thought sadly, *and now I have no idea who she is.* But she found that her memories, bittersweet and complicated as they were, did not muddy the strong satisfaction she felt at having completed the only clean course of the group.

The yard was a confusion of horses being walked and people thronging around the refreshment tables. Jane kept Lancelot away from the crowd, but she had occasional well-wishers approach, including her parents and Lily, who stood back somewhat nervously from the big horse. Finally, Lily ventured a step forward and lay a tentative hand on Lancelot's shoulder.

"I've never seen anything like it, Janoo," she breathed to her sister. "The way he just *catapulted* over those jumps"—Lily had been standing by the biggest jump and the bounce—"it was like Seabiscuit, or National Velvet, or Meryl Streep, or . . . *wow*."

"Meryl Streep?" Jane asked incredulously.

"I'm trying to think of the acting equivalent, and that's the best I can come up with!" Lily insisted, and the senior Ryans joined their daughters' laughter.

"He's extraordinarily large," her father pronounced, chewing the stem of his unlit pipe.

"And very . . . well, big," her mother added.

Jane sighed. "If all non-horsey people would please step aside, I need to keep walking the extraordinarily large and big Best Actress," she said, and they let her go with a measure of relief. Lancelot bent his head toward her and started vigorously rubbing his forehead on her upper arm. "How could anyone be scared of *you*?" she inquired of him fondly.

The full heat of the day bore down upon the festive, crowded scene, and the afternoon began to take on a glare of unreality to Jane. It was like Field Day at the end of school—a mixing of worlds that was unnerving, and on top of that a competition to worry about. The families were out of place, or the event was out of place. Should Jose really be passing plates of Benedictine sandwiches and slices of ham? Should Ben really have met Lily? Where *was* she, after all? Jane's mouth was dry and cottony and her pulse seemed to be fluttering in fits and starts. *One more thing to do,* she whispered to Lancelot. *Just one more.* Her shoulder throbbed under its tight bandage as she turned him around and headed back down the drive toward the arena.

In a flurry of discarded paper plates, reapplications of suntan lotion, melting ice cubes in watery lemonade, and the bright lipsticked mouths of mothers calling encouragement to daughters, the spectators were herded to chairs around the ring. Jane checked Lancelot's girth and tried to check her own nerves, willing herself to stay calm. She felt tired; she felt like she'd had twelve cups of coffee. She just wanted to go to the cabin and read in the cool dimness on her bunk. She wanted to jump everything in sight. Or perhaps gallop away from the farm altogether. She bounced three times and mounted stiffly.

Alyssa wasn't smiling as she entered the ring. She and Ariel looked as focused as sharks homing in on food. Now Jane had to watch. And, as before, there was no doubt that Alyssa Taylor was an excellent rider. But somehow, this time, watching her competitor gracefully zigzag from jump to jump, her neat releases, her forward-looking eyes, her judicious application of the crop, Jane didn't feel down-hearted. Instead, a strange feeling of excitement suddenly gripped her. *Yes, she's good,* she thought. *And I'm tied with her for first. How about that?*

No refusals. No falls. No faults. Alyssa's score stayed at forty, and she got a standing ovation when she left the ring.

The best Jessica could hope for now was second place, but she rode as if she were still in the running for the championship ribbon. Jane thought that if they'd been on speaking terms, she'd tell Jessica how much she admired her ride, her cool deliberation, her quick recovery when Quixotic stumbled after the combination, and her final salute, jaunty as ever, to the judges and the applauding crowd as she left the ring. When Jessica rode past her, Jane almost opened her mouth to say something, and Jessica gave her a long, musing look before turning away to dismount. But Jane didn't have time to ponder the silent exchange—she was being called into the ring.

After asking Lancelot for a canter, Jane took a gauge of his energy and stride, which seemed as fresh and lively as ever. Reassured, she looked to the first fence, an ascending oxer gaily striped red, white, and blue. "You like these," she told Lancelot, and he apparently agreed. She looked right, shortening his stride into the turn, keeping her eyes fixed on the square oxer looming directly after the curve. Up and over and she counted out six strides to the vertical at a slight right diagonal. Then a turn to the left, past her starting line, and she was squared up for another ascending oxer, then picked up a bit of speed for the longer lead-in to the combination: a vertical, one stride to an oxer, two strides to another vertical, and . . . *bonk*. The sound of hoof hitting pole. *No, no, please no,* Jane begged the pole to stay in its cups as she recovered and pointed Lancelot left and to the next vertical. She knew she couldn't stop, couldn't look over her shoulder, couldn't do anything but pray and ride and wait to hear from the audience or from the telltale clatter on the ground behind her. Nothing. *Focus,* she screamed silently to herself and counted six more strides to the next oxer, then took the following left curve wide to head for a high triple bar, sharp right turn to another triple bar, then finally six shorter strides to the last vertical and she was out, she was done, it was over, and she turned Lancelot immediately around to inspect the last rail of the combination . . . which winked innocently in the sunlight, snug in its cups. Jane blew out lungfuls of air and sagged onto Lancelot's neck, patting him over and over again.

The crowd was on its feet, and she gave a weak wave to her family as she struggled to slow an excited Lancelot down, the pain in her shoulder rising in pitch from a dull mutter to a sharp wail. When she managed to get him from the ring, tossing his head and snorting loudly, taking skittish crab steps all the way, she realized she had no idea what happened next. Did they tie? Was it over? And sudden, confused disappointment came crashing over her. *This wasn't how it was supposed to end.*

She reined Lancelot up next to Ariel, who still bore her rider, looking stubbornly at the judges and nowhere else.

"So, I guess we're still tied," Jane ventured.

"I guess so," Alyssa said flatly.

Jane felt numb, dulled, and slightly stupid with the release of nerves and the feeling of anticlimax. Robin and Jane's family would think it was wonderful. Ben would understand a little bit better, she realized, but still think she should be proud of what they'd accomplished. Susan would be pleased. None of it mattered. She probably should be pleased. *Good lord,* she thought bewilderedly, *what's wrong with me that tying for first place is such a catastrophe?* She couldn't bear sitting in this idiotic silence with Alyssa any longer, and she abruptly swung down from Lancelot's back and threw his reins over his head. All of the families and the judges seemed to be staying where they were for now, and she could at least get Lancelot untacked in peace.

"What are you doing?" came Alyssa's sharp voice above her.

"Well, I mean, I guess I'm going back to the barn," Jane said.

"What about the jump-off?" Alyssa demanded.

"What—Ben didn't say there was . . . a what?" Jane's heart revved back up again.

Alyssa's lips curled up in a smirk, and she gave an unamused chuckle. "Ben. Of course. Spying again. Didn't you hear Susan this morning? If there's a tie, we have a jump-off. So you'd better get back on, because the judges obviously think you're quitting." Jane turned hastily to look toward the center of the ring, and sure enough, the three trainers were looking at her quizzically, and Susan was making unmistakable *Get on your horse* flapping gestures with her arms. Jane needed no further encouragement. She leaped back on as if the ground were electrified, and she and Alyssa trotted their horses back into the ring, Jane's spirits lit on fire like the coat of the dancing horse beneath her.

Tom Cumbler explained the course and the rules as Jose disassembled the first jump of the combination, turning it into a double. The same rules applied, he told them, but there were fewer jumps and the course was altered. He pointed out their new route and they followed his hand with their eyes: The first jump was the same as before, then they would curve right, pass the second jump, and take the third vertical. Instead of turning left, they would head right, to jump number 8, another vertical, from the opposite direction, followed by a sharp right turn to 9, the triple bar, straight to 10, yet another vertical, then a left turn and the long stretch to the now-double combination, then a dash to the last vertical, jump 6, and the final hurdle: the square oxer, formerly jump 7. "Confusing?" He offered them a small smile. But Jane and Alyssa weren't giving each other an inch, and they both looked stoically back at him.

"Basically, it's all the most challenging jumps in a new order. And we're raising the height a bit," he finished, and Jane looked to see that Ricky and Gabriel had joined Jose in the ring and were indeed sliding the cups higher up the posts. She wondered for a moment what was so terrible about tying for first as she watched the poles inch up.

All of Jane's nobler sentiments about having a worthy competitor had dried up, and she began actively and vigorously wishing disaster (if of the fallen-pole-and-refusal variety, and not the more serious kind) on Ariel and her rider. And then at jump 9 it happened: *bonk*. But this time the hollow thud was followed by the clatter of the top rail of the triple bar dropping to earth. Ariel finished the rest of the round cleanly, though Alyssa faltered with the course direction once, having to slow to a trot to regain her bearings. Her score was now thirty-seven, and Jane was in the lead.

Jane quickly scanned the course as she circled Lancelot before the starting line, trying to visualize Tom Cumbler's hand pointing out the route. Lancelot was more than lively now. Instead of tiring, he seemed to be gathering fuel from each leg of the competition. As she shortened her reins, she wondered what memories the day's events were stirring in her horse. His tremendous pull against her was making her shoulder nearly unbearable, but there was nothing for it but to start: Any more time aboard and she was going to lose the effectiveness of her arm.

Lancelot exploded forward and Jane struggled to keep his power in check. He was champing and worrying the bit, tucking and untucking his head in a battle for more rein. Jane held as firmly as she could, but she knew his interest was lit on the hurdles before him and not on her.

They pounded over the first three jumps, but their corners were too sharp and Jane nearly lost balance as they swerved to the rail that had cost Alyssa her points. She righted herself and clung onto him as he sailed over it, anticipating the awful hollow sound, but, finally, thankfully, not hearing it. For a few exhilarating seconds, managing to control the tempest beneath her, she thought she'd won, that she'd made it, that all of the other jumps were surely easier . . . *bonk*. The last jump of the combination, the same one they'd grazed before. *Don't fall, don't fall, don't fall,* Jane chanted . . . then the clatter and the thud, and even as they breezed over the final two fences, Jane knew they had to do it all over again.

Sweat was now pouring down her face and as her eyes sought out Alyssa's, she saw that her rival was in a similar state, her face flushed and strands of blond hair sticking wetly to her neck. Jane didn't bother leaving the ring; she just waited to hear the judges' verdict. How much more of this were they going to have to do? Visions of an epic, all-day struggle swam before her eyes, and she wiped her face on her sleeve. Only Lancelot seemed cool and unconcerned beneath her, his fidgets momentarily quelled.

"Why not just call it a tie?" Jennifer's father's voice rang out somewhat irritably from the audience at the rails, reminding Jane of the existence of life outside the arena. She looked over at the small crowd, which appeared to have wilted in the blazing midday heat. Her mother was flapping her floppy straw hat in front of her face, and several grown-ups had wandered back over to the refreshment table. Jane realized she was desperately thirsty, and, seeing that the judges were still in conference, she walked Lancelot over near where her family was sitting. Lily immediately sprang up and handed her a water bottle, which Jane gulped from greedily, spilling water down her shirtfront. She didn't care: It matched the sweat stains crawling down her spine. Her parents spoke reassuring words, but the sisters were silent. Jane drank confidence from Lily's smiling, believing eyes, and handed back the bottle gratefully.

Finally the judges made their announcement. "In the interests of the riders and their horses, this next round of the jump-off will be the final one," Susan called out. "The riders will follow the same course as before, and the rider with the *fastest* clean course will be the winner."

Jane looked down at Lily, who put her hand to her neck. "Don't forget your medallion," she whispered.

Jane repeated her sister's motion and felt the cool disk resting on her clavicle. "Well, hang on, Saint Christopher," she said, and turned to leave the ring clear for Alyssa.

She paused when she heard Jill Grabel's voice: "Don't get carried away," she called to both riders, but looking meaningfully at Lancelot. "If you go too fast, you might get sloppy and knock down rails. Aim for a clean round, not a speed record."

This seemed to be Alyssa's strategy exactly, and Jane, remembering all too well her own fast-and-loose ride, thought she was probably counting on Jane's enormous horse getting out of hand and making mistakes. For

Lancelot, if he stayed under control, had the advantage of his massive stride and the speed Jane had experienced over and over again with awe. There was little hope that the stalwart Ariel would refuse jumps she'd already handled with aplomb, but maybe, maybe they'd knock a rail down. . . . The hope dimmed down to nothing as Alyssa crossed the final jump, her horse's hooves tucked neatly inches above the top bar. The judges called her time: 62.3 seconds.

Jane, having nothing to compare it against, had no idea if that was slow or fast—she just knew she had to beat it. Before she entered the ring, she bent her head briefly against Lancelot's mane, stroking his neck. "Let's show them, Red," she whispered. "Let's do this one last thing, and do it right." His ears flickered back to her and he stood perfectly still until she was ready. And then she sat back, gathered her reins, and squared her shoulders.

She glanced at the crowd, hushed and still, as she entered the ring. The afternoon heat seemed to have turned to a silent weight, and the farm was unnaturally quiet. She looked for Ben but couldn't find him.

"Ready, Jane?" Susan called.

"I'm just making sure Clay has all of his chair on the ground," Jane called back, hoping to find Ben's face among the others, but not seeing it. There was a wave of laughter, and Clay yelled, "I do! I do!" probably for Lily's sake.

"Well, come on, then," Susan said, and Jane, disappointed, turned Lancelot to the starting position. As the farm was eerily quiet, the big red horse seemed preternaturally still, his ears flickering back and forth between Jane and the jumps before him. *Controlled speed,* she thought. *He's fast, but can he be fast and careful?*

"Ready," Jane called.

It was the fastest game of strategy Jane had ever played, guessing where she could lose a stride, where she could shave the edge off a corner, how she could get from point to point square and centered but try to lose all the ground between. It felt like crazy math, painful math as her shoulder began to tremble each time she reached up into two point. It felt like she was physically hurling them over the verticals, willing her horse to pick up his feet, willing him to take off at the proper distance from the jump. It was the quickest thinking she'd ever done, and she felt her whole body reacting to her prayerful riding, making herself hold light and tight and fierce and above all up and up to reach higher, jump higher, go faster, and match speed with care and care with height until finally she heard, was it yelling from the crowd? Why were people yelling? But yelling they were, the silence smashed to pieces as she raced to the last jump and saw Ben's face between Lancelot's ears before her and he was yelling and raising his fist and Jose was thumping Ben's back and here was the last jump and when they were over Jane was not yelling, she was crying, and she knew that they'd won.

# And Last . . . the Mystery Horse

Robin brought the bucket of water closer to Jane, who insisted on taking care of Lancelot herself, though her arm was back in a sling. But Lancelot, for once, seemed close to tired, and he was calm and patient as his limping, awkward rider tended to him.

"I think this is the first time I've really seen him sweat," Jane remarked to the small group of people gathered around them, watching and, she thought proudly, admiring the mighty red horse.

"He is something else," her father mused, and Jane took this as high praise, for her parents always found words for what they felt. When they couldn't, it was noteworthy.

"After all this excitement, getting Lily to college is going to be a walk in the park," her mother commented, and Lily laughed her agreement. But Jane's tired elation sagged at the words, and she paused, sponge in hand, to look forlornly at her sister.

Lily saw her face and gave her a quick kiss on one dirty cheek. "We've still got a whole week," she whispered, and to Jane's utter surprise, she ducked swiftly under Lancelot's head and began skillfully freeing his mane from its braids. "He's really pretty sweet," she said cheerfully.

They were soon joined by the three trainers, who had disappeared to the house with Mrs. Jeffrys after presenting Jane with the satin ribbon that now hung on Lancelot's stall, its long streamers fluttering in the breeze from the barn's fan. Now they each shook Jane's hand again, and Jill Grabel gave Lancelot a pat on his damp rump. Jane's curiosity did brief battle with her shyness, and she finally addressed the Long Run trainer:

"Do you think he did almost as well as he . . . as he used to?" she asked in a low voice.

Jill smiled, but cocked her head quizzically at Jane.

"He had a rough beginning here," Susan explained. "*More* than rough, I should say. Though I thought perhaps his problems had started even earlier, when Katie Reed was still riding him." She shook her head wonderingly at the horse. "Jane's done a tremendous job with him," she added to the Ryans. "In fact—"

But she was cut off by Jill, who had turned her questioning expression now to Susan. "What do you mean?" she asked. "Katie never rode this horse."

Now Susan, and everyone else, looked perplexed. "Katie *owned* this horse!" she exclaimed. "He was stabled at Long Run!"

But Jill just shook her head. "Katie had one horse—Galahad—who she sold before she went to college. He was a chestnut, too, but more than a hand smaller, with two stockings, not three. I should know, he boarded with me for five years. I've never seen this horse in my life," she finished firmly.

Dumbfounded, Jane, Susan, and Robin stared at her, their astonishment mirrored in one another's features. The Ryans and Tom Cumbler, knowing less of the situation, looked politely interested in the debate.

Susan was incredulous. "But we picked him up from your barn!"

Jill shrugged. "I can't help you there. I've been traveling so much this summer, I haven't been able to keep track of every horse that's come through, though I can tell you that this horse never boarded with me."

"And actually, Susan, my grandsons did *not* pick him up from the barn," said Jose thoughtfully from a few feet away. He paused and put down the buckets of water he was carrying to the fields. The group wheeled around to him. Even Lancelot turned his head in an interested fashion, as if following this discussion of his origins with equal curiosity.

"Mr. Longstreet told Ricky and Gabriel to get Emily's horse from a field near Long Run, private property. I can't remember what the place was called, if it had a name. But not Long Run, that I remember, because the boys weren't happy about having to catch this horse in the field. It took them a long time, and they were late getting back." He smiled at Jane. "Looks like you have a mystery horse."

"But Susan," Jane exclaimed, "you bought him! Don't you have papers or something?" But her trainer was already shaking her head.

"Remember, Jane? We agreed to the sale, but were going to finalize the details after the Longstreets came back from vacation."

Jane's mother began to laugh. "A Lancelot for a Galahad! You got the wrong knight!"

"His name might not even *be* Lancelot," Robin said.

Suddenly Jane remembered a long-ago conversation with Jessica, when she'd told her how Emily had gotten her champion horse.

"I don't know if this means anything, but Jessica told me that Emily's parents had said that they couldn't afford Katie's horse. But then she said that Emily wore them down. What if—" She stopped, embarrassed at her own insinuation. Would Mr. Longstreet really have . . .

Susan gave her an uncomfortable look. "He did ask for a lot less than what I'd imagined he'd paid. I thought it was just because he wanted to get rid of him . . . was afraid for Emily's safety. I certainly haven't seen any papers yet." Susan cleared her throat. "Well, we won't know the truth of it till we talk to the Longstreets," she finished, "but this sure beats me."

Jane looked with wonderment at the dripping horse

beside her. She traced the long question mark on his forehead with her finger. "Who are you?" she asked him, and he blew softly to her. She thought about Emily, not even recognizing the difference between this horse and the one she'd fallen for after seeing him once in his stall. Jane felt a pang for Mr. Longstreet, if what she guessed happened was in fact the truth . . . wanting so badly to give his daughter what she desired, then seeing the danger he'd put her in with the unknown horse (though Emily certainly hadn't helped matters). No wonder he wanted to get rid of his mistake. . . .

Jane leaned her cheek fondly against Lancelot's. He was no mistake. And she realized it really didn't matter to her where he came from, or who he was. She felt at that moment that she knew all she needed to know about him, and all of it was more than wonderful.

"So, Jane," Susan asked her, "how do you feel about your mystery horse?"

"I think he's perfect," Jane said dreamily, and everyone laughed.

"Well, he's yours," Susan said gruffly.

Jane smiled and went back to work scraping the water from Lancelot's coat. But then the silence around her made her look up again.

"Wait, Susan, what did you say?" She stared at her trainer, who was giving one of her ferocious half-smile half-frowns.

"I said he's yours. If your parents agree."

Jane felt paralyzed as she turned to her parents, who

were looking very serious indeed, and more than a little wary.

Lily jumped to the rescue: "You won't have Jane's school tuition this year," she exclaimed, then, seeing their looks deepen into scowls, added hastily, "not that that's why Jane's going to MLK, right, Jane? Right, Mrs., um, Susan?"

Susan, having no idea what Lily was talking about, simply nodded, eyebrows raised. Jane couldn't speak, couldn't move. This couldn't really be happening.

"Well, it's something to think about," her father finally sighed. "But you have to know that we couldn't pay you for the horse. We don't know at the moment exactly where he came from . . . and I confess I don't have any idea how much board would be."

"It's not so much, sir," Susan said firmly. "Especially if Jane would agree to continue teaching the younger riders as she's been doing this summer. I'm sure we could work something out with the Jeffrys. And I agreed to buy him before I knew he should be Jane's. It's my choice to give her this horse. And as far as where he came from, well, we don't know. What I *do* know, and know for an almost certainty, is where he can go from here, with Jane riding him. He could be a champion. And your daughter could be a champion. What you saw here today surely must have shown you that much."

Tears blinded Jane's eyes, but she heard Tom Cumbler's laconic "Here, here," and Jill Grabel chiming in, "Without a doubt." Still, she stood frozen by Lancelot's side till she could bear it no more and words came wrenching from her in a painful plea: "Oh, Mum, Dad . . ." She couldn't finish, but everything that was Jane was in her face, and her parents saw it.

"He's a lovely horse, Jane," her mother said with tears in her voice.

"A mystery horse of your own." Her father chuckled. And Jane had to hand the lead rope to Jill so she could fling her arms around her startled trainer, pulling Lily and her father and her mother and finally Robin and Jose to her to envelop them in all the thankfulness and amazement and joy that coursed through her like a river of happiness bursting its banks.

*Jane was lingering* at Lancelot's stall, unwilling to say her final good-bye, though she would see him again, would see *her horse* again in a little more than two weeks, after the Ryans had taken Lily to college and Jane had started school. Her mind whirled with everything that had happened that miraculous day, and her heart flooded with an almost uncomprehending gratitude when she thought of her trainer, so tough, so demanding, but finally the person who believed in her most of all. And she couldn't help thinking with a kind of stunned amusement what Alyssa and Jessica would say when they found out. Both girls and Jennifer had left immediately after the awarding of the ribbons, giving over the care of their horses to the Reyes family, and disappearing in a flurry of tossed sleeping bags and duffels and wet towels and promises to see one another the next night at Jennifer's house.

As Jessica had jumped in her brother's convertible, pulling on her huge sunglasses and fiddling with the stereo, Jane had seen Ben looking after her briefly, before turning away. Their looks just crossed each other's: Jessica looked up and watched Ben's retreating back. She then glanced over to Jane, standing as sweaty and dirty and unglamorous as always, carrying the muddy length of hose to her horse, and she had smiled. It was not a very kind smile—it was knowing and a bit pitying and also a little rueful. But Jane had suddenly decided to take it for what she could, and she waved to her ex-friend, calling, "Have a good rest of the summer!" And Jessica, surprised into spontaneity, had given her a real smile and waved back. Jane thought she might have heard "You, too" as the convertible peeled off down the drive.

Alyssa and Jennifer, of course, had not said a word to her besides bright, false "Congratulations!" in front of their parents and the judges.

Jane heard a noise like a low voice coming from the stall behind her, and she turned to see Megan hanging on the bars of Beau's stall, in apparent conference with her horse, who was leaning down to catch the words being whispered up to him.

"It's hard to leave, isn't it?" Jane said smilingly.

Megan nodded, turning to her, and Jane could see that her eyes were sparkling with tears.

"He won't forget you, I promise," Jane told her, and Megan gave a shaky sigh.

"I hope not," she whispered. "But it'll be a whole two days!"

"Wait, you're coming back day after tomorrow?" Jane laughed, but tried to keep her laughter kind. "You *really* don't have anything to worry about, Megan. He loves you." Jane crossed the aisle to give Beau a fond pet between his gentle eyes. And she stepped back, startled, as Megan threw her arms around her waist and hugged her. Then the sound of a tapped car horn broke them apart, and with a final hug of her horse and Jane, Megan ran to her parents, waving at her to get a move on and get in the car.

Jane knew it was time for her to go as well. Her family and Robin were hovering around the packed car, saying good-bye to Jose. But there was one more good-bye Jane had to say, and she was wondering where she would find Ben, when he came into the barn, looking for her. He had something in his hand, behind his back. When he reached her, he held it out.

"For you," he said simply.

Jane unfolded it in wonderment. It was her T-shirt, the shredded, filthy, bloodstained one she'd worn during her second fall from Lancelot. But as he helped her spread it out, since she couldn't with one hand, she saw that he'd had letters ironed across the back, a little hard to read since they were printed in a haphazard fashion to avoid the tears: I WON THE FIRST SUNNY ACRES EVENT AND ALL I GOT WAS THIS LOUSY T-SHIRT.

Jane stared at it, then burst out laughing. "But, but," she gasped, "how did you know I was going to win?"

He grinned back at her. "I just had a feeling," he said. They looked at each other, then started laughing again.

Jane didn't know where to begin, or how to end. For this good-bye would end her summer. So, of course, she blushed. "Thanks . . . thanks for everything, Ben," she said, and felt herself turn even redder as she heard how shy and awkward she sounded. But Ben apparently couldn't think of what to say, either, and just nodded, looking with fixed interest at a nearby hay bale.

"Don't forget to keep that transistor radio buried," Jane tried.

He looked up and smiled. "Not to worry, my lady," he said in accent, and she smiled, too. It was harder to be shy with Ben than to just be themselves, Jane thought. *We sort of can't help it.*

"Oh!" Ben smacked his forehead. "I meant to tell you that if you get Mr. Gupton for homeroom you have to call him 'Guppy,' I mean, for the obvious reason, but don't let him hear you because you'll get on his bad side for the rest of the year and he'll always mark you late, whether you are or not."

"Huh?" Jane stared at him bewilderedly.

"Your sister told me you're going to MLK. Didn't she tell you that's where I go?"

"No! What?" Jane exclaimed. Ben nodded and seemed to be about to say something else when they heard the car horn.

"One second!" Jane yelled, then torn and in a riot of happiness and shock, ran to hug Lancelot one more time (which he put up with graciously), gave Beau a last pat, and, not knowing what else to do, stuck out her hand, and she and Ben shook, hard, like they had the morning after their long night in the barn. They grinned at each other. The horn sounded again, and their hands dropped.

As she climbed in the back of the car, piled in tightly with Lily and Robin, she thought she saw him mouthing something, and unrolled the window.

"See you in school!" he called.

"See you in school!" she yelled back, and waved her T-shirt, fluttering as a many-colored banner of the many-colored summer, from the window of the Ryans' car as it made its way slowly down the drive, leaving Sunny Acres.

## Note

The landscape of Sunny Acres farm—from the fields to the barns, the riding arenas to the main house and cabins—was inspired by my memories of Undulata Farm in Shelbyville, Kentucky, where I was fortunate enough to learn to ride under the expert eyes and loving guidance of the Meffert family—Bobbie and Jim, and their children, Jill and Jimmy. However, not a single character in *A Horse of Her Own* is based in whole or in part on any of the marvelous people I knew during my years at Undulata—with the notable exception of Beau.

# GO FISH

## ANNIE WEDEKIND

**What did you want to be when you grew up?**
First, a groom—until my mother said, with a touch of asperity, that that "wasn't intellectual enough" (I was ~~~ later a poet.

**As a young person, who did you look up to most?**
My sister Araby, on whom my character Lily is based.

**What was your worst subject in school?**
I failed Yearbook. I hadn't known that was possible.

**Where do you write your books?**
When I was in high school, I played hooky quite a bit and spent a lot of time reading and writing and drinking coffee at a run-down cafeteria in downtown Louisville called Miller's. When, sadly, they went out of business, my mother bought one of their tables for me, and it's still where I do my best writing and thinking, as it was when I was fifteen.

**Who is your favorite fictional character?**
A toss-up between Ivan Karamazov, Fflewdur Fflam, Betsy Ray,
Sherlock Holmes, and Long John Silver.

**What's your favorite TV show?**
My partner, David, and I are completely obsessed with *House*.
After we put our son, Henry, to bed, we eat dinner, watch an
episode, and try to spot the red herrings.

**If you could travel in time, where would you go?**
Paris in the '20s.
   Weimar Republic Germany.
   The day that the very first Neanderthal (or what have you) put
an ear of corn by the fire and discovered popcorn. I mean, how
freaky would that have been?

**What's the best advice you have ever received about
writing?**
A paraphrase from Hemingway: Writing is the art of applying
butt to seat.

**What would you do if you ever stopped writing?**
Well, if I had been born with an entirely different skill set, I'd like
to speak dozens of languages and excel at parkour.

**Where in the world do you feel most at home?**
In the Bywater, in New Orleans.

**What do you wish you could do better?**
Sing.

SQUARE FISH